This Ain't No Hearts and Flowers Love Story Pt2 by Brooklyn Darkchild

This Ain't No Hearts and Flowers Love Story Pt2 by Brooklyn Darkchild

This Ain't No Hearts and Flowers Love Story Pt 2 by Brooklyn Darkchild

Brooklyn Dreams Publishing Co
Cincinnati Ohio

Goin Back To Cali by LL Cool J	©) 1996
Touch Me, Tease Me by Case	©) 1996
Light My Fire by Jose Feliciano	©) 1968
P.I.M.P by 50 Cent	©) 2003
Stop On By by Rufus f/ C Khan	©) 1974
Lately by Tyrese	©) 1998
Excuse Me Miss by Jay-Z	©) 2003
Theme from Rocky by Bill Conti	©) 1976
Lover In You by Shalimar	©) 1981
Love Ballad by LTD	©) 1976
You Are Not Alone by M Jackson	©) 2003
Paper Thin by MC Lyte	©) 1988
Twenty-five Miles by E Starr	©) 1969
These Boots are Made For Walkin by Nancy Sinatra	©) 1966
The Closer I Get to You by R Flack/ D Hathoway	©) 1977
I Love Your Smile by Shanice	©) 1999
Can I Live by The Lox	©) 2000
50 Cent Rap Verse/Cry Me a River by J Timberlake	©) 2002
The Show by Doug E Fresh	©) 1985

Dedication

To my wonderful daughter Qiani Banks for making me believe I could actually write a book, and to all my friends at WritersCafe.org for making me believe my book was good enough to publish. A special thanks to Qa'lil and Earl for putting up with me while Mommy sat in the living room pounding out her "book," pretending she was really watching you, and to the rest of my children for not laughing at my dream. Too hard.

Acknowledgement

Special thanks to Bishop Todd E. O'Neal and his wife Pastor Linda Fay O'Neal of the House of Joy Christian Ministries in the College Hill section of Cincinnati. Their powerful Sunday morning teachings formed the basis of much of what I've come to believe about Christ, what this novel is all about, and influenced the sermons depicted in this novel.

1 OB

When I'm stressed I hang upside down; been doin it since I was a kid.

Right now I'm upside down on my porch swing, hair trailin the dusty concrete.

Far off in the distance I can barely make out what appears to be a human bein; walkin.

The figure draws only marginally closer but I can already see it's My Princess:

head down, arms folded across her chest.

Why she walkin though?

Who **does** that?

This must be one a them Non Confrontational Acts she always stressin.

My heart does a Hallelujah Jesus but my body stays still, poised.

Damn it if she can walk the three and a half miles from my gate then she must be okay.

Wasn't It **Kind** a Her To **Call**?!

I don't even wanna look at her.

Wherever she been, whatever she was doin, she home now. Safe. Sweet Jesus, she home.

After flippin upright I curl into a little ball, my back turned to the spot Cess will sit in.

Wasn't we sittin Just Like This a hundred and fifty years ago when she left last night?

Yes.

I was **upset then** and I'm **twice as upset now**.

She Coulda *Called*.

Around four I even tried to call **her** but Got No Answer.

Around three, before I started to worry, my display said Missed Call.

But my cell ain't ring so it must a been a Under Naturally Brief Attempt.

Even so Cess could a Kept On Tryin, or at **least** Left Me a Voice Mail.

Better Still she could a **answered her damn phone**, cause **I kept callin** you know.

Whatever whatever, she home now; Obie Don't Blow It.

"Hey," she says tentatively, finally arrivin at the swing.

She sits next to me, places one hand on the center a my back.

Maybe I kinda grunt back.

"You still mad, huh," she states rather than asks.

Well, DUH.

"Talk to me OB. I *need* to talk to you."

That sounds ominous to me.

I don't need no I'm Dumpin You talk right now.

"You think I slept with Einstein?"

It's a Real Question, not a Accusation; posed carefully, sorta like:

You Think It's Gon Rain?

when you planned some Spectacular Outdoor Event and the Clouds Start Formin.

"You do what you **do** Cess; you a ***woman***. **I don't control you** and I ***don't*** wanna **talk** about it."

"If we don't talk about it it'll sit between us the rest of our lives."

Oh we ***got*** that now?

A ***Rest a Our Lives***?

What ***ever***.

"Listen," Cess began, but I was quick to Cut Her Off.

Turnin around to face her I say:

"Don't start explainin. You did **whatever**, okay? It's **Over**. You **home** now.
End a Discussion."

I'm only half lookin at Princess

but she got her head down so it ain't like she Lookin At Me either.

"Sometimes a woman does what she **has** to; not what she **wants** to."

Cess says this so quietly I scarcely hear her.

"**What the Hell does that *mean*?**" I explode.

She talkin in Riddles now and it's gettin on my Already Frayed Nerves.

"What does it sound like?" she replies, barely above a whisper.

This sinkin feelin develops in the pit a my stomach.

That's when Princess raises her head,

and for the first time this mornin I get a good look at her.

Her face looks puffy, swollen; there's crusty blood in the corner a her mouth.

I'm startin to feel **Real Sick here**.

"What does that mean?" I repeat in a Kinder Gentler Tone, pressin her for a answer.

"**You** know what it means OB. Don't make me Say It Out Loud."

"What happened to your face?" I whisper,

the feelin a dismay inside me growin larger every second.

Her visage crumbles and Princess rises to go inside.

I make a grab at her arm, to make her stay and talk to me, but she **screams**, man;
such a Horrible Wail a Pain.

Stunned, my hand flies off her arm and Cess flies into the house.

Unable to move I actually let Cess get away.

Only for a second though.

That one thought: She Gettin Away, snaps me Back To Reality.

Cess was far gone, takin those steps three at a time.

If she hadn't Tripped & Fell her clumsy ass would a Made a Clean One.

She cradlin her arm, which I now see is hangin funny.

Another thing I notice is her panties is gone.

Princess would never leave her panties anywhere.

"What happened to you? What's wrong with your arm?"

I realize I'm back to screamin but I can't help it. Cess musta hit that arm cause she

let loose another screech that brings the whole family bearin down on us.

People is comin fast so I pull her dress down to cover her naked behind.

Thinkin I knocked Princess down or somethin these mothafuckas is grabbin *me.*

As *If.*

Cess makes a break for her room, slammin the door behind her. I hear the lock click.

Why would she do that?

Why would she lock me out like that?

Why would she even **go** to her room?

Shakin these niggas off I hurdle up the stairs and start poundin on Cess' bedroom door.

Nobody understands what's goin on. They all think I'm flippin out.

Before they can restrain me I grab the doorjamb on both sides and Timb the door in.

As the door splinters then gives way Princess looks at me and says:

"What the fuck OB."

She says this without anger, soundin almost Hollow and Empty inside.

Princess is seated on her bed, supportin her bad arm.

"Why won't you tell me what's wrong with you?" I demand.

Princess peers at me; miffed she Speaks Up.

"Do I have to draw you a map?" Comin To Life again she snaps harshly.

Cess signals for me to come closer, then for me to sit down. Her good hand disappears

into her bag, extracts some black scrap a fabric and deftly presses it into my hand.

"Let Me Help You Out," she attests sharply.

The Little Black Scrap is what's left a her panties.

I feel like I been punched in my stomach.

"Oh **wait**," she says sarcastically, "My **Bad**. There's **more**."

This one don't need to be opened up too tough. Any Fool Can See it's a bra

tore almost Clean In Two, a piece a wire stickin out the bottom a one cup.

"Now you got a Matchin Set. Picture Coming Any Clearer?"

Princess sounds so angry at me.

Confusion Abounds as I look from one hand to the other:

Shredded Panties, Filleted Bra.

"And now the *piece de résistance*," she announces with a flourish.

She opens the long sweater she wearin and displays a dress torn to the waist;

Bruises and Scarrin on the Over Exposed Flesh.

Somethin weird overtakes me.

The walls slide sideways and I feel like I'm sinkin.

Don't know how I got on the floor or how long I been here.

I only know One Thing:

"I can't breathe."

In a house full a asthmatics, inhalers are thrust at me from every direction.

Grabbin the one that looks most like mine's I draw two hits deeply.

The medication works,

Some, but Not Much.

"Why you ain't *call me*?" I manage to get out once my head has cleared.

In turn Cess reaches into the sweater pocket, withdrawin a Handful a Gadgetry.

"I couldn't get a call through on that damn thing. You think it's broken?"

The sarcastic tone leads me to believe I am askin too many Stupid Questions.

I don't know what else to do.

"Where'd he take you?"

"He didn't. I went to my house for a second."

Oh My God; I wanted to go there.

"What for?"

"He had some shit there I wanted to give him, and Really,

I've come to depend on you for So Long Now I'd forgotten my **Essentials**."

Oh **shit**, her pads.

"But Cess, you on your **period**."

"I didn't get the impression he **cared** OB. Caller You Say What?

Look at the panties now and tell me he **gave** a shit."

I **wish** she'd stop *talkin* to me like this.

Makes me feel like she mad at **me** somehow.

"What happened when you pushed The Panic Button?"

The facade a anger slowly dissolves. First Princess looks down, then she looks away.

"Cess?" I prod. My Princess breaks down.

"Don't be mad at me OB. I turned the damn thing off.

I can't believe I did that; it was so so very **stupid**. *Why am I so dumb*?!"

Seein Princess awash in hysterical tears I knew I couldn't get mad at her.

Not today.

Maybe next week.

I try to comfort her but she cries out in pain and shrinks away.

Then I remember that the system is designed to always be on.

"Who showed you how to bypass the alarm Cess?"

I ask in what I hope is a Neutral Tone but it was Way Too Cool & Collected.

Cess knew **whoever** Taught Her That Trick was Fi'n-a Die.

Hence she becomes Closemouthed.

"I did it," Freak Man's Up. I shoot him a Cold Hard Look a Betrayal.

"Cess kept settin it off tryna leave her own damn house," he explains;

"The police were disgusted with her so I Nigga Rigged it. I'm sorry man."

"So the alarm was off more than it was on," I conclude.

"**Basically**," Princess tearfully admits.

Anybody else but Freak would be So Dead by now.

Very Very Much So.

From the back a the crowd I catch a signal from Lee. Namin That Tune I make tracks.

"Don't **leave** me OB," Cess calls out. "*Please*. **He might come back**."

Hesitant to leave my Princess alone I stop mid stride, lookin at her over my shoulder.

Mommy comes to my rescue.

"Obie's gonna be right downstairs," Mommy lies. "You and I need some Girl Time."

She throws everybody out, God Bless Her Soul.

That Mommy's a Winner.

Me Dad Tommy Lee and Young pile into my Porsche Cayenne;

The Fastest Way to get from Here to There.

Not one a us thinks Einstein would be foolish enough to go back to Cess's.

But We Can Dream can't we?

On the way out the gate we cross paths with Hood.

Don't let Hood's Worry Wart exterior fool you:

pour two drinks into his ass and we hafta haul him out the club fore he kills someone.

At this moment we desperate to reach The Scene a The Crime

and we can't stop to pick Hood up. I honk as we fly by.

"Lee; call Hood and fill him in," I ask/ request/ hope I don't sound Too Demandin.

"Hood says there's Mad Traffic ahead on both sides. Somethin Big is Goin Down."

Great. Just What We Need.

We hit the snag and creep along while I curse under my breath.

Lo and Behold a cop stops **me**. Like most a the Industry Cats who live here

I am on a First Name Basis with most a Malibu's Finest.

This Cat I know Real Well.

"Did you lose one of your party last night Obie?"

Ding! Ding! Ding!

I know the answer to *this* one.

"Yeah, Albert Bell; drivin a silver rental. Why?"

"Sometime this mornin he ended up in the ocean. Looked like an accident to the eye

witnesses but you Never Can Tell with these things. We've recovered the car but

we've been dragging for the body all morning with no success."

"**Damn**," I mutter.

"This Albert a friend of yours?"

"Princess' ex. Showed up unexpectedly," I say, not quite answerin his question.

"Is that why you were lookin for him last night?"

Somethin in Ty's voice let me know this was Not A Casual Question.

"He ran off with Princess, we couldn't find her. Early this mornin he brought her back."

The Good Officer raises a eyebrow at my Bare Bones Explanation.

"She alright?"

"Ask me **later**. **Back at my house**. Anything **else** I can do for you?"

The Snap Crackle & Pop a static interrupts us.

"Actually there is. They've located the body. Care to ID it for me?"

"Why The Fuck Not."

Cause I gotta See For Myself *any*way.

It's that turd a'ight. News Copters buzz like flies overhead but *I'm* thinkin:

How could that bitch go and rob me a the chance to kill his ass?

"Care to make a statement?" Ty asks, notepad open and ready.

"Do I have a choice?"

"Right now you do, yeah. Later on? Who knows."

So I give him the Survey Course: An Overview a Last Night With Einstein.

Then we roll out.

We was fine til we walked through the door.

The very sight staggers everyone with me.

We stand in the entryway momentarily dazed, then one by one we fan out.

Lee goes to work snappin photos Right & Left.

As soon as he finishes we assess the damage.

There's two blood stains on the rug:

a smaller one near the door and a much larger one past the couch.

The coffee table's demolished; smashed flat somehow.

The lamps is shattered, the end tables up ended.

The couch caught the worst a it though.

Slashed beyond *all comprehension* it's what first captured our attention.

Chills sweep through me.

Princess is gonna *die*.

She was so **proud** a this house.

"Next time Freak says he doesn't believe in The Power a Prayer show him a picture a this couch. This was supposed to be Princess," Young says gravely.

Bearin Silent Witness we stand a few clicks longer with our heads bowed then move on.

The room is closin in on me and I'm havin trouble breathin again.

Wobbly, I sit down on the floor. My Dad's arm is around me, offerin me his inhaler.

Although I brought my own this time, I accept his gratefully.

From my slumped position the room looks So Much Worse: very very much so.

For some reason this whole scene reminds me a that motel room in Utah.

I feel claustrophobic. This time I hang my head down between my knees.

Huge gulps a air ain't helpin none.

I fight for control. Then my Daddy tells me to:

"Let it go son. It's better you go on and let it out now; get it over with."

"I can't," I tell him. "Cess needs me. And I'm scared I'll fall apart."

"No you won't. You'll be strong; it's already in you, and we'll be here to help."

I stumble into the kitchen, simply refusin to give in.

On one wall is a spot the size and width a' a finger.

Directly below it Princess's tampon rests on the floor.

What kinda sick animal does that to a woman?

Somebody tell me, cause I can't figure it out.

Down on my knees I attack the largest stain first. Young looks at me appreciatively.

"You're good to my daughter ain't you?" he asks semi-rhetorically.

"I try," I admit, Under Comf'table with Praise From Young.

"Once Upon A Time I thought you were The Worst Thing That Could Happen to Princess, with your Flaky Ass. Now I see how **wrong** I was."

From Young this is a Rave.

It makes me blush and I drop my head so no one sees.

The rug resists my best efforts to clean it. The harder I scrub the more smeared the rug becomes until, beleaguered, I break down and start blubberin.

I done more cryin in the last two days than I done since Dude tried to kill me.

Just that fast though my dad's arms is back around me, joined by Young's and Lee's.

Surrounded by the Men a My Tribe I give in.

The broken furniture gets carted off to the storage room, away from Pryin Eyes.

The rug gets a Super Sized Shampooin. Satisfied that the house has been set back in Some Semblance a Order I reset the alarm and lock the door.

Convinced Einstein's main motive had been to hurt me I shed bitter tears.

Barry said I'd been a bitch; delightin in pluckin Einstein's nerves like a guitar string.

I guess his String musta Snapped.

I can't begin to describe to you the level a regret I feel as I sit here.

If I'd a held my ego in check Princess might be okay.

If I'd a held my **anger** in check and done like Uncle BB **said,**

for *sure* **Princess** would be okay.

Angry…but okay.

Right about now I'd take Angry for Five Hundred, Alex.

"Why aren't you ready yet OB?"

Cess done changed into a silver lame pants suit,

brushed her hair and applied a little lipstick.

`Feelin Pret-ty Fog-gy I ask her:

"Where we goin again?"

"Where **would** we be going at 11:15 on a Sunday Morning?" Princess answers back in that same nasty sarcasm tinged voice she been usin all morn.

Okay my baby done Bugged The Fuck Out.

Oops. Sorry Lord.

"Surely you jest," I state in disbelief.

Her good hand flies to her hip; the other one hangs uselessly in front a her.

Through Chinked Out Eyes Princess glares.

"**Look,** *Fool*. Nothing has **ever** stopped me from going to church
and today is No Exception. I am **alive**. I am **home with my family**.
And, I am *going to church to Praise the Lord*.
Can A Sister Get Some **Gospel up in here**???
Or do I have to **limp over there** and **do it myself?!**"
Steppin to the side Princess motions toward the system with that One Hand.
Meekly I pick out a good burned CD featurin Kirk Franklin, Mary Mary and some
Southern Baptist choirs but I am Under Prepared for this Let's Move On attitude
Princess is projectin. She givin orders like we workin on her next video
or she blockin a stage number or somethin.
It's downright **disturbin**.
"You a'ight Baby Girl?" I ask timidly, afraid a sayin somethin that'll Set Cess Off.
"Yeah yeah yeah," she blows me off. "What A Tragedy Befell Me, right?
So What, Big Deal, can we hurry this along? We're already late."
She gotta be Trippin; I **can't** be takin this harder than she is.
Against my Better Judgment I hurriedly shower then throw on the same suit Cess is wearin.
I Love It When We Match.
Her face is swellin somethin awful even though she been steady icin it.
A pair a oversize shades hides much a the damage but every time I look at her I get that
Sinkin Feelin in my stomach, like the bottom is fallin out.
I Don't Know… The whole thing hit me so **differently**.
I got withdrawn, reflective.
I didn't wanna be bothered with **nothin**, just let me Lick My Wounds in peace.
I can't fathom Princess actin like Nothin Spectacular happened to her.
Bumpin into Mommy I start to ask her What's Up with Cess but before I can
Get The Words Out Good- Mommy puts up her hand, stoppin me.
"Let her be Obie, she's Struggling to Cope right now.
When it hits her, and it will,
she'll need you to Pick Up The Pieces."
Best I Get Ready then.

You ever gone to church **needin** to Hear A Word—and you **heard** it?
How many times has that sermon been Just for You?
If this ain't one a them Sundays then They Don't Exist.
I don't know how we did it—well yeah I do: I was speedin—

15

but we got to church in time to hear the choir's last selection,
"God's Got A Blessing With Your Name On It."
What a Great Song considerin they Marchin Song is
"The Lord Is Blessing Me Right Now."
Sometimes, in the Bleakest Moments, You Need To Be Reminded a that.
Our sprits soared, we rose to our feet in praise.
The sermon was on Goin Through. Pastor Maclean has always been a On Time Pastor,
Truly Anointed with The Holy Ghost.
If he wasn't I wouldn't **be** here.
No matter how good the choir is if the Pastor can't deliver The Word then Why Bother?
Good Music I can get On The Radio.
Pastor said that bein saved ain't the end a all our worries;
most times real trouble begins when you try to Do The Right Thing.
Can I get a *Amen* somebody?
He's Singin My Life With His Words here.
Pastor said that's cause the devil don't need to mess with those already under his control.
He just lets em go on ahead thinkin everything they doin is Krispy and whatnot.
But when a soul slides from his grasp the devil makes life hard for that person,
tryna make him or her think life was better when they was doin wrong. Pastor gave the
example in *Matthew 4: 1-11*, where once Jesus was baptized by John the Baptist the
devil immediately began to tempt Him, tryna Sway Him from His righteous path.
If the devil can be so bold as to Try & Tempt Jesus what can **we** expect, you feel me?
But just as the angels came down to minister to Jesus at the end a his trial,
Pastor said God will send us angels too,
as long as we Persevere and Don't Give In.
Pastor went on to say that prayer is the key to gettin through any trial. Sometimes God
will change your circumstances, and **sometimes** God will change *you*, so you can Deal.
If last night ain't Showed Us That nothin on the planet will.
Further on in *Matthew 26: 36-45*, Pastor used the example a how Jesus took
three disciples to pray with him on the night before His arrest.
You know those three fell asleep right?
Well Pastor said sometimes you **really need** somebody to pray with you,
but more often than not,
You'll end up Goin It Alone.
Praise God.

The altar opens for prayer. Princess heads for Pastor Julia, Pastor MacLean's wife.
She was abused as a young teen and was a promiscuous alcoholic by her early twenties
until she attended a prayer meetin run by Pastor at her college. She Got Saved and
They Got Married, provin once more that Our God is a God a Second Chances.
While Cess and Pastor Julia Get Their Prayer On, Pastor Maclean pulls me to the side.
Me and him got a Good Rapport.
And **No** that word *ain't* Report.
He knows me and advises me without Bein Judgmental and I Like That.
"How's it goin Obie; Still Keepin Strong?"
Together Pastor feels we can beat the "Demon" a Homosexual Behavior off my back.
That's not a very PC Statement but the church is not supposed to be a PC Place.
It's God's Place and I'm willin to Work With Him on that.
"Yep," I say proudly. "Been almost exactly a year."
It's true. Except for Lee I ain't slept with another man since Utah,
and don't make the mistake a thinkin I Ain't Been Tempted cause I **Have**.
I fill the Pastor in on the changes in My Love Life.
"I know it's tough Obie but y'all can do it. I think it's a good thing for young people to
realize you don't hafta have sex in order to have a relationship. That ring on her finger
only symbolizes a promise at this point. The weddin hasn't happened yet so even though
the two a you done Slipped you can still get back on the good foot with the Lord."
I promise to take this under consideration.
Really I **do**.
I ain't gon **lie**; we in **church**.
I'm a give it some Serious Thought.
Okay, **don't** believe me then, see if *I* care.
"Tell me what happened to Princess?"
I don't rightly know what to say so I Keep My Mouth Shut until Pastor speaks again.
"I'm not tryna Say Nothin Bad about you Obie but we all know you got a Bad Temper."
"Oh no," I'm quick to point out,
"I could never beat on my baby like that. Not in a million years."
Pattin me on the back the Pastor says:
"That's good; that's good."
The convo progresses no further cause Princess collapses in a heap on the altar steps,
her chest heavin with sobs.
The church evangelists rush to form a prayer circle around her.

Pastor Julia anoints Princess' head with oil and is tellin her:
"That's right child; let it go. Give it up to God and He'll take care a you."

Real weak by now Cess insists on walkin to the house under her own steam.
She wants to go to her room though.
"Come in my room with me," I try to persuade her, feelin lightweight rejected cause
she in my room **always**. "My TV is bigger and my bed is a lot more comf'table."
"I wanna be in my room with my smooshies."
"I'll bring your smooshies to you," I promise.
Princess sighs.
"I need to be in something of my own right now OB," she explains wearily.
O-**kay** Then.
She can't get outta her clothes by herself and every place I touch causes Princess to yelp.
"I feel Not So Helpful here. Tell me where it hurts so I can Avoid That Spot."
"Where **doesn't** it hurt," Cess chuckles;
"I think the fourth toe on my left foot is still a'ight."
She laughin; and that's supposed to be A Good Sign, right?
I Hope So. Anyway finally outta her clothes I can now ease Princess into bed.
"Don't go," she begs me.
I prop my back against the wall and draw one foot up on the bed.
Cess falls asleep with me caressin her head.
Moments later she squeals, jerks, and wakes up again.
She must a hit her arm in her sleep.
Young's been pressin Princess to go to the hospital,
Before Your Arm Ends Up Like Obie's Foot.
This sounds like A Plan to me.
I present it again to no avail: Cess don't wanna Deal With The Publicity.
Can't Say I'm Mad At Her. Under Fortunately the Media Mavens already done added
Princess Engaged To "Cousin" Obie with: Ex Boyfriend's Suicide and Went Amok.
Court TV posted the transcript a my call to the police on thesmokinggun.com
along with My Account a The Evenings Events As Told To Officer Tyson.
It's Gettin **Ugly** folks. I think this is why I never liked Court TV.
"I need a bath OB," Cess whimpers.
She Already Done That: *twice,* but I Know Where She Comin From.
My phone rings. It's Smoke, wantin to talk to Cess.

"Can't do that right now," I say tersely.

Smoke always been a **pushy** bitch and he's tryna Steam Roll Over Me Now.

You know how far he gon get with **that** tactic, *right*?

Worn out, my temper flares.

"Nigga I done Already Told You she **ain't** in the **mood**."

I snap the phone shut.

Less than two minutes later the house phone rings.

Hood peeps around the doorway.

"It's Smoke again Flappin his Jaws, claimin it's Important."

"**I just *spoke* to that mothafucka**."

"*I* know. I'm still **sittin** here. This nigga must be broke cause he ain't payin me

no mind at all, like he's Ei—"

My eyes widen in shock.

That asshole almost said *Einstein*.

If he hadn't **cut himself off *I*** woulda.

At the **neck**.

"You wanna handle this?" Hood asks me, Recoverin Smoothly.

"If *I* Handle This it Won't Be Good. Pass it on to Uncle BB."

Sneaky son of a bitch gets around Uncle BB too.

"He's keeps sayin somethin about a statement," Uncle BB tells me, lookin perplexed.

Callin on Holy Ghost Power I compose myself before takin the call.

"What up though?"

"*Man*, I need to talk to **Cess**. This shit's been runnin on the news all day.

What should I do? Should I make a statement?

That's Kinda Hard since I don't Rightly Know what happened."

Tell Me About It you ole **Stank** Nosy Bas–Call On The Lord Obie, Give Me Strength.

"All statements will be handled by our publicist, Dog. That's what she gets **paid** for."

"I mean as A Friend A The **Family**. Check with **Cess** and see what **she** wants me to do."

In case I ain't already told you: Smoke Ain't No Friend.

I peeped that the first time I met him. Just like **women** know *women*;

well **men know men** and **that** man wants my Princess **bad**.

I don't mean in no Good Way either.

Smoke wants to fuck my Baby Girl and that ain't hap'nin captain.

Did he Forget Somehow he got A Wife & Kids?

Believe me when I say Smoke know exactly where I'm comin from too.

That's why he always throwin some Negative Shit In The Mix when it comes to me and Princess, like if he can turn Cess against me it'll be easier to Slide Up In Her Draws. As If.

He need to learn a Valuable Lesson:

It's Impossible To Get Around Obie

"How bout you listen to **me** instead. The Princess **ain't a'ight**. A dude she was datin for *beaucoup* years Took A Header. Off The Pacific Coast. And she **Shook**.

Give Her Space."

With that I abruptly terminate the call.

"If he call again hang up," I notify Uncle BB

"That's what I love," Princess grins, "A Take Charge Nigga."

That's **Good,** cause I don't know how to be *Any Other Way*.

It takes forever to cross the hall: Princess' legs is Crazy Shaky.

Xanadi guides Princess into the toilet area while I check the water temperature.

My tub is this big Jacuzzi Type Thing with Massage Jets & Everything,

big enough to seat six (oh yeah). I ain't thrown a Wild Sex Party in here in ages though.

Not since I got Kinda Tight with Cess.

Everything's checkin out okay when I hear Princess howl and then start bawlin.

I was thinkin Xanadi was still in there with her

but I don't hear no other sound besides Princess.

I hurry to the door and knock on it but Princess wailin too much to answer me.

Worried I turn the knob.

Agony is etched into Princess' face. She doubled over with it, leanin on the wall to keep from fallin over. I reach out both hands to help.

"I can't walk anymore," she groans, all the while sinkin fast.

When I catch her she wails hysterically.

Barely, **barely** do we make it into the tub where the soothin water calms Princess down.

"Come in with me," she requests.

Not knowin about All That I ask:

"You sure?"

"Of course I'm sure. I'm **Hurt** not **Brain** Damaged."

Well… All Righty Then. Still in my underwear I climb in.

"You scared to touch me?" Princess asks, still soundin Mad Shaky to me.

"I'm scared to hurt you."

The room is silent except for a few scattered sniffles.

"Do you still love me?" she finally asks.

My heart rushes out to her. I get a little closer, reach out to lightly touch her leg.

When I try to draw my hand back Baby Girl holds it in place.

"It's all right," she assures me at the same time I'm tryna say:

"Of course I still love you. Why wouldn't I?"

Our words stumble into each other like A Buncha Drunks on Fight Nite.

"Because…," Baby Girl begins, but the thought lies incomplete.

"Because of this," she passes her good hand from her head down to her feet.

"Because of **what**," I whisper forcefully. "Because some asshole **fucked you over**?

That don't make you **Damaged**; or…or *Spoiled* or somethin."

Damaged.

Spoiled.

Ruined.

This is the Archaic Thinkin that had people Back In The Day puttin they raped

Loved Ones away in Nunneries & Stuff; cause no man would ever Touch Em Again.

What Bullshit.

"Some people are so Funny Time," Baby Girl observes remorsefully.

I rest my forehead against Baby Girl's, look deep into her eyes and hold her left hand

(cause I **know** that one don't hurt).

"That Might Be True but I'm not Some People. I'm Obie One:

The Man Who Loves You. Have I ever been Funny Time about you?"

Our foreheads still touchin Cess shakes her head and drops her eyes.

I wish I could hold her in my arms, I wish this would all **Go *Away***,

but I **begged** God tosend Baby Girl back to me In Any Condition

and **damn it** I'm a **Get** Her Better.

Now she says to me:

"OB I hurt so bad."

"Where at?"

"My pussy. My pussy is **hurting** me."

Not My Department.

"Hold on Baby Girl; let me get you some help."

My soggy underwear is drippin all across the floor, all over my bedroom rug, and

all down the hallway and the stairs, but I can't think about that now.

I gotta find Mommy.

1 ᴮᴳ

The blood pool under me has grown quite large.

And, if Einstein rapes me *one more time*, I think I'll *DIE*, **always;** right-on-the-spot.

"Kill-me-now or let-me-go," I demand.

Einstein appears perplexed, like he doesn't know what to do.

Let-me-help-you-out, Son:

***RELEASE* ME.**

"You'll tell on me," he predicts, his tone decidedly sullen.

"No, I won't," I sigh wearily.

"Promise?" he asks; almost bizarrely, surreally, childishly optimistic.

"Nigga please. *Princess Raped By Crazy Ex* is **not**-a-headline you'll see in *my* lifetime."

***Trust* me.**

This seems convincing enough; pointing to the bathroom, Einstein says:

"Go clean yourself up."

As the child-of-a-doctor I can Name This Tune in my sleep:

Wash-away-the-evidence.

This is so, so very *alright with me.*

A shower is all I can manage with one good arm.

There's a tremendous pounding in my pussy, which feels almost swollen shut,

but what on me *isn't* swollen after the night I had?

There are no words to even *begin* to describe what my behind feels like.

Best I can tell you is: it's sort-of-like I ate broken glass; it cut me up on the way out.

My whole inner thigh area is tender;

there's so much blood caked on my legs, my thighs, my snatch; it turns my stomach.

I scrub-and-scrub-and-scrub; the water at the bottom of the tub runs red.

Eventually I have to accept there is little more I can do in my present physical state.

My energy is deserting me, I hardly scrape up the wherewithal to towel myself dry.

I don't have any panties to hold a pad in place; don't feel like going to get some.

Only with the greatest of efforts do I manage to insert a tampon.

It makes me hurt *so, so very much more.*

My outfit is tattered, a blood-encrusted mess; I cannot possibly put this thing back on.

I guess I'll have to.

I rinse the skirt in the sink;

the interlock fabric should dry swiftly in the LA-summer-heat.

After redressing I risk a look in the mirror.

My face is swollen but not-badly-discolored yet; a few more hours, though...

"May I please get some ice for my face?" I ask/pray this does not provoke this clown.

Einstein hands me a bag of frozen corn.

"You ready?" he asks harshly.

I nod.

I want to go home so *badly*.

But, I remember not to say that *out loud* this time.

Obie's gate; I get dumped rather unceremoniously; Einstein hauls "major ass."

"Good riddance" to "bad rubbish."

I lean on the gate, search my brain for the magic numbers to grant me entrance.

How did Einstein get past Obie's complicated security system?

Nicole knows the code; Toya must have, also:

Obie had it changed after she tore up his Porsche.

I know the code myself; right now it eludes me.

Does Einstein?

If so, how did he get it? The same way he keeps getting my cell phone number?

Does that mean he's coming back?

Lord, I *pray* not; as long as that bastard is out there I will never feel safe again.

Not wanting to disturb anyone I stand there until it comes to me.

Blessed Lord Jesus, Holy Spirit, Heavenly Father and Savior, I am **HOME**.

I am *alive*

and *I am **home**.*

From Obie's gate to his front door is one *hell* of a long haul:

A mission, a troop, a journey, a vision quest.

Whatever the lingo of your day it's a *long walk*, **damn it;** I haven't slept in two days.

Mentally, I berate myself for not calling someone to get me, but

I've-come-too-far-to-turn-back-now, might as well keep-on-walking.

So, so very strange; but "Twenty-Five Miles," by Edwin Starr pops into my head.

That song is as old as Obie.

My Uncle BB had all that great-old-shit.

This song was on a forty-five; those seven inch circles of vinyl you had to put a piece of plastic in the middle of so it would fit on your record player.

But who remembers 45's anymore? Or record players?

By the time I was born 45's were giving way to 12 inch singles,

but these days who even remembers vinyl?

That's like saying "eight track."

No, they-just-don't-make-'em-like-they-used-to.

You figure.

When I get home though I'll have to download me some Edwin Starr.

The words motivate me; I start to sing out loud

I'm a twenty-five miles from home 'Girl/ My feet are hurtin mighty bad

Now I been walkin for three days/ And two lonely nights

You know that I'm mighty sad

But I got a nigga waitin for me/ That's gonna make this trip worthwhile

You see OB's got the kinda lovin and a kissin/ To make this 'Girl go stone wild

So I got-ta keep on/ walk-in/ uh-huh/ I got to walk on

Let me tell you now

I-I-I-I-I'm so tired

But I just can't lose my stride

Monsieur Starr had me *motivated* baby.

When my legs felt like they were going to drop *off* I kept on singing.

OB's *waiting* for me.

He's gonna make this trip worth while.

Oh *Lord,* I hurt all over; what ever natural anesthetic my body was pumping out

has worn off; once again I am suffering.

Each foot fall brings a new wave of torture, ***plus***,

These-shoes-are-*not*-made-for-walkin, child.

And: *One a these days/ these boots are gonna/ walk all o-ver you.*

Damn, Uncle BB had some great records.

My mind is wandering; one of the side-effects-of-hunger?

I'll need more than a Snickers to make *this* right.

I am sorely tempted to lie down right here by the road for a minute;

but we-all-know: I'll never-get-up-again.

So I gotta keep on…walk-in…

On top of everything else I feel hot, sticky, nasty.

So nasty.

When Einstein dropped me off the first fingers of sunlight were reaching

tentatively across the sky; the sun has now strengthened its grip.

I want to sit in my tub and **scrub/ douche/ *everything***.

You-name-it; I just want to feel clean *inside*-and-*out*.

Xena put so much effort into this dress, what a shame I'll never wear it again.

My poor house is torn up, too.

Somehow I have to get back there, clean it up, wash that ugly stain out my rug.

Oh Lord; I think I'm going to pass out.

No. I ***can't***.

I've come-too-far to die-by-the-roadside.

And I ***know*** He-didn't-bring-me-this-far-to-leave-me, but:

Lemme tell you now

I-I-I-I-I'm so tired

But I just can't lose my stride

Off in the distance now I see our house; believe me:

nothing has ever looked sweeter.

The closer (*I get to you*), the more (*you make me see*).

I have to stop this now.

The closer *I get to the house* the more *I can make out.*

Obie is *still* on the porch swing?!

Only now he's upside down: "stressing."

Poor baby; if I were Obie I'd probably have had a nervous breakdown by now.

I guess he must see-me-too: he's flipped himself upright, curled into a ball.

That Obie is "mad" flexible, Jack;

he can fold that big-ass-body into the size of an *envelope.*

It kind of reminds me of that *one* dude on "The X Files" who folded himself up;

hid on a cart. That was when "The X Files" was *the **shit***; when they dealt with

weird-human-anomalies, not that crazy, outer-space-horse-shit.

Before I sit I have to put my leg under me, take the pressure off my raggedy rectum.

Obie is all stiff—*pardon me*---***tense***; his back turned-to-me and everything.

It doesn't take a genius to tell he's upset.

When Obie went off with Toya I had all but convinced myself he had sex with her.

That's what Obie's thinking now; that I had real, actual, sex-by-choice with Einstein.

How do I know this?

I've been with Obie a long time; he acted this way when I was sleeping with Barry.

At first I was going to keep what happened to myself;

make up some lie to explain my face.

The way Obie is looking right now I *can't*:

Can't do that to *him*, can't do that to *us*.

Obie isn't getting my "message," it's so, so very *damn hard* to get the words out.

I'm pretty sure he has at least an inkling of what went down, only he's not accepting it.

I need him to make it *easy* for me, he's yelling at me, I'm afraid he's going to blow.

And I so, so very need to go lie down.

OH MY *DAMN*.

Obie grabbed my broken arm.

It is the-*worst-pain-ever*: **excruciating**.

I shriek; Obie drops my arm like it burned his fingers; under-able to face this anymore

I run-for-it; my stupid slides trip me up; I crash arm-first onto the stairs.

Ain't too-much-more of this *arm* shit I can take.

Why they all attack Obie like he tried to kill me or something?

You figure.

Me? I'm heading for my room, locking the door behind me.

Now, I've-been-told that Out-of-control-Obie is a "myth;"

something of an "urban legend."

Well the nigga **portraying** Out-of-control-Obie just kicked my door in.

Is there a Black Man on this *planet* who knows how to *leave-me-the-fuck-alone*?

I think not.

Obie demands to know what happened to me. Let's see now…

I left the house *with* the crazy-ex-boyfriend; *without* the pads.

Took "crazy" by my house, figured he'd get-his-shit-and-split.

Disabled the alarm system designed to protect my-dumb-ass.

Then got the *shit* beat outta me, raped backwards-and-forwards fifty-leven times.

All this while watching "said asshole" destroy the couch it took *three weeks to find*.

And he wants me to say *all of this* in **front of people**?!?

Really *though*.

Stop asking me *dumb* shit; I-hate-it when a nigga asks *stupid questions*.

If Obie can graduate valedictorian of an exclusive private school

he can *damn well figure out* what-the-hell-happened-to-me, know what I'm sayin?

What does he need, a *map* or something?

I'll draw him a *map* a'ight.

BAM.

I hit him with the panties *and* the fucked-up-bra that cut-my-tittie.

You know that fool slid right off the bed; onto the floor in a *swoon*?

Who does *that*?

I *almost* feel bad for him.

Almost.

But my ass is hurting too much right now.

Maybe after I finish feeling sorry for *myself*, I can work Obie into my schedule.

No telling how long that'll take though so Obie *might **not** want to* hold-his-breath.

Damn.

He's having an asthma attack.

Two hits off of Uncle BB's inhaler, we're right back to Stupid Questions 101.

Why didn't I *call*??!!

On **what**??

You try getting a call through on these little-pieces-formerly-known-as-a-cell phone

(or LPFKAACP for short).

Where was I?

Why did I go home?

Aren't you on your period?

DUH!

Check-the-rug, Buddy.

When Obie says "panic button" though?

That fucks me up; can't bluster my way through that one.

Freak gives himself up as the-person-*bold-enough*-to-show-me-how-to-jimmy the alarm.

Obie and I have been fighting over that thing since Obie first had it installed.

He always felt I took neither the alarm system nor my safety seriously enough;

he was right: I fucked that one up all by myself.

Obie's going to kill me; I so, so very can't take that right now. Undergoing a

complete-attitude-overhaul, I start sniveling like a child caught playing in traffic:

Only I got hit-by-the-car, know what I'm sayin?

Obie fixes to leave; the thought that Einstein could come back at any time

frightens the shit out of me; Mommy makes Obie promise to stay downstairs.

Mommy wants to "talk."

I-don't-want-to.

Mommy wants me to see-a-doctor.

Don't want to do that either.

Hood hollers:

"Obie's on TV."

So much for he'll-be-downstairs.

"What channel's he on?" Mommy yells back.

What channel *wasn't* he on?!?

Flick, flick, flick, flick: everywhere you turned there was Obie.

Oh *look*.

They're hauling Einstein's "rental" out of the ocean.

One caption reads:

Obie One Has Identified The Body.

So Einstein's dead.

I know I should feel some-semblance-of-relief; I-feel-nothing.

Like Einstein's death could erase, cancel out, what I've *been* through.

Nigga please.

I'm numb, empty, dead inside; the news coverage isn't helping any.

Ninety-nine variations on how "poor Albert," despondent because, after

being-by-her-side-for-so-long, Princess *dumped* him, drives himself into "the drink."

What a **crock**.

Did anybody *ask* me?

Does anybody **care**??

You figure.

"And you-want-to-know why *I won't see* a doctor," I say to Mommy.

Who does *that*??!!

That's when I realize it's Sunday.

I need help getting ready; they won't allow me to bathe.

If I ever hope to get near a drop of water again I'd better confess now.

"If you're worried about me washing away any evidence, I already did; at the house."

"Oh, **Cess**," Mommy wails, looking/sounding majorly disappointed.

In fact, it sounded a lot like how-could-you-*do*-such-a-thing, to *me*.

"He made me, Mommy, but I would have washed anyway.

I had to get that shit *off* me."

I sound perilously close to hysteria, even to my own ears;

into the tub I go.

Next Problem:

I can't get the tampon out.

Two forces are at work here. One: I don't have the strength.

Two: it just-plain-hurts-too-much; I can't make myself do it.

Can't Nobody Do You Like Jesus.

Pastor Maclean was singing-my-song when he spoke about going-through-a-trial:

if *this* isn't a trial, then, *honey*: nothing in my life will ever be.

Tired as I was I tried hard to concentrate,

making a mental note to read back over those passages in Matthew when I get home.

Pastor said sometimes God changes you/sometimes he changes your circumstances.

I think that's what He's done with me: changed me so I can "deal."

What's done-is-done; no sense crying-over-spilt-milk.

As a "survivor," Uncle Tommy says one's focus ought to be

that one has made it through,

not *what* one has made it through.

Really though.

If I keep replaying what happened to me, I'll be crazy by nightfall.

After saying that even Jesus needed prayer the night before his imprisonment,

Pastor opens the altar for prayer.

I head straight for Pastor Julia, she's-been-through-it, too. Way too many women have.

Why Lord?

Why do so many women suffer at the hands of some-sick-man?

What's *that* all about?

I'm not questioning Your Judgment, Father.

I simply seek "clarification:" a-better-understanding, that's all.

I guess I lost consciousness; the next thing I know we're back home.

Obie wants to carry me, I feel like...

I-can-make-it-on-my-own, you know what I'm sayin?

It's rough though: I have to lean on Obie several times. The turf between the-car-door

and the-front-door stretches out before me like the road between the gate and the house.

Twenty-five-miles.

My feet are hurtin **mighty** bad, y'all.

And the-journey's-just-begun; the stairs loom large in front of me.

Climbing them will be like climbing Mount Everest: daunting; yet:

I am determined-to-succeed.

I don't know who's in charge of this expedition;
but either she forgot-to-inform-my-legs or they are guilty-of-insubordination.
Too weary to go on, nothing to go downstairs to, too-damned-sore for Obie to carry,
I am **stuck**.
I seriously consider sitting right on the stairs; my-butt-would-make-me-pay:
in church I liked-to-*died*, always.
Sinking to my knees I take a few deep breaths,
gather my energy, use Obie as a crutch, make it to my room.
The room that doesn't have a door on it.
O gets pretty upset: I don't want to go to his room.
He accepts my explanation: I-need-to-be-in-my-own-personal-space quite well, though.
Everything in *here* is still in*tact;* in its *place;* I **need** that sense-of-order right now.
Need Obie with me, too.
Exhaustion engulfs me; desperate for sleep I close my eyes; every time I roll over
something hurts; wakes me up; my body feels nasty again; I need another bath.
Before I get into the tub I take another stab at removing that stupid tampon.
Can't do it.
It takes a lot of coaxing; Xena agrees to do it for me; but *Oh*:
Why it feels like it's ripping me on the way out though?
You figure.
Cause this is now way-past-unfair.
That's-not-all-that-rips-through-me: a scream does also; sends Xena scrambling for cover.
Wailing, wailing, from the pain; from despair;
I'm about two seconds from hitting the floor.
Obie catches me, gets me in the tub; calmer somehow, I look to him.
He's standing there looking terrified, under-sure; I must look a *natural* **wreck**.
I want his arms around me; I **need** this; I hurt so *much,* Lord: so **much**.
*Why won't this pain **go away**?*
I ask O if he's scared to touch me; he says he doesn't really know *what* to do;
I'll-buy-*that*-for-a-dollar.
I wonder if he still loves me; I ask: I don't want things to be *different* because of this.
If people, especially Obie, start treating me like I'm short-bus-special or something,
I'll scream. He says when it comes to me, he could never be "funny time."

I-don't-know, though: suppose he never feels "passionate" about me again?

Everything is hurting really badly now: my pussy, my butt hole;

all up by my clit is burning like it's raw or something; Obie runs to get Mommy for me.

Oh so matter-of-factly, Mommy strips down to her underwear.

This is *so, so **very** worse*:

my nakedness makes me feel *exceedingly embarrassed;*

ashamed.

"*Now*, Princess, we *have to talk*."

With Mommy to comfort me, all alone except for her,

I finally begin to describe my ordeal.

"Oh, *baby*,"

Mommy draws a sharp breath when I tell her how many times Einstein raped me.

Hesitant, Mommy asks for "*specifics*."

This is so-damned-hard.

"All together maybe five times on top and three more from the back,"

I squeak into the back of my hand.

"It was a *long night*. Please don't tell Obie," I make Mommy promise me.

She agrees on one condition.

"You have to see a doctor."

Aunty Wiz arranges for me to see her GYN on the "DL." I had some vaginal tearing that

needed stitching, trauma to my cervix, a tear near my clitoris where Einstein

snatched out my tampon. All this caused my vagina to swell up something fierce.

Groggy from the medication I try thanking Dr. Estes; the words come out slurred.

"I deal with many rape victims who are reluctant to go to the authorities.

Women aren't always treated with respect or with the sensitivity they deserve."

The next thing I know we're at the hospital.

Why these bitches wait until I'm good-and-doped-up to take me, though.

Fuck them.

Doctor Dumb-ass wants to know how I broke my arm.

"Slammed it in the car door."

I can smell the-smoke-of-speculation rising from this "cat's" brain cells.

"What happened to your face?"

"Hit it on the car door."

My ribs? My sternum? The bruises on my back and chest? The cut under my breast?

"I fell down. After I hit the car door."

You think he bought it?

Young demanded a full cataloguing of my injuries in the chart.

Something else to end up on the Internet *por la manana*.

Too tired to argue, I let my father have his way.

And here comes Officer Tyson.

I'm "too tired" to talk-to-him-too.

Believe that.

Patched-up-and-medicated, my body yearns for sleep; mercifully, this time it arrives.

Jesus-*is*-real.

The room is dark, quiet; how long have I been asleep?

Out of nowhere comes this panicky feeling: my jerking wakes up Obie.

Both his knees are drawn up to his chest; his head is slumped forward;

my head still rests in his lap.

O *has* to be under-comfortable. I'm being so, so very selfish,

but I feel like some catastrophe is right around the corner, only he can protect me.

"Flashback?" he asks tenderly.

As I nod Obie rubs my head in comfort.

"Long as I'm here, nothin will happen to you," Obie promises me.

Still, people: I can't shake this feeling of dread. Xena pokes her head into the room.

"Tugie wants to know if Princess is hungry."

"No," I tell her, but "Father Knows Best," Obie One contradicts me.

"Fix her some Soup Secrets noodle soup with toast and a cup a chamomile tea."

Obie must be fixing to eat it himself.

I haven't eaten a thing in two days; I'm not hungry yet. In fact:

my stomach is balled up in a knot.

Oh-so-patiently though, Obie spoons soup into me.

I manage to squeeze down almost half the bowl, Obie downs the rest of it: upending the

bowl, using the toast to extricate those few noodles stubbornly clinging to the sides.

We both doze off again;

the pain sends a not-so-gentle-reminder that it's time-for-my-meds.

There's no way O can sleep like this all night; I ask him to help me across the hall.

He's right: this bed is way more comfortable.

The water filled mattress alleviates most of the pressure on my bruises;

the heat is so soothing.

Should've asked Obie for a waterbed.

Full of codeine I fall asleep, Obie stretched out beside me.

I'm sleeping so much I can't keep track of time.

How long have I lain here?

An hour or two?

A *day* or two?

You figure.

It's the medicine, of course.

There's no other explanation for me sleeping so much.

Sometimes Obie is asleep beside me.

Sometimes he's sitting up next to me, caressing my head or my back.

Sometimes I'm all alone. I hate those times.

A nameless, faceless fear perches on the edge of my bed when I'm alone; suffocates me.

Knowing I couldn't make a "clean one" if my life depended on it only makes it worse.

My muscles have locked up on me; I'm finding it difficult to move.

Thank God I'm never alone for long.

This time it's the urge to pee that wakes me up.

My entire private area is tender, swollen;

when I'm finished, I have to pour some water over myself, wipe extra carefully.

The "dirty" feeling sneaks up on me, like slime or something is covering my body.

I don't want to wake Obie; I run a shower myself.

Damn it's hard to get out of this pajama under-assisted; somehow I manage.

Makes me feel sort of proud of myself.

On the ledge I discover a hundred-year-old-bottle of my body wash.

I was in O's room so often I've got mass stuff all over the place.

Wonder how he explains it to his girlies?

*Any*way…

I start out with that little bally thing; it's not doing the trick:

way too soft; the washrag is, too.

Onto the loofa we go: you can't-stop-progress, right?

This is much better, *except*…

I don't know if it's the body wash or *what*: I don't feel I'm rinsing *cleanly* enough,

know what I mean Vern?

I still feel *slimy*.

So, I try the deodorant soap: that's supposed to be anti-bacterial-and-all.

I scrub *dumb hard*, especially my breasts-and-thighs, nothing is working right.

I end up all "fetal" at the bottom of the shower stall, crying/scrubbing at the same time.

Don't even notice Obie standing there.

"That feeling don't *wash away,* Baby Girl. *Trust* me; I *know.*

All you doin is hurtin yourself; makin your skin all raw. Lemme do it for you."

Under the still-running shower Obie soaps a wash cloth, lathers me all over.

While he washes me he murmurs in my ear.

"It'll be okay, Baby Girl, you'll see. We'll get through this together; I *promise.* "

Obie cradles me until the water gets cold. Then he carries me back to the bed

where I cling to his damp body for what seems like hours before I fall asleep.

Surprise, surprise, surprise:

said somebody named Gomer Pyle.

That's what Uncle BB tells me, anyway; I don't even know who Gomer Pyle is.

You figure.

However…according to Obie I have been laying here three days; I'm sick of bed.

I *want* to go downstairs; *don't* want to suffer any "funny looks," know what I'm saying?

Obie has been selected "Town Crier;" sent to announce my impending arrival,

to instruct the masses on "How to Treat a Wounded Princess."

If anyone disobeys my royal edict: off-with-his-head.

I *mean* it.

The popcorn is popped, everyone is in place.

We're about to have a "Sex in the City" phenomenon.

Mommy-and-them stayed an extra week.

I'm not *under-grateful*; *sorry they stayed*;

I feel *guilty:*

Mommy, my dad and Uncle Tommy are all missing work because of *my* stupid ass.

Plus, you know my dad has that "drinking problem;"

is already in "hot water" at the hospital.

Oh *look*: he's knocking one back now; in a minute Young will be *fucked up.*

After three days, you'd think *something* would be easing up a little, but *NO.*

Everything still hurts-like-hell.

Thanks to "temporary insanity," I've managed to wash *all the skin off my ass* so I'm raw to boot.

Oh *well*.

Obie spread a bunch of big pillows on the floor so I would be comfortable.

Somehow I end up hitting the cushions harder than Obie intends; in pain, I gasp.

The way he's acting? You'd think he'd almost killed me.

Now he's fussing-with-the-pillows.

"*Stop fussing over me*," I bark,

(only it slips out that way before I can tame-it-into-civility).

O gives me that: I'm-trying-to-fucking-help-here look.

They're calling my number.

Halfway into the second episode, I'm hurting pret-ty bad-ly.

Way-too-proud to ask-for-help, I keep shifting around,

hoping to find a position I can live with.

"*This*," O snaps tersely, holding a pillow over his head, "is a *king size pillow*.

I have *two of them left*.

Let me know *where* you need them so I can *place them there, a'ight*?

I *can't hear my picture* with all that *moanin* you doin."

You can't hear period, *bitch:* years of loud music left your ass hard-of-hearing.

If Mommy-and-them weren't here Obie would have put the Closed Captioning on.

That's what he gets for making fun of BB, who's not even here to use as an excuse.

*Any*way…

We try a couple of things; none pans out.

Sitting puts too much pressure on my bottom.

I can't see when I lie down, plus it makes my back hurt.

Rolling on my side hurts either my chest or my broken arm.

I'm aggravated; the more helpful Obie tries to be, the more angry I become.

Why? I feel "babied."

"*Stop*," I shout, on the verge of tears;

"Stop treating me like there's 'something wrong' with me."

Clearly aggravated also, Obie draws in a deep breath; lets it out slowly.

"What do you mean 'like' there's 'somethin wrong' with you?

You *broke-the-fuck-up*, held together with a *ace bandage* and some *sutures*,

a' *course* there's 'somethin wrong' with you."

"Only my *body* is broken, not my *mind*. You don't have to act '*differently.*' If

you're angry or pissed *BE THAT. Don't* be all: I-can't-get-mad-at-Cess: she's-hurt."

A steady stare is the only response I get at first.

"Do you really think you'd feel better if I yell at you about these pillows?"
O finally asks.

"*Yes*," I answer emphatically. "Then I'll know you still see me as a 'normal person.'"

"Why I gotta act like you 'normal' all a' a sudden? Who *does* that anymore?"

I just have to laugh; all the "Queens" is coming out of his ass right now.

Obie sounds like The Nanny.

Or Edith Bunker.

"You know what your problem is?" Obie questions,

"Anything I do, you think you-can-do-better. Obie gets beat up, there you are--
all-beat-up-too. Obie breaks his foot? You gotta go-break-a-arm-and-shit.
I think you need a-life-a-your-own so you can stop-relivin-mine's."

I laugh until my body pulses with pain, then I laugh some more.

"Nigga *please. Your* problem is, you've got-to-be-the-first to do *every*thing.
Get beat up? Obie dashes for the head of the line. Break a bone? There you are,
jumping-up-and-down screaming, 'Ooh *me*! Pick *me*! *I* want to be first!'"

Okay, it *really wasn't funny,* but it *was* something for us to laugh about;
and you have to admit: it does sort of sum-up-our-relationship, *n'est-ce pas*?

"I know what'll make you feel better."

Obie puts a pillow in his lap, scoops me up, deposits me on it.

WOW, was that better; in his arms was the best place I could be.

My VDRL came back Negative.

So did my "clap smear" and my prelim HIV test.

Obie paid for that one-expensive-test all the porno stars in 'Frisco use.

It's supposed to be more "accurate."

You figure.

Anyway...so-far-so-good, right?

Even though I took the "high end" test, I'll still have to retest in six months;
again in a year.

That's a crazy long time to be under-certain but:

I'll just have to pray over this one.

Meanwhile, I've slept away another two days.

I don't want to take my medicine anymore;

when I don't it hurts so badly, I wish I had *died,* always.

That's when Obie fixes me another "codeine cocktail;"
it's off-to-la-la-land (not LA, silly) for me.
While-I-was-sleeping, (which is a different movie from *Sleepless In Seattle*)
Uncle BB and Uncle Tommy made up; they also ended up with Rahshaun's kids.
As Confucius Say: Rotsa Ruck;
they'll definitely need it; those kids are WILD.
They got the-right-one in Uncle BB though.
This will give him something to do with his retirement besides sleep-off-his
muscle-relaxants/complain that Uncle Tommy doesn't love him anymore.
Nigga please.
Mommy-and-all-them are fixing to go home. Using a couple of jumbo pillows
Obie props me up enough to make the ride out to the airport less torturous.
Do you think God is mad at me?
I couldn't make it to church; but manage to get-my-ass-to-the-airport.
I hope not, I'm on the shitty-end-of-the-stick as it is.
Malcolm leans against me; it so, so very hurts-like-hell; I keep-it-to-myself.
Doc's trip to Cali has been a total bust.
He came out here to see *My Famous Sister Princess;*
ended up seeing *Baby Girl Gets Assaulted* instead.
The poor thing won't even be around for *The Recovery.*
Next time he better check-the-ticket before he enters the theater.
What a helluva memory to leave Doc with, though:
his sissy broke-up/ stitched-up/ *fucked*-up.
One day I'll make all of this up to him.

Paparazzi dog us all the way there.
That's why my windows are tinted, man.

2 OB

Baby Girl looks Pale and Wan; **Lifeless**, you feel me?
Like she Slippin Into Darkness, only Baby Girl ain't headed for no **Nod**,
I think she **Fadin**.
Aunty Wiz assures us that her doctor knows how to Keep Her Mouth Shut.
How would **she** know?
Regardless, I take Aunty's word for it. I ain't got no other **choice**, really.
The wait seems interminable, givin me ample time to Beat Up On Myself.
"I should a never let her go," I toss out to No One In Particular
(I think he runs with that **One** Cat, Somebody).
"Well, dropping an I Told You So does **not** seem like The Move here,"
Uncle BB responds kindly.
"Don't worry; I already did that for you," I notify him.
Both he and Young chuckle.
"You always been strange," Young comments.
You ain't never lied, bruh.
They been in there for a Mighty Long Time, and it's makin me worried.
"What do you think is wrong with Baby Girl?" I ask Young.
"I Hesitate To Speculate. Let's see what the doctor says."
Fair enough.
Thinkin back on that scene at the house, and on how Baby Girl's been feelin,
Einstein might a wrecked Baby Girl's insides some.
Lord I hope not.
Sometimes girls get so messed up from a brutal rape they can't have kids no more.
That would be **Fucked**. *Up*.
Somethin **else** for me to worry bout, Like I Need **That**.
What I **need** is to Lighten Up and Sit My Behind Down:
stop Wearin A Hole in these folks floor.
No sooner had my butt hit the cushion than Dr. Lady shows back up,
givin Young The High Sign.
Next stop?
Malibu General.

Is it me or is everyone Lookin At Us Funny?

Gotta be that fuckin Non Stop News Coverage,

I peep the nurses watchin it at they station.

One a them has the decency to change the channel when she sees me.

Then she changes the channel on the set in the waitin area.

Several staff members greet me with a Hey Obie and a Half Wave,

like they Under Sure bout What's Goin On & All.

Oh **Well**.

It really ain't helpful that me and Hood still look like **horseshit** either.

At least Baby Girl is dark; you can see me and Hood's bruises clear cross the room.

The same nurse who graciously changed the TV's steps up to me and says:

"You want me to take a look at that Obie?"

My wounds is a couple days old already but Why The Hell Not, you feel me?

Besides, I had Hit That- Way Back When and was still On Good Terms with her.

"How about Hood?" she furthers.

How do I know? I shrug so she goes and asks him herself. Girlfriend sits us in Triage

while she calls for our charts. Between Bar Room Brawls and Horsin Around

we been here so many times they should Name A Wing after us.

My blood pressure is sky high. Girlfriend raises her eyebrow at me.

"Did you ever see your doctor about your blood pressure Obie?"

Silently I cuss myself out.

"I'll take that as a No. You know why your pressure's so high don't you?"

"The strain a keepin a Multi Million Dollar Operation afloat?"

Girlfriend crosses her arms and looks at me harshly.

Since I Eat Right and Exercise Daily

it must be the **same shit** she tells me **every time I fuckin come *in* here**.

"Cocaine," she pronounces professionally.

See???

What I tell you?!

"So I sniff a little," I complain.

"When was the last time you got high?"

"Yesterday," I admit.

"Sniffin is going to kill you Obie."

"So you keep sayin. Meanwhile: I'm Still Here."

But She Right Though and I know it.

My blood pressure is **outrageous** for a cat my age and in my physical condition.

The last time I was here the doc told me my heart may be affected

but I never went for the tests.

No Time.

Girlfriend, whose real name is Tracey, cleans our already crusted over wounds,

takin a Good Long Look at Hood's neck.

"Fight get outta hand this time fellas?"

You *think*?

"So what happened with the guy who drove off the highway?"

BINGO.

Me and Hood exchange a knowin glance.

Tracey ain't wanna **Tend Our Crusty Cuts**;

she wanna *Investigate*.

Do this bitch think cause I **fucked** her I'm a tell her **all a my biz?**

As **If**.

"What it *look* like Tracey?" I blurt angrily.

Put off by my sudden anger Tracey Backs It Up a little.

"I didn't mean any harm Obie. I've been in LA long enough to know the press rarely gets it right so I figured I'd ask."

No; what she *figured* was: she'd get a **Exclusive** to pass along to the Other Nurses.

Oh **Well**.

I'm Bout **Done** Son.

I rise to Make My Exit but Hood places a calmin hand on my arm.

I guess I **am** gettin Lightweight Carried Away.

Remind me to ask Hood if he Tapped This Bitch too.

"The news makes it seem like Obie beat Dude up and Brokenhearted,

he Took a Dive."

"I ain't **touch** him," I exclaim heatedly.

"Dude got pissed cause Princess ain't want his ass no more so he beat her up then Took That Flight," Hood explains patiently.

"They say the corpse shows Signs Of A Struggle," Tracey replies,

Like That Mean *I* Did It.

"Baby Girl was **defendin** herself," I tell this Stupid Broad;

"Read the chart, you'll see."

"She fights like a man," Hood adds.

"Was she hurt badly? Who's handling that one?"

Nosy **Bitch**.

Standin in the doorway is Officer Tyson, observin us.

"You about finished here Tracey?" he inquires.

"Give me a sec."

That's bout all it takes too,

then me and Hood follow Officer Tyson down the hall to a Neutral Corner.

"I just came from visiting your girlfriend," he remarks,

"She's jacked up pretty bad; broken arm, fractured sternum, couple a cracked ribs,

multiple bruises. Wanna tell me what happened?"

Not... **Really**.

Flippin it on him I ask:

"What'd *she* say?"

"**She** said she slipped and fell against the car and the car door slammed on her."

Wow. Baby Girl must still be Kinda High to come up with **that** Crappy Ass Story.

At least she didn't say she Fell Down The Stairs.

"What do you want from **me** Ty? I wasn't there when it happened."

"Well I've got a battered woman in the ER, a bruised corpse at the morgue and **you**,"

he points to me, "are the Man In The Middle Of It All. What's up?"

White people should **never** say What's Up;

even if they **do** have Southern Cracker Roots.

"I think I should talk to my lawyer," I feel at this point.

"No one's blaming you for **any**thing," Ty is quick to assure me.

Sure you're right.

"What channel you watchin Ty? Cause I been watchin the news all day now

and it looks to **me** like I'm **The Fall Guy** here."

Ty starts to say somethin else but I hafta cut him off.

Young is givin me The High Sign again. It's Time To Roll.

Baby Girl's doped to the gills.

They done put some big ole draws on her.

Some people call them bloomers, we call them **blowfers**.

She don't want me to leave her so I don't. I ain't never really been in her room before;

it's just like her room back home, in NY.

That must be why she wanted to come in here.

41

Back wedged against the wall I bend my knees and put both my feet up on the bed.

That's as comf'table as I'm a get cause this is a tiny ass bed.

Shit, it's a tiny ass **room** while you **playin**.

I told Baby Girl this wasn't nothin but a **closet** but she **insisted**.

So I made it into a bedroom just for her.

Anything for my Baby Girl; you know that.

Young told Uncle BB Einstein tore up Baby Girl's insides but she gonna be a'ight,

Thank God For Jesus. Ty told me all about Baby Girl's broken bones.

How the Hell did she walk all the way from my gate like that?

That shit is some *miles*, dog. And how did she make it to **church**?

I don't under**stand**. Baby Girl is so messed up yet she Keep On Keepin On.

Don't she realize how **hurt** she is?

And the **bruises**, man. The bruises is **visible** on her skin:

all over her **back**, across her **chest** and one on her side look like a **Boot** Mark.

There's some real bad ones on the inside a her thighs that make me hesitate to

contemplate how she got em.

And each tittie has four marks that look **exactly** like fingers.

How hard does one Hafta Squeeze in order to leave Fingerprints in someone's Tits?

Boy that bastard better be glad he's dead. What I would do to him is *Not* What's Up.

I wish I could get my Bible but I'm scared to move.

Stevie Wonder's "Higher Ground" is playin somewhere downstairs.

That's what I need, to Keep Tryin For Higher Ground.

I **know** I had said I would take Baby Girl back in **any** condition

but I been Lightweight Angry bout the condition she came back in.

I'm feelin like: If God could send Baby Girl back to me all broke up,

He could a sent her back to me Whole, you feel me?

Deep down I know I'm wrong though.

My dumb ass is sittin here **Negotiatin** with *God*.

I must be **retarded**.

This a case a Give A Nigga A Inch & Watch Him Want A Mile.

By Divine Intervention Baby Girl's couch flashes through my mind slappin me outta it.

I been **blessed**, truly *blessed*, to get Baby Girl back **at all**.

Best I **remember** that and **stop quibblin** bout the **condition** she in.

I **will** pray for guidance though cause I don't know **what** I'm doin or even if I'm

strong enough to handle the task ahead a me.

Damn.

I must-a drifted off or somethin.

Baby Girl is twitchin and cryin in her sleep.

I can Name That Tune in One Note.

"Flashback?"

She nods so I stroke her head lightly.

I been there before. Matter fact I **still live there**.

They just Ain't As Bad or Come As Often as they did at first.

After I tell Baby Girl she'll be a'ight she dozes off again. Me?

My back hurts and my legs is crampin up somethin fierce but I'm scared to leave Baby Girl; scared she'll wake up Frightened & Disoriented.

Freak finds me awake.

"Why don't you take a walk or somethin man?"

I demure. My place is here.

"If nothin else I **know** you gotta **pee**. Lemme Cover For You til you get back."

Nature **is** Callin Me, hard as I'm tryna **Ignore** Her Ass.

Freak and me Make That Switch.

As I leave I catch sight a him kissin Baby Girl's forehead, anguish carved into his face.

Then- Damn It To All Hell, when I get downstairs I find I done missed all the action.

Uncle BB **cussed Rahshaun** *out* bout dumpin his kids on us, runnin my bills up, Etc & So On.

Rahshaun got **Confrontational** on Uncle BB.

Who **does** that?

"Whatchu gon do about it? You just a Ole Ass Faggot With—"

Everyone assumes the next word was gon be Arthur-itis.

Too bad Rahshaun never got it out.

That **Ole Ass Faggot** beat the *shit* outta him.

What a **Dumb.** *Move*.

Why niggas persist in callin Uncle BB a Faggot when They Can't Win, Chile is **beyond** me. You really can't blame Rahshaun though.

Last week he didn't know Uncle BB from a can a Lead Based Paint.

Oh Well.

Besides, Uncle BB **prob'ly** whupped Rahshaun's ass for callin him *Old*.

Faggot he Relates To but Old? Now **that's** a title Uncle BB can't tolerate.

The Upshot a all this is: Rahshaun done disappeared *again*. **Damn it**.

I can't win, chile.

"You look like **shit** Obie," Lee comments. "Eat A Little Somethin and Lay Down."

"I **ain't** sleepy and I **ain't** hungry."

What I **am** is *Irritable* and right now **I Don't Care**.

"You won't be doin Baby Girl **or** yourself no good if you collapse."

True That. **Still**, I wave off his concerns and head back upstairs.

"Holla if you need somethin," Freak tells me on his way out.

Yeah, I think to myself, I need you to turn the clock back for me, bruh.

About **three days**.

Can you **Handle** that?

Early early in the mornin I roll over and Baby Girl is gone.

Baby Girl is Weak, and also Doped Up: Very Very Much So,

so I'm worried she might a Fell Somewhere and Hurt Herself.

But no:

I find her laid out at the bottom a the shower stall, **scrubbin at her thighs with a loofa**.

Ouch.

I been here **too** folks and that's a feelin she **won't wash away**, not even a **little** bit.

Crouchin down beside her I try to get the damned sponge from her and believe me:

It's A Chore.

Baby Girl is Sufferin, not just Physically but Mentally.

I don't wanna make it worse by wrestlin with her so I gently pry the loofa out her clenched fist.

Her skin is really raw, she prunin, plus

I **don't** think she 'posed to be **gettin that arm wet**.

Maybe if *I* wash her, some a that Nasty Feelin will Go Away.

This time I wake up way before Baby Girl.

Someone downstairs takes my breakfast order: Grits & Coffee, so I lay lookin at her.

This the first time we been naked in the same bed since all this shit happened and

I ain't turned on in the least.

It **is** a Sensuous Pleasure though.

Kinda reminds me a how much I useta love layin next to Baby Girl before we hooked up.

I stroke her back like I've done a thousand times before, nostalgic for those times when

everything was Easy between us and we didn't have this Rape thing to deal with.

A wave a love washes over me so intense it's indescribable.

I can't believe how much I love this girl.

44

We hafta get married soon.

By evenin Baby Girl is showin Actual Signs A Life.

"Go tell everybody that if they Look At Me Funny

or start treating me Weird or Differently I'm going back upstairs."

Fine. I do that;

put some pillows down and whatnot to make her more comf'table, right?

Then Baby Girl starts **snappin** at me, Gettin On My **Fuckin** *Nerves* & Shit.

I know this inactivity is as hard on Baby Girl as it is on me but *damn*.

I mean **Really** Though.

She don't hafta **Talk** To Me Like That, I'm tryna **help** here.

I try to Maintain but **damn it** I get Lambasted for that too.

I ask if she **really think she'd feel better with me** *hollerin* **at her** and the fool says

Yes.

As **If**.

Baby Girl just bein **Difficult**.

She refuse to accept she been Severely Injured & Concessions Must Be Made for this.

All this Carry On As Usual crap is **Annoyin**, not to mention Nerve Wrackin.

It Passes Quickly though,

in part cause I start teasin Baby Girl bout always followin behind every thing I do.

She flips it on me; teases me bout always havin to be The First To Do Shit.

The 'Girl left out one though.

First to get raped?

Well that would be Obie too.

Baby Girl made it through four eps before windin down.

She need another Cocktail but in Typical Baby Girl Fashion she refuse to take one.

I try holdin her on my lap but Baby Girl moans and groans another hour before givin in.

I never made it back to the marathon, couldn't leave Baby Girl in pain all by herself.

Round midnight somebody puts on "Eye Of The Tiger" by Survivor.

>   *It's the / eye of the tiger / it's the / thrill of the fight...*

Been there, even wrote the book. That's The Problem with America.

Too Much Violence.

My 'Girl ain't doin so well. Her stubborn refusal a her medication leaves her

Battered By Pain for Way Longer Than Necessary.

Eventually Baby Girl takes the damn Cocktail **anyway** so why is she puttin herself, *and* me, *through* this?

Who **does** that??!!

I don't wanna get outta bed no more. I just wanna lay here with my Baby,

willin her to get better. Mommy comes tryna get me up.

When I decline she gets my dad.

"You a'ight Obie?" he asks, full a concern.

"I'm okay," I answer back sorta listlessly.

"Why you don't get up for a little while?"

I explain my Under Willingness to him, same as I did to Mommy.

Shawn comes back at me with Uncle BB, who tries to Drill Sergeant me out the bed.

Closin the door on this whole ep I tell em:

"**Look**, I **ain't** Gettin Up and we **ain't** gon **Fight** About It over the '**Girl**, *a'ight*?!"

Pissed as he is Uncle BB splits. Five minutes later Freak is at the door.

"I'm a spell you so you can go downstairs and get somethin to eat."

Good One.

I ain't gettin out the bed.

"What you eat yesterday, a bowl a grits and some popcorn? Today nothin at all?

You gotta **eat**, bruh."

"Smells Like Mommy in here."

Besides, Freak might put on The Spice Channel and start jerkin off or somethin.

"Call me if she wakes up," I instruct Freak when it's clear he just ain't gon quit.

"No Doubt."

Outta bed I feel Weird & Disoriented.

It feels like everything is movin,

sorta like comin off a long cruise and touchin Dry Land again.

Although I ain't feelin hungry Xanadi stir fries me some Tofu Helper.

I pick at it half heartedly.

"You have to **eat** something," Mommy says forcefully.

You know that tone mother's get.

My reply? I look from Mommy to the plate and back at her again.

"Sweetie," she says a little more kindly,

"I know you wanna be there for Princess. That's Damned Admirable,

but if you don'teat you're gonna collapse and you won't be good for **any**thing."

Now Where Have I Heard This Before?

These people need a Script Doctor.

"Remember them So Called Football Injuries back when you and JR was ten?"
Young declares in a Playful and Good Natured way.
That was Random I think, but me and Hood start to gigglin cause *we* remember.
"They was limpin round for weeks," my dad recalls
"Guess how they **really** got hurt.
Somebody bet Obie ten dollars he couldn't jump out your window."
"On the **second** *floor*??" my father sounds Extremely Shocked.
Me and Hood is *rollin* now: very very much so.
"Yup. Obie hit the ground and fractured both his heels. Then Squared pulls a Me Too
and jumps behind Obie's ass. Well O was doubled over and didn't see Squared jump.
JR tried to scream No but you know Squared's deaf ass couldn't hear him.
JR had to catch Squared and he fell on his can and broke his tailbone."
When it happened it was The Scariest Shit In The Whole Wide World but now?
What a **Hoot**. Me and Hood can't stop laughin.
"I was on the ground tryin not to scream cause my ass hurts so bad,
and BB's dumb ass is goin Uh! Uh! cause **He Wanna Jump Again**.
If I could a Stood Up Straight I would a **whupped his ass**."
"That was Mad Fun," BB croaks, frog-like.
I'm tearin so hard I gotta wipe my eyes. BB's cacklin at the memory his damn self.
Those Were The Days My Friend.
I go to mock BB and end up duckin Just In Time: BB swung a fist at my temple.
I love to tease BB every bit as much as he hates it.
If I sounded Like Shit I'd hate folks Snappin On My Speech too.
Oh Well.
"Come on though," I continue; "that was my First Jump. Remember when Uncle
BB's mom died and he raced me up the side a his old house in Washington?
And when we got to the roof Uncle BB did some ole Wild Ass Batman Move or
some shit, wrappin his belt around the house column and slidin all the way down,
but I did a Cliff Dive off the roof instead?"
"Yeah, *I* remember. I thought you were gonna *kill* yourself," Uncle BB jokes.
"Why you always doin crazy shit like that anyway?" my dad asks me.
"Uncle BB did it **all the time** when *he* was young."
"And that's your Excuse? The BB Clone Strikes Again?"
"No, it's just Thrillin. I like the feelin a Fallin. And Goin Fast. It's Ex*ci*tin."
"It's Damn Foolish is what it is," Mommy offers her opinion.

"Squared does it **too**. We **always** jumpin off a somethin."

"We **careful** though," BB call hisself addin.

"How can you be careful jumpin off a somethin?" Mommy wants to know.

"You gotta know Where To Jump and How," I tell her.

They let this one Marinate for a minute.

"Why you take so many **risks** though?" my father asks again.

"Why y'all gotta have a That Damn Obie attitude toward me; like a *fuckin* **TV show** or somethin. It's Time For 'That Damn Obie' Again Folks. Wonder What He'll Do Today?"

I use my best TV Announcer Voice. Knowin I'm Gettin Upset I head towards the hall.

"***Get back over here***," Mommy yells sharply.

Damn it I'm Too **Old** For This Shit. I turn around slowly.

"I gotta get back upstairs," I mumble through twisted lips;

"Baby Girl might need me."

"Nice Try Obie," Mommy snaps. "Get your ass back here now."

Sullen and Moody I ease myself back into the livin room; slumpin onto the couch.

Evilness is written All Over My Face.

What else can I do though? It's Bad Form to Disobey Your Momma.

Why am I puttin myself through this shit *any*way?

I'm Doin *Fine* without these people.

"I wanna be the first to admit that when you were young,

half the time I didn't know whether to Shoot You or Jump Out The Window."

Why Mommy makes me laugh though?

Who **does** that anymore?

"Never did that mean I didn't care about you or I wished you weren't around.

You were a *Difficult Child* Obie.

Your Nobody Loves Me issues made you Harder To Deal With."

"So you're saying I was The Cause a My Own Effects."

"*Basically*. You acted an ass then pushed people away because you believed,

erroneously, that no one really cared about you."

And I'm supposed to believe it *now,* right?

As If.

Time To Go Upstairs, but when I try to get up Mommy Puts Up A Block.

Trapped by a Two Foot Dynamo I am forced to face this…this…*Inquisition*.

"Mommy even **you** —"

She cuts me off so violently my head spins; givin me The **Only** Murderous Look.

48

"Don't you **dare**. Don't you fuckin *dare* say that to me Obie Price.

I love you like I gave *birth* to your **stupid** ass. How *could* you?

If **I didn't love you** I'd have **turned my back on you** long *time* ago.

And *yes*; **I called you** *Stupid*. As your **momma** *I Can Do That*."

I can't deal with this shit. Pushin Mommy gently to the side I bolt for the stairs again.

This time she grabs me by my 'beater.

I **refuse**, I fuckin *refuse* to cry in front a these people so I swallow back my hurt.

Mommy is steady huggin me; maybe her head comes to the small a my back.

Maybe.

Anyway, I think she cryin.

"I love you Mommy," I tell her, "and I know you love me too.

I done Just Got Tired a Gettin On People's Nerves."

"So why don't you try **Not** Gettin On Their Nerves?"

"That's my whole point: this The Only Obie I Know How To Be.

Y'all all waitin for the day Obie Becomes Normal. That ain't hap'nin captain.

I ain't gon change, and even if I could: why should I?

Why can't y'all accept me for Who & What I Am? Baby Girl does."

No Answer For *That* One, Huh?

Mommy lets me pass.

I ain't gettin out this bed again.

So guess what them niggas do next? They move the party to **my** room.

Mommy crawls *in the bed with us.*

This is All Too Weird for me, specially since none a us has too much on clothin wise.

Poor Baby Girl, out like a candle in the middle a' a hurricane,

don't even know What's Goin On.

I move to the other side a her.

"What's a Born Again Virgin?" Mommy asks.

Now where the Hell did *that* come from???

"A person who gives up sex for their own Personal Growth & Development," I say.

"And you gave up sex be*cause*…?"

"Cause he thought it would make Princess fuck him outta sympathy," Freak jokes.

"Ha-ha-**ha**-bitch *NO*," I reply.

"She didn't give up sex for *you*," Hood says **one** *more* time.

And He Wonders Why I tried to *kill* his ass.

"How many times do I hafta **hear** this shit?! Change The **Record**; This One Got **Ole**."

"Is it as old as She's Gonna Marry Me & Have My Baby?" Barry asks snidely.

"What's your **point** Barry?

Cause it ain't but **one** nigga's ring Baby Girl's wearin and it **damn sure** ain't *yours*."

"You proud a yourself cause you Holdin Out For Marriage?" Hood Tag Teams me.

"Okay fellas; let's get our tempers in **check**, shall we?" Uncle BB decrees.

"Everybody in my *fuckin* **business**; All In The Toilet Bowl & **Don't Know** *Shit*,"

Disgusted, I suck my teeth.

"So tell me **your** story Obie. Mommy's listenin."

"Ain't nothin to tell. Baby Girl had a serious prob with my prolific sex life,

I tried to cut it down and I **couldn't,** so *I* decided, **for myself**, it would be **easier** to

Just Go Cold Turkey. And *Fuck You All*," I add as a afterthought.

"I see it worked for you," Mommy says in wonder.

"They **don't have sex**," Hood sneers. "Or **So They Say**. You call that **Workin**?"

"Yes we do," Baby Girl mutters from her berth on Cloud Nine. "It's The Best Ever."

"Didja hear that?" I gloat, pokin Hood in the side with my finger,

"Baby Girl said The Best Ever. That's a Rave, son. A Five Star Review."

My Inner Child sticks his tongue out at Hood. **His** Inner Child gives me The Finger.

Personally, **I'm** feelin Supremely Satisfied.

"**I thought you said y'all didn't** *have* **sex**?" a thunderstruck Hood asks. "You *lied*?!"

"Nigga, Obie Don't Lie. We ain't sleep together til Oakland," I answer proudly.

But just as suddenly it's my turn to be thunderstruck.

Me and Cess did it seven times.

Seven Whole Times.

Damn.

That was **three weeks ago**. Seems like a Lifetime.

How does one's Whole Life Change In The Blink a' A Eye?

I tune these niggas out; only a insistent tappin on my shoulder rouses me from my daze.

"So how many girls we talkin bout here?" Mommy asks, renewin our convo.

Why does she **ask** me these things? Who *does* that but a mother?

And how does one tell his momma that he *fucks* a lot??

I'm Scratchin My Head here and The Peanut Gallery ain't **helpin** much.

"Twenty girls a week," Freak calls out.

"Nigga it's Twenty Five *Easy*," Hood wagers,

"O ain't turnin **nothin down but his collar**."

What the fuck is this, a auction?

"That's cause I'm a *man*, damn it. Do **You** nigga; **Don't Do *Me*,**" I tell him.

Hood's problem is he can't keep nothin to hisself.

If Uncle BB is a Investigator, damn it Hood is a Reporter.

"**Stop actin like Obie Is Scum and You Would *Never*,**" Xanadi points out,

"**You** ain't met the pussy **you** ain't like *yet*."

"*Mind yo business*," Hood explodes.

"**You just Showin Yo Ass fo yo *momma*,.**" Xanadi hollas back.

Uncle BB and Tommy liked to fell out in the floor.

"I'm glad we ain't The Only Two People who Peeped That," Tommy chortles.

"I **don't let men** stick a *dick* in my ass though *do* I?!" Hood emphasizes.

YO-O.

Who **does** that in The New Millennium but a **Jackass**?

Do Hood- Not Know Who He Fuckin With or is he The Next Contestant on

Step Right Up & Catch A Beatdown?

You think he'd a **Learnt** By Now.

In the silence that follows, a Delayed Reaction Moment hits Hood:

it slowly dawns on him exactly what he said and he blushes **royally**.

"Oh *shit* Uncle BB," Hood bitches up, "I was talkin bout **Obie** not *y'all*."

"I don't *do* the Dick In The Ass Thing myself, but I'm *sure* you Insulted my Partner."

"At least you Got Enough Sense to be Embarrassed," Lee comments gruffly.

"I don't understand what Having Sex With Men has to do with

The Price of Tea In China **any**way," a Very Angry Freak points out.

"That's cause you a **Undercover Fag too**."

"I'm an **Out In The Open** Fag, *Thank You Very Much*."

"You need to Put Some Draws on the way you use that word *Fag*," Uncle BB warns.

"You ain't got but One More Time to insult me before I Cave Your Skull In."

Good for his ass.

Hood ain't spend the time round Uncle BB and Lee me and Freak did

so Hood got a lotta Homophobic Tendencies.

A Ass Whippin from Uncle BB might Straighten Him Out though.

While Hood sulks Mommy tries to Mend The Hole in her convo.

"I think y'all are putting your energy to the wrong use. Ever think of taking up a sport?"

"Sex *is* a sport Mommy. You're always Scoutin Out the Best Players and

the Ultimate Goal is to Score."

"You are So Not Funny."

Mommy turns her attention to Freaky next.

"So you say you Sleep With Men Too LaRocque..."

Let's see him laugh his way outta this one.

Conversation continues on its course around me yet I am oblivious.

It's funny how Baby Girl could be That Far Gone and still be aware,

at least on some level, a what's goin on around her.

Do she know when I'm gone? Do it make her worried?

To be closer to her I lay my head on the pillow, all while gazin at my Baby's sleepin face.

She So Beautiful.

My index finger traces a line down the middle a her face;

from the hairline to the jaw line.

Then I touch her lips with a almost feather like softness.

Baby Girl's lips move wordlessly, or So It Seems.

They move again, as faintly she whispers:

"Hey Obie."

She Knows.

Uncle BB helps me pack up these kids clothes.

He demanded, **and got**, Temporary Custody from Rahshaun.

This Totally Under Expected Pang A Loss rips through me.

All the time they was here I Hated Like Hell that Rahshaun dumped them on us.

Don't Get Me Wrong now, I love these kids to *death*.

They follow me around like puppies screamin Obie! Obie! Obie! like Cess useta do.

I simply Don't Have The Time anymore.

And they were like, In The Way, you feel me?

Don't wanna go to sleep at night so we can Get Our Party On.

Up early in the mornin wantin cereal when I had **just** went to bed.

Then you gotta find a damn *baby*sitter.

Where is they *parents*???

Oh *SHIT*.

I sound just like my **Grand**ma.

What The *Fuck*.

Soon as Baby Girl gets better we gonna Get Them Back.

We'll be **Good** Parents; I just *know* it.

"What's wrong O?"

Lost In Emotion.

"Uncle BB, you think maybe my Grandma loved me but

hated the responsibility my mom placed on her?"

He looks at me, surprised.

"Yes I do; and I think she took it out on you without really meaning to.

People do some Dumb Shit sometimes."

No Doubt.

In my Mind's Eye I see myself yellin at those kids Way Too Many Times these

past few weeks…and I'm shamed a myself.

"Grandma was real nice to me before Suze died.

Maybe she missed us after we left."

Rapidly, and that means *way* faster than I want it to,

the time approaches for my family to leave.

I apologize to each member individually for **Actin** So **Crappy**.

Baby Girl Emerges From Her Fog and decides to ride to the airport with us.

I Don't Know Bout All That but I **definitely** know she can't Stay Here By Herself.

After makin The 'Girl as comf'table as possible we Roll Out.

Suspectin a Princess Sightin the trail a reporters followin us is longer than

a funeral procession and about as ghastly as ambulance chasers.

Give Us A **Break**, damn it.

I mean *Really* Though; you feel me?

At least Baby Girl got to say Goodbye to everyone before the fog re-engulfed her.

That made me happy, and it made The 'Girl happy too.

It also took a lot outta her.

In the end I had to carry her back to the car.

That shot ended up on the cover a *People Magazine*.

Oh Well.

2_{BG}

It's been over a week; I thought I'd feel a *little* better by now, if nothing else.
What a letdown *this* has been, okay?
I am *so* ready-to-be-better-now; but the pain still overtakes my entire *being* sometimes.
It's so intense, I can't *think*; can't *breathe*; I **hate** this codeine, fear I
might be getting addicted to it: feels like *I can't live without it,* know what I mean?
Obie keeps *Lifetime* running 24/7; I'm in-and-out so much, I can't keep up with a storyline.
Other than that, I can't tell you much about that second week.
I was either in *pain* or in *la-la-land.*
When I begin to crawl out of my own personal-black-hole for longer stretches of time,
the first thing I notice is, it feels like I lost weight, especially in the hips-and-thighs.
Some of my titties are gone, too.
I don't mind the titties so much:
you wouldn't *believe* how hard it is to carry those boulders around every day,
but *LORD,* I don't want to lose my ass.
Ass is that "Black Star Power" for "our" women, you know?
Why I feel so *crappy* though; so, so *very* crappy.
I can't believe I'm supposed to go back to promoting my new CD next week.
Think I'll make it???
If I'm to have any-prayer-at-all,
I'll have to start getting out of this bed; wean myself off this dreadful codeine.
Since there's no-time-like-the-present, I swing my legs over the edge of the bed.
Problem.
This only happens in my mind; the reality is, my legs stubbornly refuse to move.
It takes not only several deep breaths; also all of the concentration I can muster
to get my legs over the edge. Already, I am exhausted.
In Obie's book there are "Oh *well's*" and "Oh *Hell's.*"
This is *definitely* an "Oh Hell."
Have to summon-my-chi.
More deep breaths; more concentration, then the "ultimate" attempt:
to stand-on-my-own.
Why I fall on my face though?

You figure.

'Cause there is nothing in my "repertoire" I can summon to get me off this floor.

I can't pick my *head* off the floor.

Fuck it, I can't even call for help.

Luckily someone comes in the bedroom door.

"What happened, Baby? Did you fall out the bed?" O asks urgently, sounds worried.

"Gotta get up," I manage to say sluggishly.

I feel like a "dope addict;"

or a sloppy drunk.

Obie *struggles* to get me back in bed.

Just because I lost weight, that doesn't make me a "lightweight," know what I'm sayin?

"*Please*; I don't *wanna*," I whine.

But, I'm already tucked in, safe-and-sound, head on my fluffy pillow.

"OB, *please*," I beg him.

He bends over me.

"What's wrong?" he asks softly.

"I need to get up. I have to go to work."

"There's no work today, Baby Girl."

Yes, I ***know*** this, *man.*

"Promotions next week," I force out.

"We ain't goin *no*where next week," I am thus informed;

"You get some rest and let *me* worry 'bout 'promotions.'"

What the Hell does that mean?

I *pass* out before I *find* out.

The "plan" is "simple."

Like a junkie-in-rehab, I'll wean myself off "the cocktail" gradually, taking a

little less every day until I find a dose that minimizes-pain-without-reducing-clarity.

Sounds like "a plan," right?

After the first dose, I notice the throbbing in my bones is still present;

not as bad as it could have been, but *way worse* than I had hoped.

This might not be such a "good plan" after all; what choice do I have, really?

Taking Obie's arm for support, I slowly maneuver the bedroom, which is *huge*.

That's enough for a first trip; I really-must-rest now.

I sleep, not as deeply; in a few hours I'm ready to do-like-Aaliyah and "Try Again."

Two days later I'm out on the beach.

Fresh-air-and-sunshine; the ocean smells so *good*, crisp-and-clean, know what I mean?

Obie pads a deck chair for me; we sit outside holding hands, listening to the radio.

I'm still dozing off; no where near as much as at the beginning of the week.

"You bored OB?"

"Not *bored*..."

"Antsy? Restless?"

"*Restless*. Inactivity's always been hard on me, but I *needed* this.

I needed to slow-down-and-rest-myself."

He ain't never lied.

"I'm restless, too. I **hate** this sitting-around-crippled shit; feels like

the-whole-world is passing-me-by. I'd love to say I'm enjoying your company;

but all I'm doing is sleeping. How's my CD doing?"

"Number One on the R&B charts; Top 5 on Billboard's Top 100."

"Kiss-my-Black-ass."

O rubs my neck in comfort.

"All-in-due-time, my 'Girl; all-in-due-time."

I sit lost-in-thought for a sec; after a lengthy silence, I speak again.

"Did you-all find my navel ring at my house?"

"No, Baby Girl, I didn't see it."

Obie sounds pensive, on the cusp of withdrawal.

We stop talking; his grip on my hand tightens.

Lucid enough to watch an entire program on TV,

I tune in to see what America is saying about us.

Why the "consensus" is that Obie beat me up; drove Einstein to suicide though?

As *If*.

That's some *crazy **shit***.

How could the Press vilify Obie like that without a *shred* of evidence??!!!

It's almost as if they've been *waiting* for a good-enough-reason to tear-Obie-down.

And why is this bitch, Smoke, all over television suggesting

Obie has some type of Svengali-like-hold over me?

That Obie has wrestled my career away from me; is trying to run my life?

That Obie demanded the video for "R U the 1 for Me?" be a tribute to himself?

What a *crock*-of-***SHIT***.

Oh *look*:

That fucking bitch Toya is on *three different channels* saying Obie promised to marry her;

dumped her when he found out she was pregnant.

Snatching the remote out of my hand Obie turns to "Sports Center."

Why, when "Pardon The Interruption" came on,

"Obie and Princess" was one of the topics for discussion though?

Because we-can't-win, child; *that's* why.

Weary of the lopsided press coverage, Obie snaps off the television in disgust.

We retreat to the beach; there's just something-so-soothing about the ocean.

Methinks it's time for us to shed-a-little-light on *our* side of the story.

But first...Officer Tyson pays me a visit, escorted by my-very-own-Rocky.

Obie stands; offers Ty his hand; they exchange false pleasantries, wary handshakes.

"You mind if I talk with Princess alone for a bit, Obie?"

Obie eyes Officer Tyson with increased suspicion, then slides his gaze in my direction,

where it becomes one of questioning caution.

"What if I say, 'No?'" O wants to know.

"I'll be alright," I assure my precious husband-to-be.

"You sure, Baby Girl?" he asks anxiously.

"Yeah, babe; I'm sure."

The way I see it, it's best if I get this over with now; obviously Obie disagrees.

"If you get tired or somethin wave your hand and I'll come get you."

I sign "ok;" a "very reluctant" Obie marches to the house, pushes LaRocque ahead of him.

Out of politeness, I offer Ty Obie's seat; he perches on the armrest.

We begin by discussing my relationship with Einstein.

When I get to the part where Einstein became a "bugaboo," Ty perks up.

"Did you report this to anybody?"

I grow under-comfortable.

"O thought I should have; at the time, I really didn't think it was necessary: concerns-

for-my-privacy-and-all, you know what I'm sayin?" I shamefully admit. "*God*; I feel

so, so very *stupid* now; I *really thought* Einstein would eventually fade-to-black."

"By your own admission, though, this went on for close to three years."

"Really-and-truly? I didn't feel like *dealing* with it, I thought he was just

buggin-the-fuck-out. Now I realize that might've been-a-bit shortsighted,"

exasperated, I defend myself.

"And that's all there is to it? You didn't have any underlying emotional attachments to

this Albert that might have prevented you from breakin it off with him completely?"
"No, what I *felt* was: once-upon-a-time Einstein was *good* to me. *I* didn't think he deserved to be cut-off-like-that; to have the police set on him. That was *my* mistake."
Ty appeared to understand this.
"So what happened to you?" he asks conversationally.
Here I hesitate:
his notepad may not be out, but I know this isn't a "casual convo" we're having.
Ty is *investigating Albert's death.*
How much should I reveal?
Since the-best-defense-is-a-good-offense, I barrel-ahead-with-the-truth,
(or something-close-to-it).
"Around the middle of that week I went home; Albert was sitting outside my house in a rental. That Saturday, some kind of way Einstein got into OB's mansion. I showed him my engagement ring, told him it was 'done, son,' he wanted to talk-about-it. Everybody *told* me not-to-go; I didn't listen; we ended up back at my house, and–"
Fixing to cry I stop for a minute; pull-myself-together; composed, I can continue.
"He wouldn't let me go. Albert tore up my house, beat the shit out of me all night long. In the morning he dropped me off at OB's gate, took off,
next I hear you're fishing-his-sorry-ass out of the ocean."
Those last sentences were harder to get through than anyone could possibly imagine.
The pain, the horror, the fear; simply speaking about it made me sick to my stomach.
I want my Obie.
"Was that all that happened?"
I glare at him "mad" hard; my lips pressed together until they *hurt*.
Who does this mothafucka think he is? **Huh**?!?
"What exactly do you mean by that?" I ask tightly.
Say it, mothafucka; I *dare* you.
"Did Albert do anything *else* to you? Besides physically assault you?"
My fist pumps in the air like I'm on "Arsenio," signals Obie to come-and-get-me.
I've had enough of *this **shit***.
"I'm tired, Ty," I finally say as Obie races toward me in a half-jog.
My face reclaims its former expression, eyes cold-and-hard.
When Obie sees me he becomes upset.
"Wassa matter, Baby Girl?" he asks quickly; harshly.
"I'm tired now; don't wish-to-talk anymore."

Even though I'm looking down, I sense that Obie is looking at Officer Tyson, not me.
"Let me show you to the *door*, then," I hear Obie *insist*.

O's been gone a long time; I'm getting worried sitting out here all-alone-and-such.
Suppose I have to "lose the bathroom?"
That's a *long way* from here; am I supposed to take-that-trek all by myself?
Nigga *Please*.
Oh, *look*…Obie's headed back this way, with his "jog on" again.
LaRocque is still with him, walking "double time" to keep pace.
"I'm gonna 'step off' with Officer Tyson for a bit, Babe."
Obie's announcement gives me a sinking feeling in the pit of my stomach.
"I'm leavin Freak here with you, though," he rolls along,
"He'll take good care a you 'til I get back. You-watch-and-see."
Obie is patting my hand absentmindedly; is he trying to convince *himself* or *me*???
You figure.
'Cause he's only making *me* more **nervous**.
"You gon' be a'ight 'out here' or should I take-you-inside?"
I've been outside a "grip;" I know I'll have to "lose it" soon; but for now?
For now, baby, I'm *perfectly content* in my lounge chair.
LaRocque and Obie have a changing-of-the-guard;
as soon as Obie's out of eyesight Rocky slips his hand in mine.
This is **my** "emotional attachment,"
his presence eases the anxiety I feel over O's departure.
Plus, he's good for **hours** of convo.

Today it has been three full weeks since my attack.
I feel **disgusting** again; Obie gives me a "thorough washing."
My bruises are fading; the stitches have not fallen out yet.
Might be because I slept-so-much; washed-so-little.
We seem to be gradually easing back towards some semblance of intimacy.
After my bath, we lie on the bed undressed.
O stares "mad hard" at my breasts, looks *distressed*; I'm not-quite-sure why.
"It's okay to touch me," I tell him: maybe he wants to, doesn't know how I'll take it.
Well, Obie touches my breasts, alright: not the way I thought he would.
Cupping my breasts O places each of his fingers over a similarly shaped bruise.

"This musta hurt 'somethin awful,'" he theorizes.

Actually it didn't.

I was *so enraged* at that nigga's *balls,* manhandling-my-boobs and what not,

I hardly felt any pain at all.

Revulsion I felt plenty of; *disgust* is also a "good one."

Pain? That came much-later-on;

like, the-next-day.

"Can I see your stitches?"

A "reasonable" request; first though, I have to scoot my behind down so

Obie-don't-see I have stitches there, too. He gets down between my legs like he's

going to eat-me-out or something, which is *bizarre* in a very wild-ass-way.

The only visible stitches are the two near my clit; these Obie touches gingerly.

"Did this hurt when it happened?"

Like *Hell*, Brotha Man; Like Hell.

"Does it still hurt?"

"It's tender, under-comfortable, it doesn't burn like it did at first."

At which point he "Obie's Out" on me; kisses-my-clit.

What a **HEINE**.

Instantly Remorseful, all-apologetic-and-such, Obie is quick to explain he didn't-mean-it-like-that. I'm not at all offended: I know an "Obie Move" when I see one.

It felt kind of good, though, all warm-and-tingly.

Know what else?

I saw Obie's dick jump.

Church was so **GOOD** this week.

Last week I was "conked out" (please notice the 'n');

the week before we took Mommy-and-them to the airport.

This week, *nothing* was stopping me.

Pastor Julia was in the pulpit.

One thing about Pastor Julia: she's an "Examine Thyself" preacher who *will* leave you

"spiritually bloody" if your stuff-isn't-correct. This week her sermon was on "Half-ass

Christians:" Christians-with-sex-addictions, drug-and-alcohol-problems, Christians

who curse-like-sailors (*that* cut deep), "don't tithe" (*not our problem*), "gossip."

But when Pastor Julia got to talking about Christians-who-fornicate—

say-they're-in-love/won't-get-married—I wanted to **DIE, always**.

"*Y'all know who you are*," Pastor Julia decried;

"The one's who keep sayin', '*We can always get married later on.*'"

Why that sounds-like-me though?

You figure.

Meanwhile... can somebody *please turn off that spotlight*??

Talk about food-for-thought, there was a *smorgasbord* in that sermon.

Obie's giving me that "knowing look" again, know what I mean Vern?

He knows that when I said we'd get married "one day," *I did not mean* "*to*-day."

Pastor Julia changed-my-mind; I don't want to defy God anymore.

He's been *really good* to me lately, n'est-ce pas?

The-moral-of-this-story-is: Christians can't be-like-Sinatra, doing-it-my-way;

picking-and-choosing which of the-Lord's-guidelines we wish to follow.

We have to do it *God's* Way.

Can I get an "*Amen*, somebody."

When we get home I want to take a "serious look" at our itineraries;

Obie wants me to "rest."

Obie wins again.

We doze in our underwear; at least I do: no telling *what* Obie does.

Although the sun still shines brightly when I awaken, I can tell it's getting late.

Let's assume Obie has been awake a while now.

His cheek is in its usual spot, resting atop my head, his fingers entwined in my hair.

I stir; Obie realizes I am awake; he eases away from me a few inches.

He's got a hard-on; acts like he's scared to let it touch me.

I tug at the waistband of Obie's boxer briefs; he's not budging.

"Come closer," I beckon.

"In a minute," O promises, sliding in the opposite direction.

I know where this is headed:

last night, the night before, Obie made a twenty-minute-pit-stop in the bathroom.

Clamping down on the waistband, I beg him not to leave me.

"I gotta 'lose it,'" he lies.

"Then hold it," I demand. "Or better yet, let me hold it for you."

Into the drawers, fish around a second or two and BAM: I hit "pay dirt."

Oh-so-slowly I glide Obie's "hoodie" up over his tip, back down again; up/down,

up/down; O gives in to the sensation, burrows deep into the pillows behind him.

A few more strokes, Obie puts his hand over mine, shows me just-how-he-likes-it.

Soon he's really-feeling-it.

I lick Obie's nipples; he moans; sure enough I get-him-there.

Then, I lightweight drape my crippled ass over him; we lock lips for a moment.

I want to "do it" for Obie again; he somehow knows my arm is tired now.

I-really-hurt: this trip, Obie keeps his hand over mine, we get-him-there together.

"Sorry," he whispers sheepishly.

"You're talking *foolishness*," I murmur into his chest.

Long, thin fingers stroke my spinal column, send electric waves throughout my body.
We kiss deeply one last time.

Obie pulls out his cellie.

"What are you doing?"

"Tryna juggle-some-things so I can have more time with you."

"*Don't **do** that,* OB," I shriek angrily. "Don't fuck up your career;
everything else you've worked so hard to build, just because *I* got hurt."

"Which one a them videos is gon' keep-me-warm-at-night?"
he asks like I said something-stupid.

"The one that will cause-you-to-resent-me if you give it up. Or maybe the one that'll
wreck your hard-earned-rep as an on-time-guy if you push it back on my account."

"You sound like a fool."

"You sound like an asshole."

We both have our hands on our respective foreheads; our backs turned to we'chother.
And, we're arguing now *because*...?

"Let me do this," a vexed Obie sighs. "Bein-there-for-you is more important to me
than anything else in this world. I been in 'The Industry' *seventeen fuckin years*.
If it all came crashin down *yester*day, I had a-*good-run* and made a *ton* a money. You?
You just-gettin-started, 'Girl. You gon' have more success than I ever dreamed possible."

"The Industry is your *life,* OB, it's in your *blood.* Your *career,* your *craft*: they're
who you *are,* baby; not sitting here on this beach with my *stupid, broke-up-a—*"

O grabs my chin ***hard***; cuts me off, forces me to look straight at him.

"*You are my life,*" he growls through clenched teeth,

"The Industry can ***kiss my ass.*** And you are ***not dumb or stupid***; don't you ***ever forget
it***. You made a 'costly decision' based on what you-thought-was-*right*-at-the-*time*. It's
not a price *I* think you should pay, but God is the 'best knower;' His-Will-be-done."

Feeling 'placed,' my eyes slide down toward the comforter.

"I ain't mean to yell at you," Obie continues tenderly. "You all I got and I need you

to know that. You could never cost me more than you give me *each and every day*."
He kisses my forehead; his lips trace the bridge of my nose until they meld with mine.

He didn't get the time off.

Post up in front of the computer screen, we begin to go over our itineraries.
"Me and Hood 'posed to be in Toronto tomorrow workin on that 'club scene' movie.
That'll last three months. After that, we off-to-Texas to work on that 'indie project.'"
"About the mixed kid from the 'hood who dreams of making it big in music videos?"
"Yeah, yeah; but his moms wants him to go-to-college and be-somebody."
"Only he doesn't want to leave his 'barrio' or his 'peep's'. Wasn't that written for you?"
"Most def. The best part is the parents are a Hispanic man and a Black woman instead
a that tired Black Daddy/White Momma thing. This is scheduled to run a *grip*. Plus,
I got six video shoots: one in Prague, one in London, and one in *Djibouti*."
And I have two months of promotions followed by a small, *small* role in an action flick.
Obie was able to postpone his "club movie" one more week.
Then he breaks it to me: I have been replaced in the action flick.
"I tried gettin you a extension but the producers didn't wanna wait that long.
They recast so quick they must a started lookin the day the story broke."
Shit.
I was so, so *very* looking-forward-to that role;
the "buzz" is: that film will be a blockbuster;
it might even turn into a "franchise hit" with at-least-two-sequels.
"You think I could be in the next one?"
Obie supposes so; he'll get my "people" on it.
"Who replaced me; Angela Basset?"
Obie looks at me then looks away; must be someone I hate.
"Who *was* it, OB; Nikki? *Toya*??"
"*Get seriou*s," Obie snickers at *that*. "No, they replaced you with Xanadi."
"*Little Xena*, **Warrior** *Princess*?" I am blown-away; it shows.
"It's just *The Warrior Princess* now, they couldn't clear the rights to 'Xena.' Anyway,
she didn't wanna do it and make you mad but I figured better-her-than-someone-else."
Riiiight.
"She got a 'monster followin' among wrestlin fans," Obie awkwardly fills the void.
True-that; *still*…I feel a little "Hatorade" running through my veins.

Xena's tall, thin, good looking, athletic, and light-as-hell (light *skinned*, not *weight*).
And that skinny-yaller-bitch got my part.
Is it *in **you***?
"You a'ight, Baby Girl?"
"*No*," I sob, "*I wanted that movie*," and the "downpour" begins.
Obie hugs me; kisses my forehead; that's not much of a "consolation prize."
This shit just isn't fair; my whole *life* is falling apart.
*Why am I paying such a high price for leaving a **bad relationship**?*
"There's 'good news,' Baby Girl," O says. "Your agent sent over a script, it shoots in
three weeks. It's *short notice* but you're replacin Chante Pierce, who got 'knocked up.'"
"Oooooo, I *heard* about that."
Her "baby daddy" is a big-name-rap-star who's married-with-children.
How many ways can *you* spell "ugly"?!
"*Hold on*...the *rapper movie*?! I'm not playing *some rapper's* chick-on-the-side."
"It's not-that-kinda-role. You play a female-squad-member and it's a 'pivotal role.'"
"OB, it's a *'drug picture.'*"
"*What's-your-**point***?!" he questions in irritation;
"We watch *every single nigga picture that comes out, good-or-bad;*
and we *enjoy* most a' em. It's not some big-Hollywood-production; **big damn deal**.
This flick targets *your* audience, Princess; *your* 'fan base.' *Therefore,*
this movie will offer you *far better exposure* than the one you missed out on."
"You already said 'yes' didn't you," I say rhetorically; dry my eyes, reach for the script.
"*When have I ever done that to you*?!" Obie explodes;
"You watch too-much-TV. I run neither your *life* nor your *career*."
"My *bad*, OB; I'm *sorry*. The way you're talking it's like you *know* I'll do-this-one."
"*Basically*; but it's *still your decision*. I simply '*recommend*.'"
"Did you *'recommend'* to my agent I would do this one?" I sulk.
"No, I merely expressed a *sincere*, most *heartfelt* confidence that you would
probably-*choose-this-project*."
What a **Dick**.
Still...it's not like I have anything else going on.
I begin to peruse the pages.
Next Problem:
"Hey O? This is a five- to six-month shoot in Chicago. When do we see each other?"
"I ain't rightly worked-that-out-yet," O admits, looks crestfallen. "Now that we

hooked up I don't feel the same about seein we'chother only every couple a months."
I know exactly how he feels.
"You not in the-best-shape-a-your-life, *either*, Baby. *Who's gon' take care a you?*"
"I'm a 'big 'Girl,' not a 'Baby Girl;' I can take-care-of-myself."
Talk about "false bravado."
That's what my *mouth* is saying; my *heart* is screaming *please-don't-leave-me*.
"Under-most-circumstances you *could,* but *right now* you need somebody *with* you.
You need *me*."
I lean over; our foreheads touch.
"Yes, I do," I whisper softly. "I need you so badly."
"Very, very much so?"
"*So, so **very**.*"
He ain't never lied.

Today I went the whole entire day without one cocktail; I feel good about that.
It's been a long-hard-day for me though, even with the nap Obie makes me take.
Emotionally exhausted, physically drained, I cannot manage my clothes;
Obie has to help me.
The stitches around my clit are gone; I wonder about the internal ones.
Cautiously, prudently, I deliberate the merits of checking-it-out.
I am afraid to put my fingers in there,
consumed with the fear I might discover some hideous deformity:
A rip/tear/hole/etc; something under-naturally-aligned in my pussy.
Rational Princess knows I am being "ridiculous;"
Ravaged Princess prefers not to find out Einstein's done-me-some-permanent-damage.
Swallowing my fear until it lodges like a lump in my throat I take-the-plunge
(no pun intended).
Everything kind of feels the same as it always did.
Yes; my hand has been in here before: it's-my-pussy, I'll touch-if-I-want-to.
I don't feel any sutures; I don't actually know where Dr. Estes put them,
there's not a lot of room in here for them to get lost in, know what I mean Vern?
Satisfied all-is-right in my reproductive-world, I wash my hands; head for bed.
O is stretched out in his drawers;
bummed he couldn't finagle his way out of any commitments.
I feel panicky; I keep it to myself; O already has a lot on his mind.

Lights off: we're pressed up close to we'chother, I feel so safe-and-warm in O's arms.
Can't I stay here *forever*, God? *Please*?
Now-that-I-know precisely how Obie felt earlier, I regret having yelled at him.
No amount of *adulation;* no *accolade*, could replace *this*;
this blissful feeling, this peace-of-mind.
I would throw my career over in a *second* to spend the *rest of my life* with this man.
What we have is one week.

It's "official."
Obie's in love with my *hair*, not *me:* he has his hands twisted up in my mane again.
I predict he's going to turn himself on in 3-2-1—BINGO.
The-easing-process begins; I make a pre-emptive-strike.
"Stop moving away from me," I grouse. "You hurt my feelings when you do that."
"I'm tryna be *'sensitive'* here."
"'Sensitive' to **what**: what **you** think I'm feeling?! I'm not *scared-of-your-**dick***, OB,
it wasn't *you* that hurt me; it was ***Einstein***."
He ponders this a moment.
"I need to know you still want me; that I still turn-you-on."
"***Quit*** wit' that *'damaged goods'* shit, *a'ight*?" Obie shouts.
"Tell you *what*," I propose, "*You* stop acting like your dick will make me
run-for-cover and *I'll* stop acting like 'damaged goods.'"
His silence leads me to believe Obie has acquiesced on that point.
That plus the pressure on my *back*, the hot lips on my *neck*, the hand on my *breast*…
You get the picture.
Since I still can't roll over, I motion for O to come around in front of me.
I reach in his unders; free-his-'Willy' (WOW that was awful), press it against my
exposed midriff. When I throw my leg over O's hip a spasm of pain wracks my bod.
I have to fight the urge to wince; otherwise I might never get near the dick again.
We embrace tightly; kiss passionately.
It feels good except:
it doesn't turn me on like it use to; I am "greatly disturbed" by this.
O begins to moan; his hands explore my body.
Under-able to "reciprocate," all I can do is let Obie rub against me until he's through.
We lay wrapped up in we'chother for a ***grip***.
I'm hurting all over; after the speech I just gave, I won't say a *thing*.

Mercifully, O rolls me off.

My bones are throbbing; after I lie back, relax, the pain eases; is *much better*.

My eyes are closed; when I open them Obie is "stiff" and ready-as-ever, poor baby.

Since I'm feeling so-so-very-much-better, I scoot towards the end of the bed.

O cocks an eyebrow at me: it takes me *so long to do this* it's *ridiculous*.

Then I **pain**stakingly roll my "broken ass" over onto my stomach.

Facing "the mic" I smile, say:

"Hey baby! How's it hangin? Things are on the 'upswing' I see."

"Why you always do that?" O gasps, forfeiting control to a fit of giggles.

"I *have to* say 'hello' to my-*mans*-and-them. We haven't spoken in for*ever*."

"You's a *fool*," he cracks. "A *real* **nutcase**."

"You want mommy to give-you-a-kiss, slip-you-some-tongue?" I ask "the mic."

Now, you can't tell me O doesn't know what I'm about to do.

He knows just as surely as I knew he was heading for the bathroom to hit-himself-off.

Quickly, I stick my tongue ring into the opening; twist it around.

"Oh **SHIT**," Obie pants heavily. "What the fuck you *do*in??"

Guess-who's-not-laughing-*now*???

He grabs two fists-full of sheets, bends his knees, pushes himself up/away from me.

Still panting like he'd run from the police, Obie stares down at me;

eyes/mouth wide open with surprise.

"So-good-you-can't-take-it?" I taunt.

"Somethin-like-that; yeah," O admits.

With my good hand, I move to draw him into my mouth; Obie pushes me off roughly.

"*QUIT, GOT-DAMN IT*," he yells brusquely.

"What the *fuck*, O; I'm quitting **because**...?"

"'Cause, I ain't **about** to let the **rape victim** go **down** on me."

WHOA.

No the **FUCK HE DIDN'T**.

Did that *Ungodly Bitch* just call me The **RAPE VICTIM**???

He must be out of his **mothafuckin mind**.

Seething, I literally tremble with rage; my anger boils over uncontrollably.

"**FUCK** your big, dumb, ugly, gay, *White* ass, Oscar Price; the **rape victim** has a

name, **damn it**. My name is **Prin-cess** Davis. My **ability** to **make decisions for myself**

has **not been damaged** in any **way, shape, form, or fashion** by *my ordeal. Therefore*;

I **do not need you to make them for me**. It is **my** choice to go down on you, so *please*

don't feel like you have to *not-let-me* for **my-own-good**. I had a **mind of my own**
BEFORE I WAS RAPED, and I'll have a **mind of my own** on the **very-day-I-die**."
Somebody "call" **THIS** nigga's "number" now: he has made-me-feel-like-*shit;*
and I'm passin-the-stick *straight back to him.*
Disgusted, I move to get off the bed, only I move-too-fast; hurt myself.
I can't make this stupid body do ANYTHING anymore.
Reflexively, Obie jumps to my assistance; violently, I brush him aside.
"*LEAVE ME ALONE*," I yell. "**I DON'T *NEED* YOU. I CAN *DO IT MYSELF*.**"
Of course I am tired-and-upset; I *can't* do-it-my-self; that's never stopped me from
trying before. Angry, I drop down in the rocking chair "dumb hard," hurt my behind
"something awful," send a chain-reaction-tidal-wave-of-pain up through my ribs to my
breastbone, out to my arm. The pain jolts my body like a defibrillator except,
instead of shocking me back-to-life, it shocks me back-to-agony.
As I have *basically* done-this-to-myself,
I will not cry…I will not *cry*…I will *not cry*…
I can't even make myself do that.
My knees draw up to my throbbing chest, I stifle disconsolate wails with folded arms.
Obie sits on the edge of the bed staring at me the whole time;
forlornly, I rock myself until I doze off.
In my sleep, I can feel Obie's arms enfold me; lift me up; carry me towards the bed.
Thank God: I'm way-too-tired to fight anymore,
"eternally grateful" I don't have to spend the night in that hard-ass-chair.

The sun shines brightly, *crisply*, through the glass-paneled eastern wall of
Obie's bedroom. There's no telling what time it is.
One thing's for sure: it must be time-to-get-up.
I have always loved this view; from the bed you can
contemplate-the-ocean in all-its-glory, as well as its "many moods."
Like the ocean, my Princess-self is calm this morning;
tempestuous state left behind with the darkness.
Behind me Obie stirs, shifts, awakens, touches my hair; I snuggle in closer to him.
"I wanna apologize for last night, Baby," he murmurs.
"It's all-good," I demure. "I kind of flew-off-the-handle myself."
"I just wanna do everything **right**. I want to…"
I wait for Obie to find the right words.

"Don't worry about it," I say in the meantime. "I know you 'meant well.'"

"Yeah; the road-to-Hell and all-*that*-jazz…"

Blanketed by silence, calm-and-serene, we take pleasure in the feel of we'chother.

"I want to make love to you, OB," I murmur passionately.

Feeling him stiffen, *not like that either*, I pray this doesn't turn 'ugly' like last night.

"You sure about this? You don't haveta do this for *me*, you know; ain't-no-*rush* here."

Peeved, I make a "great effort" to remind myself that Obie is *concerned* about me.

Someone *else* might not have **cared** so much.

"I *need* this, O; I feel like I'm 'ready.'"

"What about your stitches?"

"I *think* they're gone, I'm-*not*-really-sure; check for me?"

"How I do that?" Under-certainty clouds Obie's demeanor.

*"Stick your **fingers** in my **pussy**, see if you can **feel** them."*

DUH!

He doesn't look "too sure" about *that* one, folks.

As a matter-of-*fact*; Obie looks like that's the last-thing-he-wants-to-do.

He goes-for-it-anyway;

like a quarterback throwing a "Hail Mary Pass" with three seconds on the game clock,

Obie bravely inserts his fingers,

"In Search Of…The Missing Sutures."

"What do they feel like?"

"Like *'not-pussy,'* OB."

"That's *very helpful*, Cess," O replies dryly. "Very, very much so."

"Well, how the Hell would *I* know??? You *do* know what pussy *feels* like, don't you?"

"Heh, heh, heh," is O's sarcastic reply.

"I mean with your fingers, not with your dick."

"I *been there* a couple a *times*, Princess; come **on**."

"Just 'checking.'"

Obie grumbles something under-intelligible in return.

"You so nasty," I tease.

"You love it, though."

Yes-I-do.

Obie has stretched out, his head on my stomach while examining me;

seemingly listening to what my organs have to say.

I run my fingers through his hair; methinks we *both* have a "hair fetish."

"I want to apologize, too; for calling you all those names last night."

"Oh *yeah*? What names was *that*? Big? Dumb? Gay? White?

Did I leave *out* somethin? *You* know; anything *designed to hurt me*?"

Think O is upset?

You figure.

"That was *totally* under-called for, I *apologize*."

His head nods atop my stomach, all-is-forgiven.

I half expect Obie to get up; he doesn't. Instead, he put *his* tongue ring to "good use,"

erases all-previous-doubts about my under-responsiveness from my mind.

I'm "almost there;" Obie stops; maneuvers himself on top of me;

That's when it *hit me:* my heart starts racing; inexplicably I can't breathe.

I open my mouth; gulp deeply;

O's towering frame above me makes me feel like I'm suffocating.

What's *that* about?

Who *does that* anymore?

"You a'*ight,* Baby Girl?" O sounds suddenly distressed.

Oh *sure*… I *hear* Obie,

but I'm busy squinting my eyes shut, trying to recapture-the-mood.

*Why is this **happening** to me*?

"What's *wrong*??" Obie demands.

"I'm okay," I lie, all *squeaky; odd*-sounding.

"No, you *NOT*," he refutes my bold untruth, rolling off of me. "Talk to me, Baby Girl."

"It's okay; it's okay," I stand by my statement;

"I'm just winded; alright? Let's-keep-going."

"As *If*. Look at you; you all balled-up-in-a-*knot*.

Talk to me; *open* your ***eyes; let me know what's goin on.***"

"I don't know," I'm compelled to confess, my eyes obediently open;

"My heart is 'beeping;' I can't catch my breath."

"That's called a '*anxiety* attack;' it's cause you 'speedin'.'"

"I am *NOT SPEEDING;* I feel so *'ready.'*

I mean, I *thought* I was ready. It's so ***fucking unfair***."

On his side, head propped up in his hand, Obie gently strokes the hollow of my throat.

"You can get ***mad if you wanna***," a no-nonsense-Obie firmly states,

"have a 'screamin meanie' again like last night; pitch-a-bitch-down-a-flight-a-stairs if

you have to. I. Don't. Give. A. ***Fuck***, Princess. It has only been *three weeks* since you got raped. Somehow you got this twisted notion you can rush-your-recovery: put it on some type a 'artificial timetable' like a item on your *itinerary* or somethin. It. Don't. Work. That. Way. *Face* it; you **gonna haveta allow yourself** some *time*-to-*heal*. But no matter *how long it takes*; I **promise** I'll be-here-for-you."

Easy for *him* to say.

Nobody raped *Obie*; *I'm* the one with the "issues" here.

Personally, I am sick-to-death of "recovery,"

wish-to-move-on to another stage in my life.

How long will my body continue to betray me this way,

operating as if *it* is "in control," *not* **me**?!

"You don't understand how much I need to find out if it can feel good again, like it used to.

I don't want to be scared to make love the rest of my life; I *don't* want to *lose* you."

"You really think I would leave over somethin like this?"

"Sex is very important to you."

"NO, fool; *you* are really important to me. Can-you-get-that through your 'thick skull' *sometime-this-millennium*?! I gave up a fantastic-sex-life 'cause *pleasin* **you** *meant* **so** *much more.* In return you showed me not just the joys-of-non-sex, but the best-sex-of-my-life. If we gotta start-from-scratch, well: so-be-it; I already know the outcome."

"Sex is important to *me, too*; *I* want it to be the-way-it-*was*."

"Give it time, Baby Girl. If you build up to it, it'll come."

"Can't we please try again?"

"You *hard-headed*, you know that? Very, very much so. "

"Wouldja have me any other way?"

I think not.

So we start again; end up the same way; except *this* time, I start snotting-and-tearing.

I *hate* what's happening to me; I am convinced *nothing* will *ever be "right" again.*

Like so many times these past few weeks I find myself being rocked in Obie's arms.

It's becoming a "bad habit."

Obie sits straight up; helps me to an upright position.

The sunlight illuminates my chest;

in the harsh daylight my fading bruises seem especially stark.

I watch Obie swallow; his hand moves involuntarily; each finger matching a bruise.

His hand slowly drops to his side.

"My bruises turn you off, don't they?" I ask ruefully.

"You know, only some kinda *freak* could make love to a battered woman and not be

bothered by her scars," Obie says quietly, head hanging, brooding for a moment. Then
he raises his head; looks at me sorrowfully. "This'll work a lot better if I don't look."
Above my head, O spins a finger; I turn my back to him;
with two "false starts" under-our-belts we take-some-time to reorient ourselves.
Obie's head seeks familiar ground; he palms my breasts gently.
I lean into a muscular body that seems smaller somehow, as if he, too, has lost weight.
"It's possible, I ain't been eatin much lately."
He *barely* gained back the weight he lost last year, if at *all*,
now he's losing more weight??!!
Nigga *please*.
"You lost 'mad' weight, too, Baby Girl;.even your titties is smaller."
As he's saying all this Obie is fingering my nipples with a feathery-light touch.
"It doesn't look bad, does it?"
"You had plenty to spare. Now you won't haveta squeeze them 'D's' into a 'C' cup."
Big Yuk. I slap Obie's thigh playfully.
What does he know anyway?
Just because he's sucked thousands of titties, that doesn't make him an expert-bra-fitter.
In the meantime passion is building inside me.
I lean closer than ever to Obie, caress his thighs with the fingertips of my bad hand:
something (at last) I can do with minimal pain.
"***Stop using that arm***," Obie chastises me.
Oh *HELL*.
"I want to touch you," I whine like a baby. "I love you so much; I want you so badly."
For a split second Obie releases one breast, moves my curtain of hair out of his way,
nibbles and sucks on my neck, massages my breasts simultaneously.
"I love you, Obie," I moan in sheer delight.
"I love you, too, Baby Girl," he moans back. "I love you *so much*."
I can feel him jump once or twice against my back, dick practically *leaping* to life.
I grind into Obie; he grinds back into me; one of his hands moves between my legs.
"Pleasure filled" in three separate places,
they combine to feed the fire growing steadily within.
Not knowing how much my body will withstand I don't want this orgasm wasted on O's hands.
"Hold up," I pant, pray this will work, turn to face Obie; ease him into me.
It feels *weird*; not exactly *right*.
I flinch from discomfort; at least I can breathe, I'm not "panic stricken."

"Hurts?" asks Obie anxiously.

"Tender is all," I answer honestly.

"Want me to stop?"

"No, no; I'm fine."

And I *am*: this-time-it's-gonna-be-okay.

Obie disengages his lips, holds me ever closer, rocks me some more.

This is a different rhythm: the sweet surrender of the afterglow.

We two are *so close* I-can-feel-his-heartbeat (and he didn't even say a word)

right through his chest wall. One of Obie's hands slides to the nape of my neck.

He kisses me again: softer, sweeter, gentler;

far less urgent than in the heat of our lovemaking.

"You okay?" Obie makes sure.

"Yes; I am; thanks, Babe."

"*Anything* for you Baby Girl."

He doesn't ask "what for:" he *already knows*.

It is Tuesday. The clock is winding down on me at "breakneck speed,"

putting me under incredible pressure to get-well-soon.

Three-more-days, Lord.

Since I'm up anyway, I might as well go for a walk on the beach.

My mind believes I can do it; my body is preparing another "massive insurrection."

What asshole said: "If the mind can believe it, then the man can achieve it?"

What *horseshit*. Then again…

Maybe I'm not "believing" *hard* enough.

You figure.

Anyway, the "lightweight jaunt" from the house to the shoreline wears me *out*.

I literally have to *sit down* to *catch my breath* (it has gotten *away* from me).

If I ever hope to increase-my-stamina, I'll need to *walk farther*,

but what if I can't make it back on my own?

Sure, I've got my cellie; I can *always* call the house;

how **embarrassing** that would be though.

Hello…This is Princess; I've-fallen-and-I-can't-get-up???

What the *fuck???*

I so, so very *refuse* to stray-from-my-plan; that doesn't mean I can't *alter* it.

Maybe instead of *one-long-walk*, I'll take several-*short*-walks instead; how-you-say...
Build-up-to-it.

That'll work; back-to-the-house-for-me.

And guess who *I* run into, standing out back with his arms folded, *waiting* for me?

I'm not-in-the-mood for this shit.

"Where you been?!" he demands.

"I met my lover down by your 'rock;' hope-you-don't-mind."

"*Hi*-fuckin-*larious*, Baby Girl; now, *where you been*?!"

So, *so* very tired-of-being-grilled like a "holiday burger,"

I shove my hands into my sweatshirt pockets; face Obie defiantly.

"I went for a *walk*, O; o*kay*? That *a'ight* with you?"

It *better* be.

But, of-*course*-it-*wasn't*.

"By your*self*??" he exclaims. "Is you **crazy**?? Suppose you *passed out* or somethin."

"I would have called the house; said: 'I've-fallen, and-I-can't-get-up.'"

Which is *so* funny to me; I mean, wasn't I just *thinking* about that?

Even when we're mad, our minds travel in the same circles.

"Go on and laugh-with-me, OB," I coax him "You know you want to."

He turns his back on me, hiding (I'm sure) a smile.

"You scared me to death," he continues less frantically. "Why didn't you wake me up?"

Another sigh-of-oppression escapes me.

"***What***," Obie's "irritated ass" spits out; "Am I gettin-on-your-*nerves* or somethin?"

Bingo!

"You're crowding me again.

I wanted to go by my*self*: the whole 'needing space'/time-to-think thing."

Because I *know* this is such a *difficult concept* for Obie, I soften my tone substantially.

"Sometimes, I want to be alone," I tell him; slip one arm around his waist;

"That doesn't mean I'm getting tired of you.

I can only take *so much solitude* before I-want-my-Obie again."

See how easy it is to make him smile?

Our impending separation looms larger-than-life in our minds;

doesn't help our appetites at all.

We end up eating *toast*.

Toast and *coffee*.

Who builds stamina on *toast*?

Who does *that* anymore?

The TV watches us for another hour or so; I decide to brave-the-beach-walk again.

Obie gets that panting-puppy-dog, take-me-for-a-walk-too look on his face.

However; he's trying on the give-the-'Girl-some-space thing.

It's a lit-tle-bit *snug* on him; *especially* around the *neck* area.

He better be *damned glad* I-feel-like-company.

Tall-blonde-stud and I stroll with our arms around we'chother's waists like lovers do.

Oh *wait…My* "bad."

We *are* lovers, *n'est-ce pa*?

I want to say like "real lovers;" damn it, *we're that, too.*

Sometimes I'm so "flighty" I astound *myself.*

Let's just say we stroll with our arms around we'chother's waists and leave-it-there.

We have passed the point where I wound-down this morning; I am growing weary.

Don't know if O is reading my mind or my posture; he advises me to:

"Let me know when you get tired, a'ight?"

That pisses me off, I don't know why; the dumbest shit usually does.

"Stop fretting over me," I snap.

Beside me Obie begins to simmer quietly. I glance at his profile; his jaw has tightened.

"I don't want you to wear-yourself-out," he just as quietly explains.

"*I know what I'm doing, okay*?" the angry words spill out in a jumble.

"And *I* know you'll walk a mile, and half-*kill*-yourself, to *prove-me-wrong*."

"*No, I won't*," I vow viciously.

O stops dead in his tracks, makes *me* stop awkwardly.

"You hate for me to tell you what to do, don't you?"

"Yes, I do; I really do; it's nothing personal: it's how-I-am. Although, I'm grateful you do: at times, I desperately need your advice, don't know how to ask for it."

Oh *look…*I made Obie smile again.

"*I love your smile...*" I sing to him.

"O-*kay*, 'Shanice,'" he says shyly; blushes a little; graces me with the-*only*-Kool Aide-grin.

"Sorry I'm so bitchy."

"You-do-what-you-do, Baby Girl; you do-what-you-do."

Tugging Obie's belt, I steer us back to the house.

I caution you against assuming this signals-a-surrender;

Obie better not be thinking that, either.

From way-out-of-left-field-somewhere comes the urge for steak-and-potatoes.

"You can't eat that," O says flatly.

"Why not?" I have to know.

"You ain't ate nothin solid in weeks. You gotta build-up-to-it."

What the *Hell* am I building; a *pyramid* out of *Pringles* or something?

'Cause if Obie uses that phrase **one-more-time** *I'm going to*—

I'm going to get my *attitude* in check, that's what I'm going to do.

"Don't take nothin to make you mad, do it?" Obie observes.

"Must be genetic," I jibe, then delight as a sheepish grin spreads slowly across O's face.
Touché, baby.

My "White Knight" kneels in front of me; I squeal: I get to ride-the-Obie-train.

"Full-speed-ahead, Captain," I give the command.

"Aye, aye, Sir," Obie responds.

Arms spread out, head thrown back, O running as-fast-as-he-can, we head-for-home.

After way-too-much-debate for my taste, Obie cooks me Chicken Creole;

throws some hot-turkey-sausage in for good measure.

The food is cooked to *death,* it's almost *soupy,*

but soupy is good… soupy is good… and so is this damned Creole.

So good I ate two bowls full.

"You gon' puke" Obie predicts.

Nigga please.

Obie made himself some Creole, too, with soy sausage; minus-the-meat of course.

Believe me it is much better than it sounds.

The whole "steak" thing has me boggled 'til it hits me:

it's been almost a month since my attack.

Shit; just in time for Obie's departure;

this is getting more-and-more-depressing *every day.*

"Mind if I sit here with Baby Girl for a while, bruh?"

Into this blissful domestic scene enters my man, The Latin King.

It took a *lot* for Barry to approach Obie like that:

O gets cold-and-distant at the *sight* of Barry.

After they toss a few disposable banalities at each other, I notice Obie is being a ***bitch***.

I give him this insistent stare;

he gives me a Kelis: I-hate-you-so-much-right-now stare back,

like I *give* a flying fuck.

Obie turns this same gaze on Barry, only now it is so, so very much-more-*intense*;

so *very*-under-necessary.

"Barry has as much right to talk to me as *any other motha fucka in* **town**," I caution O.

Chastened; full-of-hate, Obie slinks off.

You know the old if-looks-could-kill line?

Let's just say I'm lucky-to-be-alive and leave-it-there.

"You take care now, *nena*," Barry rises to go. "Don't let nobody make you take on more than you can handle. By the way, *Mami* says to tell you 'hi.'"

He leans in; kisses me softly on the cheek.

Guaranteed somewhere Obie is watching; plotting-a-murder.

That Barry still cares is touching; that he ever cared at **all** is a "serious surprise."

Men and their inability-to-show-their-emotions.

Obie slouches back to the couch, "bitch mode" in "overdrive;" I-don't-care.

"He ain't haveta *kiss* you like that. I'm *sorry*, but he *didn't.* That was *'mad'* disrespectful."

"To *whom*, Obie? Not to *me: all he did* was *kiss me on the cheek.*"

"Looked like the *lips* to *me.*"

"That's what you get for *"investigating."* Don't you *trust* me?"

"Of *course* I trust you, Baby Girl. I don't trust *The Latin King*; far as I can *throw* him."

"The both of you are **dumb**-together. Who fights over a girl when it's *her* decision which nigga she wants to be with? Who does *that* anymore?"

"Every man believes he can change-a-woman's-mind, specially when the woman's hot as you."

"You *figure*?" I ask, incredulous.

"I *know*," Obie responds emphatically. "Women is the same;

they believe if they do everything *just-so*, then some nigga will *love-them-for-ever*."

"And you believe *what*, OB?"

Without moving his body, Obie's eyes turn towards me; fix me in their stare.

"I believe you're the only woman for me; and any man that tries to steal you away will meet with a **untimely end.**"

O-**kay then**.

Obie wants to "do it;" I can tell by the way his fingertips traipse my spine, only: yesterday was *plenty* for me. Not that it wasn't *great,* mind you.

I wanted to *prove something to myself;* we *did all that;* now I just-don't-feel *very sexy*.

I don't want to be selfish about it, though, especially since I was the one who *started* this crap in the first place, so I go on ahead, give-it-to Obie.

He makes it so-damned-good, I almost forgot I didn't want to.
Almost.
Two-days-to-go. I try to eat a good breakfast; can't get it down;
still can't make it much farther than Obie's rock, either.
This is *so*-not-**good**, people.
Titi (as Barry calls Aunty) comes thanking me for smoothing the way for Barry.
Titi's a funny breed of woman: no *way* am I furthering *my man's cause* with his *ex*,
especially when we all live in the same household.
That's taking the "non-jealousy" thing a-bit-too-far, don't you think?
Or maybe she understands Obie and I are tight-like-that;
and Barry doesn't-have-a-*prayer of* getting back with me.
You figure.
I have call-in appearances on several radio morning shows, including Doug Banks.
Unfortunately, my handlers have gotten pret-ty-sick-of "The Obie and Princess Show."
Who *cares*, man?
I *ought* to pull-an-Obie: tell them to kiss-my-ass; I agree to do these appearances solo.
Fighting is *such hard work;* I don't have it *in* me right now, know what I mean?
Later that evening Dionne blows by with the baby.
I get a sudden inexplicable longing for a Baby Girl of my own;
to dress in Armani, Tommy Girl.
Brushing this aside I figure: what kind of parent would *I* make?
Young, selfish, never-had-a-mother to pattern-myself after.
What a "laugh riot."
Barry and Titi arrive; we pop popcorn, chill; someone sparks a blunt.
Since I am off-the-cocktail, I take-a-few-hits.
What the Hell, it's a "party," right?
I'm feeling "mighty mellow;" all-is-right in my world.
Until Obie and Barry get into it.
Now that we're high, Barry demands a dance with me.
Who does *that*?
"Back up off my 'Girl, son," Obie tells him, grabs Barry roughly by the arm.
"She was *my girl first*," Barry corrects him.
"*Was* nigga, *was,* and *why we back on **that** crack, **anyway**?!* That's *old news, claro?*"
"Why don't you niggas grow *up*?!" I explode.
Suddenly I'm *so, so very tired;*

if you ask *me*, The Latin *King* is acting like a Latin ***ASS.***

Titi's not all-that-pleased with her "so-called man," *either.*

"How you gon' push up on Baby Girl with me right here in front a you," Titi goes off.

"We ain't *married*," Barry informs her. "Ain't that what you always tell *me*?"

By her facial expression I would guess Titi is developing a "'tude"-of-her-own.

"I may be old, Black *and* toothless but, ***bitch,*** I *don't need a nigga like* ***you,***"

Titi declares, heads for her room.

In a moment-of-clarity, Barry realizes he has *fucked up again*; he hurries after Titi.

Rots of Ruck, Chief.

Since the room is actually *Barry's*, I wonder how long Titi's going to be in there.

Oh well, another-one-bites-the-dust.

Can't-we-all-get-***along,*** *though*?

Geez; ***you*** figure.

'Cause if we had *one* ***party,*** where there *wasn't a fight,* I would just about ***die,*** *always.*

What I *really* want is to go check on Titi.

If *my* man made a play-for-his-ex in front of *me*, it would be *so, so very* ***on.***

That's the problem-with-men: they talk a "good game;" treat-you-like-shit *any*way.

Today is our last day together.

Coming-down-off-of-his-cloud, Barry confesses he still-has-a-thing-for-me.

Well, *DUH*!.

He's sorry he didn't treat me better when we were together.

Haven't I been here *before*?

I mean, let's-move-***on***; this is *so, so very* ***over,*** already.

Actually, Barry isn't a bad person, he just doesn't know how to *treat* a woman.

So many men missed *that* class in "Manhood Training,"

there must have been a "Hooky Party" that day.

Obie and I take a crazy-long, leisurely walk on the beach.

Instead of turning back when I get tired, we stop; chill for a spell, then continue on.

We talk a great deal; not about anything serious, though.

Don't want to spoil-the-mood.

When we get back to the house Obie turns to me, murmurs quietly:

"Do you mind if I go out to my rock for a sec?"

I putter around the house aimlessly. Obie is only at his rock, yet I miss him terribly.

My meandering brings me out to the pool deck;

off in the distance I see Obie sitting with his legs crossed facing the ocean.
Just looking at O makes me feel close to him; I sit there watching for quite some time.
I figure he's out there meditating or what-have-you;
but something doesn't seem "quite right."
His shoulders are shaking way too much, gradually it dawns on me: Obie is crying.
As a rule, no one is allowed to mess with Obie when he is on his rock;
unless, of course, you want to *die,* always.
I am stuck between the urge to reach-out-to-him; the desire to respect-his-privacy.
I decide upon the latter, as difficult as it is to sit here: to watch my baby cry.
His bags are already packed.
We don't do much the rest of the day except sit up under we'chother half naked.
I might not feel sexy but I *definitely* feel the-need-to-bond with O;
to feel him move inside of me.
It will be a-moon-and-a-half before we see each other again.
The hands on my hips guide me firmly forward, except
Obie has neglected his "coverage."
"Condom," I murmur, reminding him.
"Uhn-Uhn," he moans, persistently tugging at my hips.
Okay, he's really-blowing-my-mood here.
Time to bring *this* shit to a *halt.*
"*What!*?" he growls angrily.
"Come *on,* O: I don't want to get *pregnant.*"
"You *won't*, Babe, I **promise**," he sighs in my ear. "You fi'n a get your *period.*"
Nigga please.
"I don't know what the *hell is on your mind.*
A girl can get pregnant at *any* time; *I* can't **afford** a baby at this-point-in-my-career."
"*Anything* is possible *theoretically*, but it's *highly improbable* you'll end-up-in-trouble this close to your period. *Besides*, is that the worst-thing-that-could-happen?
Our baby would have *plenty a company* and two *very famous parents.*"
How long has this been on Obie's mind?
I "hesitate" to "contemplate."
However, what he said about the probability of my getting pregnant *does ring true.*
Breaking into my thoughts, Obie places his lips on my neck, begins stroking my breasts.
"If we gon' spend the-rest-a-our-lives together, we gon' haveta take the condom off
*some*time, you feel me? I ain't had 'raw sex' since I was *fifteen,* and I wanna make

love to you the way it's *supposed* to be; not *bound-in-rubber*."
Maybe he's right, I sure *hope* so; either way,
his tongue on my breast convinces me to proceed.
We make love over and over again, storing up "nuts" for the long-cold-winter ahead of us.
I've gotten tired; I hurt all over; Obie is in "Energizer Bunny" mode.
I don't want to break-his-heart; plus: one day *soon* I'll be missing his big beautiful body.
After our fifth or sixth go-round Obie breaks down; squeezes the life out of me
(clearly forgetting about my ribs); bawls like a baby.
"Oh, God, why do I haveta go? I don't **want** *to;* I wanna stay here with *you; forever.*"
"I don't want you to go, *either*. After all this time I can't imagine being without you."
We have been together the better part of two years;
seeing each other every single day, sleeping together every night.
"*Why* can't I go with you again?"
"Your career would go down the *toilet bowl*;
you would *hate me for the rest of your life,* **remember**?
We talked about this *before*."
"The only thing I'll hate right now is leaving you."
I understood completely. I hated him leaving me too,
straight up until the time he went through the door, two hours later.

And then I hated it even more.

3 OB

You know that nigga Hood told on me, right?

He called Mommy and told her I wouldn't get out the bed.

And he wonders why we call him The Mommy Clone.

I spend several Long and Under Necessary Minutes on the phone with Mommy,

reassuring her that **yes**, I **am** a'ight and **yes,** I'm a get outta bed **Real Soon, okay?**

This shit is **worse** than livin with your fuckin mother, **that's** what it is, you feel me?

Fuck HIM.

I'm a **kill** this bitch for **real** this time if he don't Get Up Out My Biz.

The house is quiet, ain't no kids to tend to, so what I'm gettin up for?

The 'Girl is Out Cold; she only wakes up to take her Codeine Cocktail.

Every so often I heat some soup in the microwave and feed her, best I can.

Really, she's not eatin much **at all**, but then again:

Neither am *I*.

I hope I ain't lost no more weight.

It was hard enough puttin the weight back on the **first** time.

We done run outta juice and stuff so I make a run down to the kitchen and Re-Up.

I ain't been down here **five damn minutes** yet I hear a loud THUMP.

I know the Name a **This** Tune:

The 'Girl Done Fell Out The Bed.

This is why I don't get **up.**

If there was **anybody here at all** to send on a run I wouldn't a got up **this time.**

Upstairs Baby Girl is layin like a lump on the floor.

I'm The Fool Strugglin to get her Big Black Ass back in bed, you feel me?

But **she** keep carryin on bout Gettin Up;

Beggin and Pleadin and sayin She Gotta Go To Work.

I'm thinkin she mean **Today** but she mean Next Week.

As If.

We ain't goin **Nowhere** For A While so I Hope She Packed A Snickers.

Do she Understand Me or **what**?! I don't know cause she passed out again.

With The 'Girl sleep I watch TV.

Why I **bother** with this shit I'll never know: It's Such **Bullshit.**

Our "E! True Hollywood Stories" is on **Non Stop** like a F'in **Marathon** or somethin.

Our differences is **definitely** reflected in our "Hollywood Stories."

While mine's was a Two Hour Epic, The Girl's was hardly worth The Hour It Filled.

A Big Stink was made about Baby Girl growin up with money.

Big Shit.

Like Niggas Can't Have Money **Too**.

They scraped up some girls from our school to talk about how

Baby Girl Didn't Have No Friends and was Screwin her Own Damn Cousin.

Where do they **find** these people?

With nothin else bad to say they fleshed out the rest a the hour

speculatin on her relationship with The Infamous Obie One.

I'm Her **Cousin** too damn it; First Foremost & Always.

Now **my** True Hollywood Story? **That** was some **shit.**

They dug up enough crap on me to make that bitch a **miniseries**

but they managed to Cram It into two hours.

What did they include? Well, what did they leave **out**, dog?

Mother a Junkie (**boy** they worked **that** one), Lived On The Streets, Left With Father

At Age Six (I was **seven**), Problem Child, Discovered On Street Corner With

Half Brother (I really hate that term), Stint With Male Prostitution In His Teens

(now **there's** a Good One), *Alleged* Drug & Alcohol Problems and Numerous

Brushes With The Law.

Oh. And **By The Way**;

He's a Pretty Good Dancer and Shoots Great Music Videos.

See where I'm goin with this one?

My Life has Overshadowed My Career, which is Quite Stellar Thank You Very Much.

The way they make it seem all I am is Some Fuck Up who Got Lucky Cause

He Can Dance *A Little*. Well I was Famous **WAY** before I Started Shootin Videos.

How many famous dancers **is** there *anyway*?

Fred Astaire?

Gene Kelly?

Obie One?

Fuck Em.

Some *Clearly* Hastily Thrown Together show came on chroniclin me and Princess'

relationship from the time she first hit Cali to our engagement.

Now this is more like it: reminds me a all the Good Times we had.

Another crappy show interviewed people, mostly in The Industry, who supposedly **know us.**

As **If.**

Smoke made a Complete **Ass** outta hisself, and not cause he was Talkin Bout Me:

He Ain't Know What He Was Talkin Bout *period.*

And where the Hell did they find **Toya's** Dumb Ass?

Why is she on TV *Insistin* She Havin My Baby?

As *If.*

To think I actually **liked her** for a minute.

Oh **Well.**

She gon be **migh-ty** up-set when Survey Says: **Obie One; You Are** *Not* **The Father.**

The one person who **could a** acted a Natural Ass didn't.

A reporter cornered Nikki somewhere and asked for her comment.

"Leave The Girl Alone," Nikki replied in a huff. "She ain't done nothin to nobody."

I have **got** to do somethin **nice** for that girl.

My **favorite** show was Style Watch: Top Ten Obie & Princess Outfits.

My Inner Clotheshorse is **particularly pleased:**

I put A Lotta Effort into them Matchin Outfits.

Sick a watchin Media Sanctioned Obie Bashin I sneak downstairs and call Nikki.

"I just wanted to let you know I appreciate you not joinin the Shit On Princess Party."

"'S All Good, Obie. You know You My Nigga."

"Well Yo Nigga wasn't that Kind & Sweet last time we met so you really didn't hafta Go To Bat for us like that."

"I got what My Hand Called For, you smell me? I ain't Mad At All. E'ryone knew Y'all Was Gon Hook Up eventually. I shouldn't a Put My Heart In It to begin with."

"You got a Lot More Class than I Give You Credit For.

I'm sorry for the way things went down between us."

"Yo; Stop **Apologizin.** We had a Good Run."

Yeah,

Like Freak said: Fond Memories.

"Who this bitch runnin round talkin bout she havin your baby though?

I mean if you was givin One a Those away…"

"OOOH! Don't get me started on **that** one. **You** know she got bout as much chance a bein Pregnant With *My* Child as Dan Rather got a Fuckin Lil Kim."

I ain't mind layin round the bed with Baby Girl,

but this Sittin On The Beach shit is drivin me **crazy**.
Baby Girl feels like The Whole World Is Passin Her By Too.
Oh **Well.**
My Tranquility Needed Work **Anyway**.
The 'Girl is Comin Along **Nicely**, only Not As Quick as **she** would prefer.
I don't see what the rush is no how, it ain't like her CD ain't Sellin **Itself.**
We **sure** Don't Need The **Money**, with what we made and our investments
we set for *a little* while a least.
Why The 'Girl don't just Slow Her Roll (Playa) and Concentrate on Gettin Better?!
And Who **Says** That anymore???
Late In The Day Officer Tyson stops by to interview Princess.
I don't think it was such a Good Idea for Freaky to let him in here,
OR for her to submit to this type a questionin, but he **is** a Officer a The Law.
Draggin my Angry Black Butt back to the house I instruct my 'Girl to
Signal if she Need Help.
I'm So Upset I can't get past the slidin doors, for over half a hour I just Stand There
watchin Baby Girl and Ty through the glass, my stomach churnin anxiously.
Then I see Baby Girl pump her fist like she on Arsenio or somethin.
"Wassa matter?" I ask My Baby, glarin at Officer Tyson.
"I'm tired and I don't want to talk anymore," she says fretfully.
Baby Girl is **Really Upset,** and I am **Hatin** Ty for **botherin** her.
"Let me show you the **door,**" I offer, All My Hatred showin.
He better be glad he's a **cop,** I know **that.**
"Tell me what **really** happened," Ty asks at the door.
"We been through all this before. Ain't nothin else I can tell you," I answer curtly.
"Did Albert rape Princess?" Ty asks me pointedly.
He must be Out His Mothafuckin **Mind** to ask me some shit like that.
Now I know why Baby Girl got **tired** on his ass so fast.
"What did **she** tell you?" I ask cagily.
Ponderin his answer for a moment Ty says quietly:
"If the answer was **no**, you'd have said so right away."
"You **figure?!**" I counter swiftly, not wantin Ty to know he Hit The Mark.
"Why don't you guys report it? If it'll help any I'll take the report myself."
What a Dick.
"Is today Report A Rape Day in Malibu?" I ask sarcastically,

85

"**Come on**. She Goin Through Hell as it **is** Ty. I mean, you watched the **news** lately?
You think that girl wants The Whole World to know what happened to her?"
Both a us is Occupied with Our Own Thoughts at this point.
"Later on you might be sorry you didn't," Ty predicts.
One thing I can say for sure: Ty's about as Decent and Fair Minded as a cop can **get**.
He ain't out here tryna Make A Name For Hisself by Breakin The Princess Case.
Some Official Person **should** know The Truth,
but I would **never** Drop Dime behind my Girl's back.
I think.
"Come out to Laurel Canyon, I wanna show you somethin. Off The Record."

Her gorgeous body still bears the bruises a her ordeal; horrible discolorations that
cling obstinately to her back and breasts, defiant in the face a time like a placard
Einstein holds up from the grave emblazoned with the words FUCK YOU OBIE.
What kinda monster **does** this to a woman he **claims** to *love*?
Who **does** that??!!!
With The 'Girl's permission I put my fingers over the marks on her breasts.
My hand's bigger than Einstein's,
my fingers extends a inch and a half past the bruises' borders.
The 'Girl said she ain't feel much pain durin the attack itself, that came later.
I been **that** route myself.
Curious, I ask to see her stitches.
A Raggedy Lookin Tear winds upward from the mouth a her 'cat to her clit.
That looks **Extra** Painful, she says it was.
I feel so bad for her; I could **die,** always.
So of course I go Pull a Obie and kiss the poor girl's pussy tryna Make It Better.
I **swear**, if I don't **Astound Myself** *every single day* then I Ain't **Truly Breathin.**
Now I gotta trip all over myself Apologizin &All
but The 'Girl takes it in the spirit it was given.
Thank God **Somebody** Understands Me,
cause I Don't **Understand My** *Self* Too Tough.
Last thing I needed was to Kiss The 'Girl's 'Cat though.
Now my Hormones is Jumpin All Over The Place.
It's been A **While** Jack, and although Intellectually I know My 'Girl Is Hurtin & All,
my **dick** wanna Do A Little **Actin.**

It's so ri*dicu*lous.

I try to have a **talk** with him but he's payin me **no mind whatsoever.**

He **know** what he **want**; only **I can't give it to him** and this aggravates me To No End.

I wish I could Flip A Switch and not hafta be **bothered** with Petty Ass Desires.

Like **that'll** happen.

Forced to do the Next Best Thing I Flog my Log.

Constantly.

My arm hurts and I done lost a layer a skin on my dick but **Here I Am Again.**

My self-esteem goes **right down the toilet with my jism**.

Can I **die** *now* please?

Went to church, church was good; still wanna Get My Dick Wet.

I want to **die,** *always.*

The Big Beautiful Black woman by my side ain't helpin matters none.

She sleepin so peaceful that I press myself against her for a little while.

I bury my fingers in her hair, lovin the Melon-y Smell and the Soft Silky Feel a it.

I need her body **so** *bad*, which to me is like a Betrayal a Our Situation.

Who knows when Baby Girl will feel like Makin Love again?

I would Never in A Million Years try to rush her into Havin Sex and I **sure as Hell**

wouldn't dream a Steppin Out On Her, that would be *Too* **Under Fair:**

very very **much** so.

I can handle this situation As Long As Necessary, even if I hafta Handle It **five times a day**.

Just make sure I got enough baby oil, you feel me?

Baby Girl is wakin up.

I ease my dick off her back so I don't upset or offend her or whatever,

but she keeps pullin at my draws and beggin me to come closer.

Oh **Boy**.

Maybe if I go Release Some Tension first...

but: Hell No, She Won't Let Me Go.

What she **does** is reach in my draws and start playin with my joint.

Good **God**, dog. Feels So *Good* but she don't know My Rhythm.

Rhythm is **important** to a dancer, you know.

Everybody's got A Rhythm; I gotta help her Establish The Right One For Me.

Baby Girl puts her tongue on my nipples and it's **Over.**

My greedy self wants Another Go Round but The 'Girl is **tired**, I can tell.

Her hand feels a thousand percent better than mine's so I use her hand to get off a second time.

Afterwards I feel **pret-ty slea-zy**.

"Sorry," I whisper guiltily.

"You're talking foolishness," a very groggy Baby Girl rebuts on her way to sleep.

Sure You're Right.

I still gotta make **more time** for us. I don't wanna **leave her**,

I **can't**: we been **together** too long.

I'm just about ready to Chuck All This and follow Baby Girl on her rounds.

Get us A Few Good Outfits, maybe some Matchin Arm Slings,

you know, do it up Ghetto Style.

I don't need the rest a this crap; I could be her PA:

I mostly fill that role **anyway**, only I do it outta **love.**

Wonderin if I can Pull Some Strings, I reach for my phone.

Then the Earth Shifts On Its Axis somehow and Baby Girl and me end up

fightin over my efforts to dump some a these Upcomin Projects.

She under the Misguided Belief that In The Long Run

I will **resent** Givin Up My Work for her.

As *IF*.

What the Hell is she smokin; **Crack**?

Do she really think Any **Job,** Any **Where**, can replace What We Have Together?

Or Make Me Feel As **Special**?

Cause she **tryna** act like She **Don't** Need Me, and That's **Bullshit.**

Losin It, I Tell Her About Herself.

She looks Crushed and *I* feel like A **Heel** for **talkin to her like that.**

Still; she should know **better** than that by now.

I say sorry anyway, what the fuck.

The first call don't Go Too Well.

Instead a choreographin one or two scenes a this Club Movie

Me & Hood is doin **The Whole Flick.**

Two months ago I would a told you it was the **Best Thing** That Ever Happened To

Me outside a Baby Girl, we got **roles in this bitch** and *everything*.

The director let me delay *this*-one-week but won't Let Me Slide any longer.

Too Integral To The Production & All That.

Fuck.

Who Do I Hafta Bone To Get *Off* This Picture?

It's turnin into One Great Big **Obstacle,** a **Impediment.**

Do you believe I can't dump any a these videos, either?

Three Outta Six Producers threatened to **Sue** Me for Breach a Contract.

I can't figure out why this is **happenin** to us, Baby Girl deserves **Better.**

Me? I been a Fuck Up my **whole life**; Why Should This be Any Dif?

But if a man's Primary Responsibility is To His Family then

how can I go to work knowin my 'Girl is *sick* and she *needs me*?

Bein on The Horns of a Dilemma is a **Rough Ride** Jack.

Why nobody gives a Flyin **Fuck** though?

How would they feel if it was **they** girl?

Then again, these is people who would Run Over They **Mommas** for a contract.

Oh **Hell.**

The last call I don't even wanna make.

I been in plenty a movies but the ones I want I can't never get cause I'm Too Light.

You Don't Look The Part is what I hear most often.

Well, I Don't Look The Part in Real Life but I'm Still A Black Man, **a'ight**?

What the **fuck**.

So anyway, about three years ago I got to talkin with this producer who

failed to hire me forThe Same Old Reason.

I Vented My Frustration at bein constantly turned down solely because a my skin color.

He listened sympathetically but I figured we had Left It There, you feel me?

A year later I get this script in the mail:

Young Light-Skinned Kid Fights For Acceptance In The Hood While Dreamin A Bein

A Video Ho. The Post It Note attached read Make Any Corrections You Like.

So I did.

Reluctantly I close my phone.

There is no **way** I can call and beg off this movie; it was Tailor Made For Me.

Every bit as much a my blood went into that script as the original writer's.

That script went back and forth between us for seven months before it earned my satisfaction.

Now comes the moment I dread the most: The Itineraries.

We don't even Pass In The Night for the next **six months**.

Who's re*spon*sible for this shit?!

Damn it, that would be **me**.

Tears well up inside a me cause I feel Defeated By My Circumstances.

Depression grabs me by the throat, cuttin off my Air Supply.

It's Only Six Months I tell myself. I can make it; I **know** I can.

We been apart longer than that. Baby Girl can **too**, if I get her some **help**.
The 'Girl's mind has not yet alighted on this particular problem.
She concerned about her movie role.
You know.
The one that she ain't **GOT** no more.
Ever the Bearer a Bad News I break it to The 'Girl as gently as I can,
tackin on at the Last Possible Moment that Xanadi got her role.
That went over like a **bomb.**
There's no good way to take news like that so I let her cry for a sec,
then hit her with the Good News—I got her another role.
Okay so it's a 'Hood Flick instead a the Hollywood Blockbuster she had originally,
but why she dis the picture like that, yo? We watch **every nigga picture made**, Good
Bad or Ugly, so why wouldn't she wanna be **in** one? Shit, if I wasn't already Makin A
Movie Myself I swear I'd Roll Over and Take One For The Cause to get on **this** one.
I'm tellin you I'd Suck Someone **Off**.
Every nigga **in** The Rap Industry's in this, they all got a cut on the soundtrack too.
Freak and BB got small supportin roles,
and I just heard from A Source they gon enlarge BB's part from a Integral yet
Non Speakin role to one a along the lines a his Wrestlin character:
a deaf kid everybody makes fun a, only this one grows up to be a Cold Hearted Killer.
It's Very Few Lines and it'll explain why he Sounds So Awful.
Princess is replacin Chante Pierce. The part is **huge**, third female lead I think,
and they givin Baby Girl Chante's songs too. I encourage her to **think** about this one.
Ditzy believes I already Accepted The Role On Her Behalf;
like It's A **Oscar** or somethin.
That 'Girl makes me **so mad** sometimes.
If she wasn't **already hurt** I'd choke the livin **shit** out her ass.
Oh **Well**.
In the end she agrees to take the part.
Wise Choice Baby Girl.
Another night finds us snuggled up together in the bed chitchattin.
I'm layin here playin with Baby Girl's hair, feelin her warm body next to mine.
And you **know** what that does to me.
I back away from her and she **lays into me** bout how I'm **hurtin her feelins** and all.
Like **I Meant To Do *That*.**

Or my day has **not been** *crappy* **enough.**

Apparently, The 'Girl is offended by my Assumption a What Will Offend her.

What should I do, Ask Her?

Excuse Me, but Can I Press My **Dick** On you?

Who *does* that??!!!

Don't I at least get Bonus Points for **Tryin**?

Come on…Twenty Five Points at **least.**

Anyway, she want Dick On Her Back, I'll give her Dick On Her Back;

I won't complain.

I give her Lips On Her Neck and Hand On Her Tittie too; The Whole Shebang.

YO!!! What am I *doin* **to myself**?!?

Baby Girl beckons me and I rub myself on her stomach til I come, Just Like Old Times.

Still Hard but Maintainin My Cool,

I am Bowled Over when Baby Girl rolls onto her stomach in front a me.

Then her Silly Ass grabs my dick and starts talkin to it.

I never seen a girl talk to a dick like it has a Actual Brain and not just a

Mind A Its Own; cracks me up **every time.**

Slidin my foreskin up with her hand Baby Girl giggles.

"Look! I'm puttin his Hoodie on."

O-**kay** Then.

Three times the hoodie Goes On and Comes Off.

She may call it Puttin On the Hoodie; **I** call it What A Hand Job.

Oh **Boy.**

While I'm ridin this Wave A Ecstasy Baby Girl says somethin bout givin my dick a

kiss or **somethin** but before I get a grasp on what she sayin her tongue ring is **on me.**

Or more like **in me.** Right in that little hole in the tip.

Couldn't get away from there **fast** enough, I almost **came** in the poor 'Girl's **mouth.**

Why she won't **stop** though?

After all Baby Girl's been through I can't bring myself to let her do that.

Pullin a Clarissa I try to Explain It All To Her, only:

I **mighta** made The **Slight Mistake** a referred to her as The Rape Victim.

I **mighta.**

I ain't sayin for sure.

But can you imagine the Shit Storm I mighta created **if** I had actually **Said** Such a Thing?

Okay.

I said it.

And **BOY** am **I** *SORRY.*

WOW.

What a **Screamin MEANIE** that 'Girl had.

Damn.

She did everything but Throw Plates.

Ain't nothin I can do but Wait This One Out, which looks like it could be **all night.**

When she Finally Falls Asleep I carry her weary bones to bed.

TRUST ME, I won't be makin **that** mistake *again*.

The Mornin Sun makes everything seem Fresh and Brand New.

After we both Express Regret for Last Night's Actions

Baby Girl wants to make love to me.

I'm Under Certain about the whole thing: Very Very Much So.

In fact I'm **convinced** she Rushin again: Everything This Girl Does is at Warp Speed.

We debate the issue briefly but why did I **Go** There? I Can't Win, **Chile.**

So I try the What About Your Stitches tack. The 'Girl wants me to check for them.

Up in her snatch.

With my fingers.

She must **really** wanna Get Laid Bad.

Okay, *that* was Insensitive.

Ashamed a myself *el otro vez* I rest my head on Baby Girl's stomach and Take The Plunge.

Feels Okay to **me**, *especially* with Baby Girl rubbin my head.

Givin her a Clean Bill A Health I figure: While I'm **Down** Here…

Suddenly we hit a Snag.

When I go to Put It In, Baby Girl freezes up.

I **know** I done **Somethin Wrong,** only Baby Girl won't tell me **what.**

Nervous about The Act to **begin** with,

Apprehension Comes Of Age in a heartbeat and is now Full Grown Fear.

"Keep going," her Dumb Ass insists.

As *If.*

The Fool Don't Even Know she havin a Anxiety Attack.

I remind her it's cause She **Speedin** but **she don't hear me though**.

A Hard Head Makes A Soft Behind Every Time, right Uncle BB? So we Try It Again.

You think it works **this** time?

Oh **Well.**

Only **this** time Baby Girl starts **cryin**.

Oh *Hell*.

Luckily she mentions in passin that she panics when I get on top of her.

Shit--we can fix **that**. Like the Late Great Aaliyah said:

Change Position.

Next Problem: the sunshine highlights her injuries unbearably.

My stomach rebels, forcin me to swallow back my bile.

"My bruises turn you off, don't they?" Baby Girl solicits.

Oh My Fuckin **God**, yo. What kinda man **wouldn't** get Turned Off?

Unable to look I ask her to turn around. This is like my Favorite Position anyway;

Remember the Cure For The Cramps?

This time we Take Our Sweet Time and Gettin There is No Problem.

I make love to every inch a my Baby's body, bruises and all, cause

I Love Her That Much.

I have the most **Powerful Intense Orgasm** a my **life,**

and she got the nerve to thank **me???**

As *IF.*

What we got, three—four days left?

The Closer It Get the Worser I Feel.

You think it made me feel better to wake up and find Baby Girl gone?

Frantic, I search the house but there ain't no Baby Girl nowhere.

Runnin past the back door I **happen** to look out and there she is,

Sittin At The Water's Edge.

Who **does** that, Otis Redding??!!

What in the **Hell** is she **doin**?! Did she **collapse**? Stiflin the urge to bolt out there and

strangulate her I wait rather impatiently for Baby Girl to return.

Don't take long; whatever she did burnt her out completely.

Ass draggin, Baby Girl damn near **limps** back to the house.

Riot Act in hand & Ready To Read it I demand to know where she been.

Why she tell me Out By The Rock Fuckin Somebody?!

Who DOES That??!!!

Pursuin this line a questionin The 'Girl not only reveals she went for a walk but also:

I am Crowding Her. I guess I'm supposed to let her Go & **Fall Out somewhere.**

Every day it's Some **New** Shit.

Okay, this is **Old** Shit but Everything Old Is New Again, you feel me?

I feel A Tude comin on.

More than **that** I feel **wounded** like she Don't Want Me Around.

What's **that** all about, I ask you?

Noticin my Injured Feelins Cess do her **best** to reassure me I am still Very Much Wanted.

Believe me that was a Under Natural amount a work.

A lite lunch, a little TV, and Baby Girl is ready for another walk.

Oh **Goody**, I **get to go** this time.

No *really*.

I'm Really Enthusiastic about this.

For dinner she want Steak & Potatoes, the Period Thing hard at work.

Where Does The Time Go? Somebody Help Me here.

After almost three weeks on a soft diet Baby Girl ain't gon digest no steak yet

true to form, she don't hear me on **this** issue either. Resigned to her contrariness

I don't even **attempt** to argue with her. Instead I cook her some Chicken Creole,

Soft & Soupy. Relishin the flavor she polishes off three bowls full.

Meanwhile Lack a Appetite done Staked Its Claim on me

and the best I can do is pick at my food.

At this rate I'm gonna Dry Up & Blow Away.

The problem is, all I wanna do is hold her: Get It While I Can, you feel me?

I bet once I'm gone I'll miss Baby Girl's Relentless Arguin and her Crappy Mood Swings too.

Ain't **that** some shit?

Why The Latin King Disrupts My Reverie though?

Hator.

Baby Girl invokes her right to talk to whatever piece a shit she wishes to.

Whatever.

Fuck This Bitch **Barry** though; I'm stayin **Right** In The **Hallway**.

Where I can **Keep A Eye** on The **Ugh** Couple.

Okay, that bitch is Kissin My 'Girl. **Somebody** owes me a **Ex-pla*n*ation**.

Right before he ends up **In A Body Bag**.

The only explanation Baby Girl is willin to give is that:

Outta Respect for the Relationship she and Barry once shared I am Obliged in some

way to allow Barry to Speak To Her In Person about her health.

Help me now; how does that include him **slobbin all over her?**

"That's what you get for Being Nosy," Baby Girl informs.

No *that's* what I get for lettin Barry's Triflin Ass sit next to my girl Under Supervised.

Let's watch **that** happen again.

Next night Hood, Dionne, Baby Girl and me gather round the Big Screen to play The Game.

The 'Girl is wildly animated, and for the first time since this tragedy befell us

I have a glimmer a hope that Everything's Gonna Be All Right.

Then Barry and Aunty arrive.

Can't You Feel The Hator In The Air?

Under pressure to Maintain My Center **for The 'Girl's sake,**

I **ignore** his ass, even when he **insists** upon **playin The Game with us**.

After we get High this nigga Flips The Script and tries to **make Princess dance with him**.

What an Appropriate Place for a Obie Tude, don'tcha think?

Cause His Cheese Musta Slipped Off His Cracker **Big Time**.

Bein Far Too Proud to allow herself to be Played Auntie Takes That Step.

That's when it dawns on this mothafucka that he done stuck a quarter in his ass and

PLAYED HISSELF, so he scurries off after Aunty.

Definitely **not** The Brightest Candle In The Monastery.

Takes me almost fifteen minutes and half a blunt to Calm My Black Ass Down.

It's o-*kay* though cause I had A Lotta Rage to vent and welcomed the opportunity to

Dump It On Somebody I **Absolutely Hate.**

"Yo," Hood captures my attention,

"I asked Dionne to Go Wit Baby Girl on her Rounds."

"*Son*," I reach out to hug him. "I can't thank you enough."

"**Kill** that, yo," embarrassed, Hood Brushes Me Off,

"It's that old Brothers Is Down For Each Other No Matter What thing. **You** know."

"Well Brothers Appreciate All A Nigga Does For Them so Smoke Upon **That**."

I know this a Personal Sacrifice for Hood: he was gonna take Dionne to Canada.

I worry The 'Girl'll Take A Rain Check though since she don't actually **know** Dionne

but Dionne musta Presented Her Case Well cause it's All A Big Go.

Our last day together sneaks up on me and I'm so down I could just die, always.

We been up all night and did some Radio Call Ins early this A.M.

so we crawl into bed and doze for a while.

I **Absolutely Positively** do **not** wanna Get Outta This Bed but Baby Girl is barrelin

Full Speed Ahead and I'll be **damned** if I get Left Behind in her wake. Besides:

The bed ain't nowhere near as much fun when she ain't there.

Princess has a Hearty Breakfast, part a her Fitness Trainin.
I don't know how she squeezes it down cause I can't eat a thing.
I think I'm gonna be sick.
Our Power Walk on the beach devolves into a leisurely stroll and that's Fine By Me.
The more time we spend together the better, you feel me?
It's comin down on me though, the tears and all. Not wantin to cry in front a The 'Girl
(that **Manly** thing) I get her safely to the house then double back to My Rock.
My Rock is my place for Meditation & Reflection, which I need **plenty a** Right About Now.
Reachin Deep Within Me I summon Holy Ghost Power,
the only thing that can Give Me The Strength to Walk Out On My 'Girl.
Legs crossed in front a me, palms outstretched, I face the settin sun and begin to pray.
I need answers I'm positive will Not Come Today; resolve I Surely Hope Will.
I'm stuck like a motha on the total Concept a Responsibility.
I'm not a Jackass I just Play One On TV so I know I done made The Wise Choice.
Even Baby Girl recognizes Throwin My Career Away Don't Make Much Sense.
So why do it keep **Tuggin** At Me, Demandin to be Accepted?
I been around this Mulberry Bush Ad Infinitum Ad Nauseam and I **still** can't reconcile
my decision with the feelins in my heart. Overwhelmed I burst into disconsolate tears.
The Crying My Heart Out thing lasts A Millennium. I don't feel One Damn Bit Better.
Ain't cryin supposed to be **cathartic** or somethin?
I'm feelin worse **now** cause my **head** hurts and my *nose* is all stuffy.
I gotta Face The Girl **lookin** like I been Cryin Like A **BITCH** too.
Oh Well.
Splash A Little Water On Your Face & Move On Obie.

Lonely Already and I Ain't Even Gone yet, I coax Baby Girl back into bed with me.
Semi Nude and Semi Conscious we lay explorin we'chother in a Lazy Hazy Way.
If I say I Don't Wanna Go again Would That Be Redundant?
I Thought So Too.
So I'm just gonna Enjoy This Moment long as I can.
Tracin the ridges a Baby Girl's spine with my fingertips over and over makes me
wanna grab two handfuls a hair and…
Only, I Don't Get There cause Baby Girl moves my hands to her breasts.
To quote some Dumb Commercial: I am Alive With Pleasure.
Okay, that was *Tres* Corny.

But **still**... **You** know how I'm feelin.

Our lips pressed together, The 'Girl's beautiful titties in my hands,

I'm Ready &Willin to go; Sans Condom. Couldn't Slip That Past Baby Girl though.

Worried about Gettin Pregnant she Freaks Out on me.

Need I remind you not only is she gonna Marry Me, but she **is** gonna Have My Baby.

In her mind however this is a concept Best Left Under Explored.

O-kay Then...Survey Says:

She most likely won't be Gettin Pregnant Tonite **anyway**: Too Close To Her Period.

Besides, I am sick to **death** a rubbers. In all honesty I wanna feel Baby Girl round me

Raw & Wet like that **First First Time**- Way Back On Her Couch.

You know; That One Time me and Baby Girl keep Pretendin **Never Happened.**

As **If**.

Conquerin Baby Girl's Misgivins I am In There Like Swim Wear,

over and over and over again.

I can't get **enough,** yo. Some Small Part A My Brain **knows** I should be Takin It

Easy on Baby Girl, Respectin her Condition & Whatnot, but I can't Stop Myself.

The Girl ain't complained yet, and that Same Part A Me wishes she **would**.

It's not **like** Baby Girl to let me steamroll over her.

She always Understood Me Better than I Understood Myself so maybe she just

Knows Where I'm Comin From.

I Sure As Hell **Hope** So.

My dick is Shootin Fire again, from **every single cell in my body**.

Snottin like a **Bitch** I collapse on top a Baby Girl.

Fuck Redundancy to all *Hell;* **I Just Don't Wanna Go.**

And leave all this behind??? I ain't *never* been as happy as I been the last two years.

It's as if my heart is bein Ripped From My Chest, Soul To Follow Shortly.

I would rather **die on the spot** than catch that flight to Canada but no one on the

Decision Makin Committee bothered to Ask For My Input.

Can't even sue em, Right a First Refusal wasn't Specified in The Contract.

Have to talk to my Business Manager about that Oversight.

Satirical Banter ain't helpin either. I'm screwed.

You know that song "Leaving on a Jet Plane," by Peter, Paul and Mary?

That's **exactly** the way I feel, been **here** before too.

When me and Baby Girl got high I wasn't so high I didn't know what I was doin.

Figurin she'd stop me eventually I was determined nonetheless to Ride The Wave as far as it would take me.

Who knew it would take me All The Way Home?

You could a bought me for two cents.

All my condoms was in my luggage cause I was with **Baby Girl**, **RIGHT?**

Oh My **God**.

I ain't wanna Stop and Go Get One, she might Come To Her Senses, you feel me?

Why did I **do** that to myself? Goin Raw with a girl you **Care About** is *Intense*.

Too Intense.

Musta been the same for The 'Girl

cause in the mornin we couldn't look we'chother in the eye.

It wasn't Shame; it was Lover's Remorse: that *OH*; What Did I *Do* feelin.

Why didn't we **talk** about it, I **wanted** to, but Baby Girl kept Cuttin Me Off.

And Deep Down Inside I guess I was afraid.

But I kept callin her just to hear the sound a her voice.

When I went to sleep I dreamt a Baby Girl Hot & Naked under me, legs wrapped around my waist, lips on my chest. Still, that second time Baby Girl put her feet in my lap I was kinda scared to touch em. Honestly Folks after the way the First Ep went over I ain't think I had a Snowball's Chance In **Hell** a Hittin That again.

I was Way Better Prepared though, condoms tucked Safely In My Pocket Just In Case.

Well a nigga can **Dream, CAN'T HE?**

At first I grazed her toes very lightly with my fingertips a couple a times,

kinda like Testin The Water. Believe me I knew Where To Take It from there though.

Our first time I admit was **not** My Best Performance, we ain't even get outta our clothes.

But this time? This time I undressed Baby Girl **myself**.

When we finished I carried her to her bedroom where we slept naked, braided together.

You already know what happened the next day.

My flight was scheduled to leave at four a.m.

Normally flights fill me with A Sense a Anticipation as a New Adventure Spreads Out Gloriously before me. For the first time in my life I actually dreaded my departure.

Baby Girl was sleepin so peaceful I ain't wake her up.

Kissin her on the forehead I headed for the door.

Outside the cabbie honked his horn. Inexplicably Peter Paul and Mary popped into my head.

All my bags are packed/I'm ready to go/ I stand here waitin/outside your door

I hate to wake you up/ to say good-bye

But the dawn is breakin/ it's early morn/ The taxi's waitin/he's blowin his horn

Already/ I'm so lonesome/ I could cry
So kiss me/ and smile for me/ Tell me that/ you'll wait for me
Hold me like/ you'll never/ let me go
I'm leavin/ on a jet plane/ I don't know when/ I'll be back again
Oh babe/ I hate to go.

Notice who I said now cause that song was covered on the Armageddon Soundtrack,
but for Sheer Poignancy you Can't Beat The Original.
I left a note thankin The 'Girl for a wonderful time and promisin to call.
Didn't Happen.
As warm as Jamaica was it felt Cold & Lonely without Baby Girl.
Partyin, Drugs, Authentic Jamaican Foods, Ho's By The Layers, **Surfin**:
this was my Dream Vacation yet I felt **empty** inside, you feel me?
So why didn't I call?
My head was fucked up that's why.
So much had happened I didn't know What To Say or How To Act.
Afterwards I wished I had Swallowed My Pride and Had That Talk
way back after the first episode but by then it was Too Damn Late for that shit.
Okay, okay, I'm Lyin out the Crack A My Ass again.
 I was terrified Baby Girl was gonna do me like the first time and
Act Like Nothin Happened and my **heart** was All In It.
I might a lightweight Fucked That One Up but my God is a God a Second Chances.
So I'm Leavin on **this** Jet Plane *because*....?

I Hold This Truth to be Self Evident:
The Glow has Worn Off This Lifestyle for me.
It was a **Great** Life when I didn't **Have** a Life, you feel me?
Globe Hoppin don't mean nearly as much when All You Ever Wanted is
Sittin Back At Home.
Well they can **make me get on this fuckin plane**;
they can make me **shoot this stupid ass movie**,
but **GOT-DAMN IT** they can*not* make me **Like It.**

Pardon me, but my cab is waiting.

3 _{BG}

Minutes-seem-to-hang-like-hours when you're missing someone.

This moment in Princess Davis Price-Davis's life is brought to you by Timex.

Now that Obie is gone time seems to be going tick...............tock.

Get-the-picture?

I putter around the house aimlessly: don't eat, don't sleep, don't take-my-walk.

Of course, now that there's-no-Obie to sneak-away-from I cannot *imagine* walking-without-him.

The good news is, Dionne feels every bit as out of sorts as I do; together we commiserate.

By three p.m. we, too, are on a plane, to diddy-wa-do, who cares?

I don't.

This stupid ass promo tour rushes by in a blur of I-want-my-Obie.

So much to do, so little time; and my label keeps trying to pile more appearances on top of me.

I am bone weary; exhausted from my ordeal, the rigors of "self-promotion."

I broke my right arm, am left handed;

that's supposed to make-it-all-right for me to sit, sign autographs for three hours.

Well, damn it: my *body* hurts.

My business associates are seemingly insensitive about my health issues;

I end up inviting them all to kiss-my-Black-ass;

they respond by saying I'm starting-to-sound-like-Obie One.

No, I sound like a mad-as-fuck-*Princess,* but if *that* makes them feel better, *fuck* 'em.

Dionne is a *lifesaver*: she reminds me to eat, encourages me to rest,

keeps me company when "loneliness" threatens to drive-me-out-of-my-mind.

Way-too-often I forget that Dionne lives-in-that-boat, too.

In that weird biological pattern either God or Mother Nature has developed,

we both get our periods at the same time.

Twice as much Bitch to go around.

Dionne jokes; says God was against that plan, but Mother Nature figured if all women

caught their periods at the same time men couldn't fuck around on them that week.

Somebody give Momma Nature her "props" for thinking like a real-woman-should.

She must be Black.

Anyway...every three cycles or so I actually have a normal period,

so Mother Nature must be working *double time* on my behalf.

The first week Obie and Hood call every day; by week three we're down to three calls a week.

Or less.

Since the fellas are at *least* as busy as we are, if not *more* so, we can understand this.

Besides,

"It's not like we don't call them, too."

"I know girl; my cell phone bill is *outrageous*. Don't know why, Obie says he'll pay it."

"And you *complainin*?! Who does *that*? If it makes-him-feel-better why-fight-progress?"

"That's some *real* Mommy-like-advice, Dionne; since when does paying-some-woman's-phone bill make *Obie* feel better? He's the cheapest-nigga-in-town; doesn't believe in giving a woman anything that doesn't shoot-from-the-end-of-his-dick."

Nicole puts things in the-right-perspective for me:

"Maybe it's 'cause Obie don't *see* you as 'some woman.'"

You figure?

In ATL we end up at a wild-ass-party; *boy*, could I use some partying.

I get higher than I should; "hook up" with some dude.

The sex was a'ight—nothing spectacular, it wasn't a *Waiting To Exhale* moment either.

Dionne "hooked up," too; a guy she obviously knew/had fucked before.

If she likes it, I love it.

It's like six-in-the-morning now; I've got a seven-fifteen radio spot.

We're rushing back to the car; I grab my cell phone out of the glove compartment; the banner reads 17 Missed Calls.

Why they're all from Obie though, the last one only fifteen minutes ago.

I'd locked my phone in the car: didn't want Obie to fuck up my "party mood."

All these missed calls have me sorry I-*went-there*.

Understanding the situation, Dionne drives while I climb in the back; make-that-call.

"Sorry I missed your calls, babe. I left my phone in the car."

Silent for a moment, Obie says:

"Where were you last night?"

Here, I am tempted to lie; I don't.

"And you left your phone in the car."

"You know how I am," I offer as an explanation; it's plausible, right?

"So how was it?"

"The party was *bangin*, baby, we had a *great* time."

"I meant the *dude* you 'hooked up' wit'. How was *he*?"

Stunned into silence I ask myself why Obie had to take-it-there; then I ask *him*.

"You gonna get all irritated-on-me and *lie*, Princess? I wanna *know*. How *was* he?

Did-you-have-a-good-time?"

"O-*kay*; *you* sound upset. This might-not-be such a 'good time' to *have* this convo."

"I am **not** upset," Obie back peddles. "Talk to me; please; I won't fuss no more."

We're at the hotel, engaged in a "mad dash" for the elevators.

If I don't get off this phone I'm *going to be late*.

Three hours of "phone tag" later we reconnect.

"What makes you think I was with some dude?"

"What makes you think you have to lie about it?"

Uhh… I care about your *feelings*?

"OB, you know I love you," I begin instead.

"And who-you-fuck-has-nothin-to-do-with-how-you-feel-about-me, right?" he finishes.

I was only going there in my *mind*.

"Babe, I don't want to fight," I sigh.

"Then *talk to me*; like I'm a *person*."

I can't continue this line of conversation, I just can't.

We agreed we didn't have to remain "totally true" to each other;

somehow I feel I've done Obie a disservice.

"Remember night-before-last when you called me and I said I was in the bathroom?

Suppose I told you I was with some girl I met on the set."

Under-predictably my stomach plummets.

"And suppose I told you I was 'kinda busy,'

but when I saw it was you I stopped and went to call you from another room.

How would you feel about me; would you still love me?

And would you still stick to that story you're tellin?"

It must have taken a lot for Obie to admit that to me.

My-number-gets-called.

"I ain't mad atcha Cess; I ain't mad at all.

I admit it hurts to think of you with another 'brotha,' but I understand, I really do."

"Oh, Obie," I blurt out, the words/emotions rushing out of me,

"I'm so, so *very* sorry. I don't know how it happened.

I was so *lonely*; I didn't want to hurt-your-feelings by telling you."

"So how was it, though?"

"It was a'ight; nothing-to-write-home-about."

"**Good.** I'm *glad*."

"What about your girlie? Did you really 'pull out' on her?"

"Right-in-the-middle. She was a'ight, too, but nobody-does-it-like-you."

Stop Playin.

"Baby Girl? I know if I'm not gonna be true then I don't have a right to ask you to be; but I still hate it."

"That's good: I can't stand the thought of you with some other chick, I *never could.* I *can't* tell you what to do, I *won't,* but I wish things were ***different.*"

"So do I. They got us 'grindin' *todo dia* 'til we can't get away but we got to *do somethin quick.* I need to see you *so bad*; my body *aches* from missin you: very, very *much* so."

An unbearable sense of loss sticks-to-me-like-duct-tape long after I hang up.

Dejected, I cry myself to sleep.

"*I do* NOT WORK ON SUNDAYS. *PERIOD*."

First my Business Manager, then a Record Exec call me to "request" two appearances from me *por la manana.* Slamming the phone down in disgust I turn to Dionne, ask: "What's **wrong** with these people?"

"Nigga *please.* Don't compromise your integrity, 'Girl; give in on somethin important to you as this and the next thing you know, they *own* you. Ask-me-how-I-know."

"You know what we should do?" I ask excitedly. "Let's catch a flight and go to church."

Going from ATL to Cali you're actually in the air five hours; get there two hours later.

Bizarre, until you get used to it.

The down side is: the return flight will *cost* us a couple hours.

Oh *well.*

And guess who we run into at church the next day?

Can you say World Famous Davis?

I stare at Nicole; try to see if she set this whole thing up.

Her face isn't giving up any clues, I'm so happy right now, it doesn't even matter.

After church Obie and I steal-away-home.

We aren't in the house ten seconds before we are buck-naked.

I haven't seen Obie in almost two months; I'm hungry for him.

After we explore we'chother's bodies with our lips/ tongue

I take a ride on The Obie Train and I don't mean his *back.* I like this ride much better.

Time burns quicker than a gasoline thong in Hell.

Much as I enjoyed our little respite, it was like ripping the Band-aid off my wounded heart: it's bleeding again.

This time I may-not-recover.

This movie is a *gas*, man.

Everybody who is anybody in the Rap Industry, half of the R&B talent, is on this flick.

The Media would have you believe all-rappers-are-animals;

thrown into a room together, they'd proceed to attack one another until no one is left standing.

What a load of Bullshit.

Almost everyone on this shoot is getting along *great*; those who aren't are mature about it;

"petty beefs"/ "lightweight static" gets squashed swiftly.

We all know the-country's-eyes are upon us;

we'll be good-and-got-damned if we fuck-it-up (*too* much) for Black People everywhere.

What would make this shoot *perfect* is Obie One; too bad my order got delayed.

By three months.

In the future, if O can't coordinate the itineraries better than this, I'll *fire* his ass.

The first week we are delayed by script rewrites.

BB takes his first look at his newly enlarged role: he's the Enforcer for a gang that

stages a series of robberies at our Safe Houses to disrupt our operations.

In that whole art-imitating-life thing the former stash-house-thief offers some

pointers on authenticity.

Another round of hasty rewrites; production rolls.

My feelings about this shoot are deteriorating at an alarming rate.

The stunts are so, *so* very demanding; most of us feel pressured to do

as many of our own stunts as possible. As a whole we are in great physical condition;

if we feel stretched beyond our limits, methinks something-is-rotten-in-Denmark.

I'm not *in* such-great-shape; *I* feel **wrecked**.

Last night Dionne and I cried for *hours*; I want to go home **badly**.

Another weird thing is: every woman on this set got her period at the same time.

You've never seen so many thugs run-for-cover in your life.

It would be *hilarious* except: *I didn't get mine*; it's scaring the **shit** out of me.

We're working on yet another complicated stunt.

After a massive shootout Nicole, Dionne, X, and Drag-on are cornered in a back room;

the only way out is through a window.

Fantastic, right?

We shoot the scene; the director yells cut; Nicole lies on the ground motionless.

She missed the safety bag; landed on her head; a puddle of blood grows steadily under her body, she dies at the hospital; no one can figure out what went wrong.

I call Obie; tell him; he and Hood are here within hours.

At the funeral Hood sits between Dionne, her mother; supports both women as best he can.

Obie does his part; the whole funeral scene, Alicia's grief, overwhelm Freak.

During the funeral we get word that Big Momma died.

Hard hit, our-senses-reeling, we drag ourselves to NY.

We all end up at Big Momma's Harlem brownstone, and what a *crappy **dump*** it is.

Obie and I spent "mad" energy trying to convince Mommy to move.

Which one of us thought about buying Big Momma a nice house somewhere?

True, we are only the grandchildren; she has two "music icons" for children;

does that absolve us of our responsibility?

Nigga please.

I feel like we let Big Momma down.

DNA fixed up *their* momma's house up *"lovely;"* WFD did the same for Mommy.

I can't remember the last time I *called* Big Momma; I barely *knew* her.

She was my grandma-and-all, but we-didn't-interact much.

When Freak and I used to stay at Big Momma's she was always in her room.

Drinking.

Turns out Freak was very close to Big Momma; he's taking her death very hard.

Obie and I bounce to Park Ave, where Uncle BB has "our" kids.

Obie looks so at ease sitting cross-legged on the floor with them;

for the second time, I'm hit with that urge to have his baby;

although, I don't think I could ever have one-*tenth* the patience Obie possesses.

Two days after Big Momma is laid to rest Uncle Truth drops dead:

cocaine-induced heart attack.

If anybody else is going to die this week *please let me know.*

Better yet: see if you can't *postpone* for a minute.

Who's on the Scheduling Committee *anyway*?

Don't they know that *three* deaths in *two* weeks is a little *hard on the nerves*?

Also, and *I'm not trying to be mean or anything,* if Uncle Truth had died *last* week;

it would have saved us at least *one* cross-country jaunt.

'Cause, damn it, back-to-Cali we go.

East Coast is up in Obie's mansion, only this time it-ain't-no-party.

All this death has made us *numb*: we are walking around like zombies.

Obie works closely with Aunty Cay to coordinate press releases from our respective publicists.

Mommy-and-them have never seen Obie at work before;

their jaws practically have road rash from all that dropping-to-the-pavement.

Guess "the fam" is still having a hard time seeing Obie as *grown,* not some *goofy-ass-kid.*

By far the hardest person to deal with is Uncle Truth's wife.

One-quarter Puerto Rican, Aunty Passion's stunning to look at, but: *what-a-bitch.*

Don't know how Uncle Truth stood it: must have been *great sex;* they have like *six* kids.

Oh *well.*

"She reminds me of my *mother,*" I mention the night before the funeral.

Everyone except Mommy and Young stares at me in amazement.

"When did you see your mother?" Uncle BB grills me.

"Back when I was six," I retort.

So: Mindja Bizniss.

"And?" he demands.

"And *what?*" I counter. "She called me a bitch; slammed the door in my face."

What's notable is *not* Uncle BB-and-them's reaction, it's Young's *lack* of reaction.

"You *knew,*" I accuse my father angrily. "You *knew* that bitch *treated me like shit* and

you *still* continued to be-with-her. How *could* you?"

Young atypically meets my gaze; says nothing.

"You *bastard fuck,*" I explode. "You got your life broken down into these

neat little compartments so you don't have to actually *deal* with any of it.

You got the: faggot-lover-box, the: good-doctor-box, the: I'm-*a*-drunk-box,

the: I'm-fucking-my-brother's-wife box; what box do *I* fit in? Oh *wait; my* bad:

You *stuck the kid in the box with the fag; killed-two-birds-with-one-stone.*"

On a roll, I find I can't stop myself, while Young accepts my tirade wordlessly.

"That's why you hated O all these years, isn't it? He took me to see my mother."

"Sure you're right," this he *responds* to; "You think Obie *asked* somebody?

'Excuse me; should I take Princess to see her momma?' *No.*

Nobody *told* Obie to *do* that, he just *took it upon himself,* like he was *grown* or somethin.

Obie was *always* doin *dumb shit* like that, like *he*-got-a-better-plan-than-*Ford*

or some shit. If it was such a 'great idea' don't you think I'd a took you my*self?*"

"You *cocksucking*—"

Obie's hand clamps down on my mouth, cutting me off.

"BB's the 'cocksucker;' I'm the 'butt boy,'" Young has the nerve to joke.

We wrestle violently until Obie takes me down. Enraged, I attempt to scream;

the sound is stifled by his palm. I keep thrashing; Obie tries fruitlessly to calm me.

The expression on Young's face never changes.

"She sorry Uncle Young; she don't mean it, she can't help herself is all."

That is a *fucking lie*. I am *not sorry at all*; Obie has *no right* to apologize for me.

I'm so mad, I fight back twice as hard; the struggle finally wears me out.

As soon as I stop Obie releases me; draws me onto his lap; I begin to cry.

"How did I end up with such *fucked up parents*? Who does *that* anymore?"

"You know how you always askin how come your mother didn't just give you away instead a tryna kill you? Well, that's what Young *did*, he gave you away *'cause* he *loved* you, *not* 'cause he *didn't*. He was just a kid tryna get through school and raise you at the same time, only he couldn't *do* it, Princess; he couldn't *do* it. *He ain't know how*; no one ever took care a Young like they was *supposed* to. When he saw how much Uncle BB loved you, he knew he'd never haveta worry 'bout you again."

I listen to Obie; try to picture in my mind what it must have been like for my father.

Being young myself, I can understand the position my dad might have found himself in, a little baby under-expectedly thrust upon him.

What I can't for the life of me fathom is:

"How could you *be* with *Sally* when you can't even *look* at *me*?"

"I don't know why I stuck with your mom, except to say I loved her.

Don't care how she treated other people, Sally was always good to me.

You look *so much like* her; every time I look at you, it *hurts*."

Now I *know* he's lying.

"I don't look anything like Sally Walker. That bitch was 'fugly'."

"No, she wasn't," Uncle Shawn cut in. "Once-upon-a-time Sally was *stunnin*, like you.

She was the prettiest Black girl in the neighborhood, and one of the nicest, too."

Nigga *PLEASE*.

"But, she *hated* me. If it wasn't for Hood, Sally would have watched me *starve*."

"I can't explain that away; I only know I did the best *I* could for you."

"Your momma was very sick, sweetheart; please don't personalize her actions.

Sally probably had a severe case of post-partum depression," Mommy adds.

"She made some serious mistakes, and she felt Cancer was her punishment,"

Uncle Shawn expands. "When you young-and-beautiful, watchin your body disintegrate is *not a easy thing*. Sally *suffered* and she took-it-out-on-the-world."

What about me??? Like *I* didn't suffer at *her* hands?!

You figure.

But don't get back to me, I *still* won't care.

Every dark cloud has its silver lining. The bright side to this unholy-spate-of-death is: Obie and I are together again.

An added bonus: sex is a great-tension-reliever; after a day like today you've got-to-believe we're at-it-like-rabbits. Obie touches me in a way I didn't even know *existed*. Great God *Almighty*, what an orgasm. Oddly though, right after I come, I catch these horrible, period-like cramps, only they're way worse than any cramps I've ever had. My stomach hurts so badly we have to stop-and-chill.

"What's up," Obie asks, since: "It's still too early for PMS, ain't it?"

See now, that depends on your *perspective*.

It might be way-too-early for my *next* period,

but it's definitely on the *late* side for the *last* one.

It's o-*kay* though; better-late-than-never, I always say.

Eventually the pains pass; from there it's *on*.

I'm lying on my stomach, Obie's tongue working untold magic all over my back. Then I feel him grab himself, try to enter me. I freak the *fuck* out; start screaming; my entire body gets *rigid*; I mean *stiff* as a *board*.

"What's the matter?" Obie is clearly upset. "I was just gonna hit-it-from-behind."

Okay, see, I *knew* that. So why do I go and lie, saying:

"I got scared with you lying on top of me like that."

You figure.

Absurd as it sounds, a part of me so, so very *really thought* O was trying to hurt me; don't know where that came from. Obie changes his mind about having sex.

"It's okay, O, honest. I just freaked for a minute."

"I just wanna hold you," he decides.

"Not that one, it makes you look like an old lady."

I'm dressed for the funeral, I'm ready to go, Obie doesn't like my dress.

"I *know* he didn't just tell her to *change her dress*," I hear someone mutter.

Yes, he *did*, *AND* I *changed*, so "do *you*," okay? Let-me-worry-about-me.

Fine, whatever, only he doesn't like the second dress either.

"Look, OB, tell me what dress you have in mind so I can go put it on."

"You gonna do somethin with your hair?" is Obie's next complaint.

Nigga please.

For the record, I do not style my hair if I can help it:

Long-and-straight works *fine* for me, thanks; Obie, however,

likes fancy hairstyles as much as he likes designer-dresses-and-Jimmy Choo's.

Not **hardly** in the mood to spend-an-hour with the-curling-iron, I say:

"Oh, yeah; hold on a minute."

Grabbing the right half of my hair I throw the whole section casually over my shoulder.

With a Hollywood-head-toss, I smile brightly; say:

"How's that?"

"Go bring me the irons," Obie instructs, *not* impressed with my bullshit.

"Now he's gonna do her *hair*???!!!" came the same hateful voice.

Who **is** that bitch? Must be Aunty Passion: *who else would care*?

"You didn't know Obie was a 'gay hairdresser?'" Hood quips.

"How's your *neck*?!" Obie snaps back maliciously.

Obie picks out my shoes, my handbag, we are ready-to-roll.

How abso-fucking-lutely depressing.

As the only "ink-spot" in his high-yaller family,

Rahshaun practically grew up in Uncle Truth's house;

I guess this was like losing his father, whom this nigga doesn't know *anyway*.

The Aunties never stopped crying; Uncle Shawn was damned near right behind them.

The only sibling with a "dry eye" was my father, "the stoic."

When we looked around, Rahshaun had evaporated.

I recognize he's upset-and-all; but how do you disappear on your own *kids*?

Who does *that* these days?

Back at the house we grab a few drinks; attempt to unwind; I put my feet in O's lap.

"Nah; *nah*; **nah**," Uncle BB jokingly chides,

"None a that 'footsie' shit *here*. Y'all know what *that* leads to."

"You *told*?!" I shout/know Uncle BB can*not* be talking about what I *think* he is.

"Lightweight," Obie admits/looks down at the floor/semi-nods his head.

"Oh **Hell** no; you *didn't*," I fume; stare angrily at O; jerk my feet off his lap.

"*Yes*, I *did*," Obie counters, grabs my feet, drops them back harshly in place.

How *could* you?!" I ask, my anger rising.

"How could I *what*?" Obie comes back at me.

I *want* to say: how-could-you-tell-everybody-I-fucked-you-on-my-couch,

but I can't make the words come out my mouth.

"*Bastard,*" flies out instead.

"Wasn't no ring on *your* parents' finger when *you* was made, *either*," Obie snaps,
"'cause *that* was **before-she-married-my-dad, right**?!"
"You big-fucking-dumb ass-White-*faggot*," the tirade begins.
"*Fuck* you, you stupid *cunt*; *triflin* **bitch**."
"I *know* you didn't just call me a *bitch*."
"*Yes I did*, and you ain't got *near 'nother time* to string that group a insults together at me. Who the fuck you think you is? You think the sun rises-and-sets on your Black ass?
No, it *don't*, and let me tell you somethin *else* that might-not-be-too-apparent from the way niggas is *throwin* theyselves at you. *Sun-shine* does not em-ma-nate *from your pussy*.
Ain't *nothin* you got so good it's gonna make me put up with *this SHIT*."
Obie's head is bopping, accentuating every word he says.
Overcome by anger I jump him. This is the first fight we've had since I promised myself
I wouldn't treat O like this again. The sane, rational part of me is appalled by
my behavior, I lack the control to stop myself; the situation devolves to where
Obie and I are practically fist-fighting in front of the whole family.
People are yelling at us to stop; hands reach out to grab us, are knocked away.
Obie tries to take me down; I fight him like a tiger;
by mistake he falls on me *hard*; knocks the breath from me.
Winded, I draw air into my lungs deeply, gather my strength for a fresh attack.
Reading my face, Obie pins my legs with his knees; my hands up over my head.
I'm still struggling; *damn it, I can't move.*
"You haveta *stop*," Obie yells in my face. "I'm *sick* a this shit."
Let's-not-act-like I don't *know* this, *man.*
I *really do want* to *stop,* only *I don't know how.*
"You act like we did somethin dirty or nasty, Cess." Obie continues.
Well, if he wants to calm me down, he might abandon that line of convo, because:
"I DON'T WANT TO TALK ABOUT IT."
We lie here for an interminable length of time.
You know O isn't letting me off this floor until I calm my Black Ass down;
you know I'm stubborn, too.
Finally the whole process wears me down;
I stop struggling long enough for Obie to peel his body off me.
As haughtily as I can, for I *am* a Princess, I rise to my feet, head for the stairs.
"You gotta stop this," Obie begs me. "I can't do this no more."
My response is to flip him the finger.

At the top of the stairs I turn right, head for my room;

Obie's supa-dupa-long-ass-legs get him there in three seconds flat.

"Out the fuckin room," he orders me.

"Or else what; you'll kick the fucking door in again?" I quip.

"*I'm a kick your fuckin **head** in. GET OUT THE ROOM.* You belong with me."

"A pig will drive my SUV first."

"I'm sick a your *shit*, Princess."

He ain't said nothin but a word.

Hurrying to our room, I throw some clothes in a bag.

"Where are you going?" Obie asks me wearily.

Good. **Question**: I'm sure-not-going back to *my* house.

Running down the stairs, I ask Dionne if I can go home with her.

"Nah, 'Girl. You need to stay here and work-this-shit-out."

Trifling *Bitch.*

Surveying the room, I gather I'll get the same response from anybody I ask.

Fuck 'em *all*; they can be on Obie's side if they *want* to; I'll get a Ho*tel* room.

Back upstairs one more time, grab my bag, head for my car.

Obie stands by watching me listlessly.

Halfway down the driveway I'm seized by another cramp,

this one so vicious I double over, almost crash my car.

The squeal of the tires as I frantically hit the brakes draws a crowd.

Obie is at the front of the pack, wearing his concern on his face.

"Wassa matter Cess? Is it your stomach again?"

My stomach has been acting up all day, not "lightweight," either:

brutal pains so severe at times, I couldn't even walk.

Obie puts his hand to my forehead, checks for fever.

Our fight is forgotten, he carries me back to our bedroom.

I guess I lie in bed maybe half an hour or so before the bleeding starts.

This doesn't feel like a period though;

I'm scared something bad is happening inside me.

The bleeding becomes a hemorrhage; I pass a huge clot.

I can *pass* some *clots*, this is the biggest-one-ever, almost the size of a small egg.

Obie examines it under the bathroom light for a spell, then says:

"We goin to the hospital."

4_{OB}

This Jam would **not** a been Complete if the weather wasn't *disgustin* in Canada.

I mean, that's The Icin On The Cake, ain't it?

I leave my Beautiful Woman in Warm Sunny California

to be All Alone in Arctic Ass Toronto.

WHY AM I HERE?

It's Cold & Crappy and **already** I want to *die*; always.

It's Gonna Be A Great Day folks.

Even Hood looks Beat Down By Circumstance and he's **always** been The Anxious Type.

Who's **responsible** for this shit?

He better not let me Catch His Ass.

I'm not in a Good Mood, can you tell?

First day on the set don't make it no better.

They shootin a **NY** movie in **Toronto**, *AND* it's a **Club** **Movie** with **No Niggas.**

I didn't know they still **made** All White Movies.

Who **does** that?

Ain't there a **law** against This Type a Thing?

Shocker Number Two: They want Hood to straighten his hair.

He ain't had to do that since The **Eighties**, **MAN**.

I'm gettin **heated** here.

Me and Hood deliberate for **hours** about whether to Pack Our Shit & Go,

but we (**HE**) decide to Stick It Out.

Good Career Move & All.

As *If.*

Hood looks Damn Near White with his hair pressed.

He could Pass just as easy as me. Which got us to **thinkin…**

On Closer Inspection there's some Mixed Kids on this set who's either Passin or

was chosen cause Like Us they **can** Pass.

People think that whole phenomenon a Passin- Died Out in The Sixties.

Ungawa; Black Power right?

To those a you who think that, let me direct your attention to Mariah.

Just cause she Open about Her Black Daddy **do not mean** she ain't **Livin & Actin**

112

Just Like A **White Woman**.

That my friends is **Passin**.

Mommy was Passin too, cause Until Recently, **Mommy** thought she *was* **White**.

You know **Hood's** Black Ass useta *Embarrass* Her??!!!

In fact, Mommy in*sisted* she was White, and no Amount a Persuadin convinced her otherwise.

She useta say: If A White Momma Don't Make Me White

then A Black Momma Don't Make Her Black.

As **If.**

I **hate** that shit. I hate the whole **emphasis** on skin color.

Why is White Skin supposed to be So Much More Desirable?

I'd ask Who Made That Shit Up but I Already Know.

Well I been Trapped In This Skin my whole life and it's **never** done much for **my** Self Esteem.

I could Pass more easily than the majority a Light Skinned Folks.

I choose not to.

First, I would Lose My Family, and that's simply Under Acceptable:

I love these niggas.

Second, I was raised in a Black environment, steeped in Black culture.

My Whole Entire Identity is in my Blackness.

Even if I tried on White Culture it would be Foreign to me.

Like a Ill Fittin Suit it wouldn't Serve Its Purpose nor Meet My Needs.

I adored my White momma yet I don't identify with either **her** Whiteness

or with **Whiteness in General**.

I need to be **surrounded** by Loud Vibrant Dynamic People of Color.

Lotsa mixed kids Pass, either Pro Actively or Re Actively.

Even the one's as dark as Halle Berry demand to be called Bi Racial,

as if you could be **both** at **once**.

They just tryna Distance Theyselves from they Blackness.

Like that's not **The First Thing A Person Sees.**

They may not know what country you from or how deep your pockets is but they **know**

You're A Nigger.

That's For Sure.

I ain't never Proactively Passed in my life but I **have** Reactively Passed.

Once I was on a bus in Bensonhurst when several White kids pelted a Black kid with The N Word.

The second time I stopped to pee in a Cracker Bar and a bunch a rednecks was laughin and

tellin Nigger Jokes.

You just don't fuck with a bunch a Dumb Ass Crackers cause In Groups They Can Be **Lethal**.

This the spot where I'm supposed to tell you how much I hate bein Light Skinned right?
Under True.
I **hate** lookin like a **White** person.
I would **kill** to be Light Skinned, even light like Freaky and Hood.
At least people can More Or Less **tell** they Black.
A Once Over Lightly with The Color Brush would a **sufficed**, *very very much* so,
but if I had came out Lookin Like Baby Girl I would **not be cryin.**
You can never be Too Rich or Too Black Sayeth The Fabulous BB Johnson.
I however am not **Light,** I am **White.** Light Skinned is this Lovely Euphemism
Black people created cause ain't no other polite way to describe me.
Looks Like a White Guy is **Not** Polite.
So here we are stuck in this Hell called a Movie Shoot, a Hell a My Own Makin, and
the producers is Workin Us To Death. Production starts at The Ass Crack a Dawn and
continues almost until The Moon Calls It Quits, which is Fairly Typical for a movie.
Me and Hood hafta teach The Principals all these Complicated Dance Steps.
Most a these people can Master The Steps but they can't Breathe **Life** into them, you feel me?
They **Look Like Actors, not** Club Mavens.
If they target audience is *anybody* connected to The Club Scene they bout to be
Sorely Disappointed. Plus, Hood and me's got **parts** in this **Piece a Shit.**
I don't wanna Show My **Face** in this Stinker but Hood said:
Everybody Makes A Bad Flick Now & Then.
We ain't bonded with the cast or crew either so there's no one to hang with.
"You think it's cause they Sense Our Disdain for this project?" I ask Hood.
"No, *I* think it's cause you asked Where All The Niggas On This Flick At?"
We giggle despite ourselves.
That **was** some funny **shit.** You should a **seen** them crackers' faces hit the floor.
"You Too Damn Outspoken for Your Own Good."
"Oh **Well.**"
"Why you ain't eatin nothin?"
"I don't know, dog. I ain't been hungry lately."
"Well you startin to **Look Bad.** Like a 'Head or Somethin."
"Well **you** suckin up every pound I lose so I know where to go when I need em."
I'm jokin and we laughin but I can't have people thinkin I'm **Smokin** so
I fix a plate and force myself to eat it.
"You wanna go out?" Hood asks me.

"Not really, maybe next time."

"This's why I Don't Subscribe To all this Love Bullshit. It's Painful," Hood complains.

"But it's cool when you with her though, a'ight?"

"No Doubt," he confirms, "but She Ain't Here Now and I'm **Lonely,** yo."

That folks is Hood Speak for Horny.

I commiserate with Hood, my Partner In Gloom.

I think I- Live There Too.

"Let's Hit The Clubs," he suggests.

I beg off though, not In The Mood for Casual Sex. Instead, after he gone I call Princess and we have Phone Sex. For me this A Whole Lot Better. Only…

Stressed, a week later I end up in bed with some chicks I don't even **know**.

My Dick Was Happy, That's About All.

Tired a my grousin, the next mornin the Director lashes out at me.

"Graduate from High School first and then come talk to me about my film."

"Mothafucka I graduated Valedictorian a one a the most **prestigious** private schools in New York City. There ain't a **damn** thing I hafta prove to **any White man on this planet**. I got a 1700 on my SAT's and I can Read Write & Speak a more perfect English than Webster himself. I also speak four other languages. I speak a dialect **comf'table** for me and easy for Those In My Circle to understand. You don't **understand**; *therefore* you **must not be in my circle**. Too Bad For You. Let Me Help You Out and Express This in a language far more to your Personal Liking. In my Professional Opinion, a film about the club scene in New York City that totally omits Black people is not only **Insulting**, but is Racist Propaganda. I say that not only as a Life Long Club Hopper and as a Fellow Director but also as a Black Man."

By the weekend four Black faces was added to the cast and they let Hood braid his hair.

I try to hold out as long as I can but I get tired a jerkin myself off every night and find myself with a production assistant from the set.

We Hit The Sheets and while it ain't the Best Sex Ever it **is** Sex so I Ain't Complainin, you feel me? On the **other** hand Girlfriend is carryin on like **I'm** the Best **She** Ever Had. You know That's Possible: very very **much** so but I ain't even **tryna** be Spectacular.

I wanna be **Good Enough** so she won't Complain but **Not So Good** she becomes a Cling On.

I Got A 'Girl you know.

My cell starts to ring, fuckin up my concentration.

I try my best to ignore the damn thing but subconsciously I glance over at the nightstand.

Damn it, it's Baby Girl. I feel Caught and **she ain't even in the room**.

Finally the phone stops ringin.

I try like Stella to Get My Groove Back but I can't.

"Sorry. I gotta make this call."

Wrappin myself in a blanket I go in the next room and call Baby Girl back.

We talk for three hours, and Surprise Surprise:

"Wow, you still here," I manage to say, *tres* awkward.

"You must really love her to get up and call her back like that.

My boyfriend would never do anything that thoughtful."

She sounded Sad & Wistful when she said that but:

"Maybe you with the wrong guy."

Oh **Well**.

"Yeah I **should** be with **you**."

OH. She **Fuckin Up Now**. She **know** it too cause she adds:

"I know that's not possible but you can't blame a girl for dreamin, can you?"

"No, I 'spect not."

"Come back to bed. We don't hafta do anything, I just don't wanna sleep alone."

Fair Enough.

Why she feel **so good** in my **arms** though?

One thing Girlfriend is right about: I'm Sick & Tired a Sleepin Alone too.

Girlfriend's body fills up that empty spot where Baby Girl **Should** Be but Ain't.

This must be what kills ninety-nine percent a all long distance relationships:

Desperate People clingin to Someone Else tryna Fill The Void created by

a Loved One's Absence.

Won't be Happenin *Here*.

Girlfriend need a New Man and *I* need my Baby Girl.

That chick felt so good in my arms I barely spoke to her again.

Hope she Understand: it's Back To Anonymous Sex for me.

The next night I try to call Princess.

When she don't answer I'm **convinced** she with The Next Dude.

It's six a.m. before Cess calls me back and I'm upset.

Intellectually I know whoever Cess fucks don't affect her love for me

but emotionally it Hurts Like Hell.

I don't want Some Other Guy kissin on Princess:

touchin her Spots, makin her Moan & Groan.

That should be Mine & Only Mine.

The flip side is: I should be Hers & Only Hers and I Ain't Got There Yet.

But not cause I Ain't Tryin.

Shootin goes on for*ever*, during which time I miss Cess's call, call her back,

leave a message, then miss her call again.

It's called Phone Tag, one a the most annoyin games known to mankind.

Late that evenin I ask Cess again if she hooked up with someone.

You know how women always say it's **worse** when you lie about it?

Well it's true.

Cess lies and it ain't makin me feel no better.

Breakin down I Lightweight Admit I Been Under Faithful too, even though we ain't got

That Type a Commitment. This frees Cess's tongue and we begin to talk about it.

We both can't stand the thought a The Other bein with Another

but we Recognize ain't much we can do bout it right now.

I wanna Take This Op to emphasize the Right Now aspect cause:

Best You Believe I ain't Livin Like This Too Much Longer.

Know what I need?

I need me some **Jesus**.

Sunday we goin to church.

I **Love** The Lord cause He First Loved Me.

Jesus knows what I need too; otherwise He wouldn't a sent Princess to church in Cali.

Dionne's here too: A Blessin for Hood.

After service Hood & Them go They Way and Cess & Me go Ours.

Bet we all End Up In The Same Place cause Me & Cess couldn't **wait** to get in bed.

Back pressed against me, magnificent boobs in hand,

What More Could A Dude Ask For?

But when she Put Her Lips Around Me, takin that Downtown Route?

Oh my **damn**.

We end up screwin away a couple a hours, which is all the time we had.

Just Like That it was Over and I was Back On A Plane to Toronto.

"Hope I don't look as bad as you do," I tell Hood.

He slumped down in his seat lookin all Dismal & Overcast.

"You look bout Bad As I **Feel**," Hood snaps.

Ouch.

Time Moves Along and we're Off this Fugly Picture.

Don't Tell Mom The Movie's Dead.

I can't believe I left Princess **behind** for this shit.

Oh *Well*.

On to Houston.

This is more like it; Warm Sunny & Niggas Everywhere only now Princess in Detroit.

I was closer to her in Toronto.

I can't win, chile.

When Cess calls in the middle a the day I **know** it can't be Good News.

But when she tells me that Nicole just *died*? What kinda **shit** is *that*??!!

Nicole wasn't **All Bad**; we actually had some Good Times.

It's a shame The Bad Times overshadowed them. Still, I feel like a *truck* hit me.

The sisters is **so distraught** we can **barely** get them on the plane.

What *I* can't believe is **Princess'** reaction.

Cess don't Make Friends Easy so to make a friend and then lose her in so short a time musta been one Helluva Blow.

Seein Nikki lowered into the ground does somethin *foul* to me.

I can't wait to get **outta** here. Toward the exit Shawn comes runnin up to me.

"Big Momma dropped dead in the C-Town on 145th."

"What the **fuck**?! Who **does** that??!!!"

"Don't Ask **Me** Son, I Ain't The One."

If Death Comes In Three's who the Hell's Gonna Be Next?!

I Hesitate to Speculate.

Big Momma's place is Smaller and Dustier than I remember.

Don't look like she was Managin On Her Own too tough lately.

I feel **bad** cause I ain't really called Big Momma that often these past few years.

A moon or so ago I asked Big Momma if she wouldn't like me to Buy Her A House somewhere Nicer but like Mommy- She'd Been In Harlem too long.

She resisted all my efforts to fix up her Dinky Little House too so after a while I just Left It There.

Now I wish I had Paid Her More Attention.

Walkin round brings back some Memories &A **Half** though.

I had some **Damn** Good Times in this house but it's also the place where my momma Ran Off & Left Me.

Freak was extremely close to Big Momma and sits in the corner cryin his eyes out.

I offer Freak a much needed Shoulder To Cry On.

Why he's the only one in this room **cryin** though?

Who **DOES** that??!!!

I **still** cry for my momma.

Pissed at **every Davis that passed through Big Momma's body**

I readily follow Princess to Uncle BB's.

Oh my *babies* is here! It's been so **long** since I *seen* them.

They look like they done growed about a foot apiece.

Jay, the baby, is walkin now, which gives me a Pang a Regret.

I missed his first steps. What **else** am I gonna miss?

Maybe I'm a hafta Rethink this whole Uncle BB Can Raise Our Baby thing.

It **Sounds** Good On **Paper** but two or three movies, a tour or two and the kid'll be Grown.

Will he even **know** us? Other than what he sees on TV?

Not The Life I want for **my** kid.

Me and Squared wrestle with the boys for a while then I read them all a story.

Princess sits in the corner watchin me with admiration.

A Hundred & Fifty Years Ago this was Me & Her.

Who'd a thunk Way Back Then she'd Grow Up to Be My Wife?

Squared done got **massive** durin his stint with WWF.

Xanadi's put on muscle mass too, along with somethin **else**.

The girl got a Boob Job.

Hell *No*; Xanadi looks just like a **woman**.

She showin off The Boobies to anyone who'll peek which of **course** includes **me**.

Anybody showin a tittie, I'm **lookin**.

They look **natural** too not like those Overblown Hard Ass Baseballs so Popular in Cali.

Crazy chick even lets me Cop A Feel and they **pass that test too**.

You can Always Feel The Bag though.

Although none a Big Momma's kids is Cryin Over Her Death they all Got a Opinion on How The Funeral Should Go.

The Biggest Mouths is the One's From Outta Town.

The Ones With The Long Green.

Don't Take Long for them to be at each other's throats.

Pardon The Interruption but these **same** niggas ain't done *shit* for they momma since Moses Parted The Red Sea.

They just Showin They Ass cause the funeral's gonna be a Media Event.

These niggas make me **sick**.

Somebody should take pictures a this *dump* and put them in "The Enquirer."

See how they like **that** shit.

Fed up, Shawn and Young Opt Outta the fray. I don't know who **won**, but:

I did a better job than **this** with *Nikki's* funeral.

Like roaches they pick over the few little belongins Big Momma had.

I grab some pictures a me Freak Hood and Cess when we was kids.

There's very few pictures a Squared and most a those show him scowlin.

I forgot how **Angry** and **Unhappy** Squared useta be.

Oh **Well**.

Back to Houston.

Me & My Big Mouth.

Two days later Uncle Truth completes Death's Triple Play, sniffin til his heart gives out.

Wasn't like he was a Head or nothin,

Uncle Truth just liked his Sniff every Now & Then.

Don't we **all**?

His death scared the *crap* outta me.

I can't even Enjoy My Cocaine no more.

Another Oh Well Moment and:

We're Goin Back To Cali (Cali...Cali...).

I'd **love** to say I Don't Think So but **this** is gettin **R***idi***culous**.

Poor Uncle Truth's wife is Overwhelmed By Her Situation so

I offer to make the arrangements for her. Princess thinks Aunty Passion is a

Mean Spirited Bitch but Cess ain't takin into consideration the woman

just lost The Love A Her Life and is Under Attack by her Pushy In Laws.

I'd be a Bitch **Too**; you feel me?

She accepts my offer **basically** because Aunty Cay and them tried to

wrest control a the funeral **from** her, and I Asked Nicely.

Best I Get This Thing Movin.

Before Uncle Truth's funeral ends up One Big Fiasco like Big Momma's.

Aunty Cay and me end up Workin Together.

She just would **not** accept bein Cut Out The Picture.

I'm **amazed** at what a Powerhouse she is but **Hey**,

I impress the shit outta **her** ass too.

"I never worked with you before cause I always thought you were a Cracker Barrel.
Guess I was wrong. You wanna shoot my next video?"

I don't know what to say: **partly** cause I just can't get past the Cracker Barrel remark.

"You don't like me, do you?" Aunty Cay asks. "You think I ran your mother away."

Davis Clairvoyance?

You Make The Call.

"That and the fact that you called BB Defective," I let her know.

"He's a *Crack Baby*," Aunty states flatly.

"What's that make me?" I ask tryin not to be annoyed.

"I *told* you; a **Cracker** Barrel. But it seems you can Pull It Together when You Hafta."

"BB's a **sweetheart**," I say defensively.

"BB's on *medication*. Wasn't he A Monster before they Doped Him Up? How's Xanadi
gonna handle it if he forgets to take his pills or just plain old decides to stop? And what
if they have babies? Them bein cousins Ain't So Hot to **begin** with but he's **Deaf too**.
You & Peanut's Daughter should **think** a that you know. How's **that** gonna turn out?"

I can't believe this bitch.

Once Aunty Cay was the most Down Ass Chick you could ever meet.

Now she a Hag.

If she wasn't my Aunty I'd **Bust Her *Ass***.

"What happened to you?" I ask, in shock.

"The wrong **man**," she answers bitterly. "Can You Feel Me Now?"

Very very much so.

"So you gon Shoot This Video or **what**," Aunty presses on.

What I'm a **do**, say *No*?

Princess compares Aunty Passion to Sally Walker, which sparks a Real **Shit Storm**.

But guess what we found **out** though?

Sally was not only **Pretty** once but **Nice Too**.

As *If*.

After Cess goes to bed Bobby Brown tells us Sally's mom useta beat her for
hangin round with That Tar Black Nigga With The Milk Stain On His Face.

Sorta made me feel **sorry** for Sally.

Sorta.

But Not Really.

After a day like this I need some lovin **bad**.

Cess gets the wrong idea when I try to Stick It In though.

I can tell by the way she screams No No Don't Hurt Me.

Then she lies and says it's cause I was on top a her.

Enough a **that** already. My Baby is Terrified and I done Lost The Mood.

Holdin her close we fall into a fitful sleep. Shit don't improve the next day either.

All those Davis's who ain't cry at they **own momma's funeral**

boo-hoo-*hoo* over Uncle Truth.

What a bunch a **Crack**heads, and **this** includes my **father**.

Big Momma might not a been The Greatest but they never failed to call her to

Watch They Damn Kids so how bad could she had been?

I *loved* her, and if I was the Tears In Public type **I'd a cried**.

My Heart Is Bleedin for her right now.

After all **that *I*** need a **drink**. Absentmindedly I rub Cess's feetie-toes and

Uncle BB makes a Smart Ass Crack about it. Cess flies off the fuckin handle ***again***,

stringin together Big Dumb White and Faggot into her Favorite Mega Insult.

Coppin a King Size Tude I tell that Simple Bitch off and she **slugs** me.

If I hadn't seen it comin Cess would a busted my lip **wide open**.

I am *so* got damn **Sick and Tired a All This Fightin**.

VERY VERY MUCH SO.

Cess is in Battle Mode, *I'm* tryna Wrap Her Up and Take Her Down.

Somethin goes **wrong** and we end up fallin.

My Full Body Weight lands on top a Cess.

That's **gotta** hurt.

But like a Timex Cess- Takes A Lickin & Keeps On Tickin.

I hafta pin her to the floor in order to subdue her.

Why she wanna act like what we did was Dirty or Wrong?

Cess don't wanna talk about it, and Therein Lies The Problem folks.

We got this Huge Event we was involved in that we

Both See in Different Ways but Can't Talk About.

It's drivin me *nuts*.

That night was Special to me and **I'm not gonna treat it like** some Deep Dark Secret.

Who **does** that??!!!

Calmin down Cess heads **straight** for her room and packs but what's a nigga to do?

Tomorrow I'll Miss Her Like Crazy but Tonite?

Tonite I'm so tired I'm **numb** and I can't argue no more, it's wearin me down.

Princess runs past me and out the door.

Not two minutes later we hear the Squeal a Tires.

Crazy Fool done prob'ly **Ditched** herself again.

O-*kay*...

I ain't **got** no ditches.

What The Hell Has She Done?

Back in the bedroom Princess clutches her stomach.

The pain intensifies til she begins to bleed.

Cess passes a tremendous clot which gives me chills when I look at it.

First a' all, *I don't think this is no clot*.

Whatever it is it's shaped like a egg 'cept it's only bout a quarter- to a half-inch thick.

It's surrounded by some kinda membrane or sack or *some* shit

with a perfectly round openin dead center.

I hafta stretch the openin some to get a good look at what's inside.

Why'd I *do* that?

It **seems to be** a solid mass a pinkish grayish Bead Like Thingies like them Ice Cream Dots

with a white streak shootin out the middle like a twisted radius or somethin.

I think I'm holdin what's left a my kid in my hand.

"We goin to the hospital," I tell Cess.

4 BG

They say you can't miss what you never had; but
in a few short hours I have become obsessed with this child I will never know.
It was *my* baby; I miss it *terribly*; it was gone before I had a chance to know it was here.
How could I have a miscarriage when I didn't even know I was pregnant?
How could I get pregnant if Obie and I are always careful?
That one time that we weren't was *so **long** ago.*
I had my period after that, remember?
I just don't understand.
I *know* I said I didn't want any babies;
if *I had known I was **pregnant***, I would have taken better care of myself.
What would it have looked like?
Dark like me?
Light like Obie?
Creamy brown like BB with killer grey eyes and dark curly hair?
I am all "deathed" out, can't take any more. A wave of *grief* engulfs me;
like at the ocean, it pulls me under; in its wake, I am unable to talk to anyone.
Are you listening God?
It's me, Princess.
I'm sorry for the wrong I've done, beg Your forgiveness in Jesus' name,
ask that you please don't heap any more on me right now.
I know if I hadn't started that fight with Obie my baby would be alive today.
I made a promise, I broke it, but the cost is so ***high***, Lord.
So ***high***.
They wanted to do a vacuum aspiration to empty the contents of my womb.
Isn't it empty enough?
I knew it would hurt so I "threw one;" they *made-me-anyway.*
Afterwards the nurse comes in with a RhoGAM shot.
"I don't need that," I tell her.
"You've never been pregnant before and you're RH negative.
You *have* to take this so your body doesn't attack your next baby."
"Miss," I repeat impatiently, "I don't need that thing; I'm DU positive."

"The doctor said--" Nursey began; I cut-her-off-at-the-pass.

"Get that thing away from me," I order her, tired of farting-around-with-the-help.

Nursey runs out of the room like her ass was on fire, probably to get the doctor.

"You really need that shot," Young advises me.

Nigga *please*.

"Don't you think I know my own body?" I snap. "I don't *need* it. I'm DU positive.

Bring me an OB who knows what the Hell he's doing; watch him agree with me."

What they send me is some bullshit resident; I flip.

What is it about the male species that has them believing they know

more about a woman's body than she does?

I'm getting *damn* frustrated here; you *know* what that does for my mood.

Young has them sedate me; says I'm not "acting rationally."

How rational *is* one in the midst of a miscarriage?

I can't tell you: this is my first.

I *can* tell you the Head of the GYN Dept confirms that I *do not need a RhoGAM.*

The hospital moves me upstairs to a private room;

one by one, family members come in to sit with me for half an hour;

Obie comes in last, stays the-rest-of-the-night.

He doesn't sleep, neither do I; in the morning I recover my ability to speak.

"Why you ain't tell me you missed your period?"

Obie asks in a non-threatening, non-accusatory tone of voice.

"I was scared," I explain. "I thought something had gone 'haywire' inside me."

Although I don't say it out loud, I thought I had Cancer like my mother.

"You okay?"

What a *dumb question*; I can't bring myself to answer that one.

But he means well.

"What about you?"

Answer a-dumb-question with another-dumb-question? Get-no-reply in return.

You-know-how-it-goes.

Here I am, on every channel for the third time in six months; we sit-in-silence as the

television watches us; I'm becoming a regular evening-news-staple.

Didn't that used to be *Obie's* job?

That was a *joke;* if I had *any sense of humor left at all,* I *might* even *laugh.*

Might.

Somewhere along the line I doze off; dream of a beautiful, chocolate baby; awaken in tears.

Oh-so-softly Obie brushes them away with his thumbs.

He, too, has been crying.

My eyelids flutter-and-close; when I open them again it's morning.

They say I lost a great deal of blood; it needs to be replaced.

Both Obie and Young question the doctors at length about alternatives to a blood transfusion.

"She's at a five-point-six, which you know is critical," the doctor defers to Young;

"It's almost impossible for a normal person to rebuild his blood volume,

and even if Ms. Davis could, it may take several months."

Which we don't have.

"Given her GYN history a transfusion is the only viable alternative.

In fact, another heavy period will probably kill her."

The family lines up outside the lab in order to donate;

there's no *way* I'm accepting blood-from-a-stranger.

Which is what the doctors want me to do.

Under normal circumstances, I would have been released after twenty-four hours;

I have to stay until my condition stabilizes;

while I'm here they run some tests to find out why my periods are so heavy.

I have fibroids.

Nothing can be done that won't compromise my fertility;

the doctor prescribes a birth control patch to regulate my bleeding.

Cool.

On the third day, I rise phoenix-like from my latest tragedy to leave the hospital.

As we walk out the front door, flashbulbs go off in my face.

When a celebrity talks about the high-cost-of-fame, this is it in-a-*nutshell,* folks.

Despite Obie's campaign,

and the one thousand free T-shirts he gave away on our website declaring such,

the whole "Leave The 'Girl Alone" thing is quite-obviously-lost on these people.

Back at the house my very shaky Princess-self prepares to pack my bags.

Obie has to get back to work; this movie means-the-world to him;

now he's *twice* as anxious about leaving me.

I assure Obie everything will be "okay;" encourage him to "move on."

Our movie has begun to roll again; I'm pret-ty ea-ger to get back to work myself.

A lot of time-and-energy has been invested in this flick, *as well as* one-girl's-life.

Sitting at home will give me too much time to think, *anyway,*

which at this point is not-a-good-thing.

Besides, another day of Obie hovering over me might drive-me-crazy.

In the kitchen Obie keeps staring at me with sad, doe eyes.

The sadder he looks, the worse I feel; I can't bear the sight of him anymore;

I turn away; Obie puts a hand on the small of my back.

"I'm so *sorry*, Cess."

"It's not your fault, O. If I hadn't picked a fight, you would never have fallen on me.

I promised myself I wasn't going to *do* that anymore—"

Tears well up inside of me; I press my head against the wall to hold them back.

"It's okay to cry, Baby Girl."

No it isn't; if I start to cry, I might not ever stop.

I hold up my hand, palm side out, to let Obie know I need-a-few-minutes.

A little closer now, Obie puts his other hand on my back, leans in close.

His lips brush the back of my neck;

his hands slide around to my stomach; his head rests on mine.

Almost simultaneously we begin to cry.

"We'll have another baby," Obie promises me through his tears.

I turn to face Obie; reach up on tippy-toes to kiss him comfortingly.

Soon we are kissing with intense ardor that morphs straight into messing around,

in the kitchen, up against the wall, with the whole family out in the living room.

We straighten our clothes, cry in each other's arms some more.

At the airport the next morning, the family gathers one final time.

After exchanging heart-felt-goodbye's we board separate planes to our

separate sections of the continent.

This movie shoot does the trick; keeps my mind occupied;

I don't have a chance to dwell on my miseries.

The cast and crew are very sympathetic; on we go, business as usual;

I make it clear I don't expect any concessions just because I lost a baby.

I'm here to do my job, *period*.

Let's-get-this-shoot-underway.

Instead of socializing I find myself moody; floating back towards my trailer.

LaRocque surprises me by showing up five minutes later.

Boy does he look ***shook***.

I am on my back; LaRocque lies down next to me on his stomach; taking my hand he says softly:

"You know I'll love you forever?"

"What's wrong, Rocky? You've been acting weird since you got back this morning."

"Nothin; I just ain't told you I love you in a long time.

You been through some *shit,* you know."

"Nigga **please**. You *figure*?!"

Rocky wouldn't say anything else, but he was so down he made *me* look *chipper*.

The following week Obie comes to shoot Nicole's tribute video,

which will run over the closing credits. At least everyone's all in one place.

All day long I cling to Obie like white-on-rice; that night we make wild, crazy love until

the sun comes up; I don't think we're supposed-to-yet.

Oh well.

Obie has to wrap quickly, get back to his set; once more I'm left feeling like

we-didn't-have-enough-time-together. Obie's movie is taking longer than planned;

last minute rewrites have improved the story line tremendously;

Obie is so, so very excited about the film's potential.

My shoot wraps in two weeks. I'm looking forward to hanging around with Obie,

and of course we'll be together for a couple of days when my next video shoots.

Knowing this isn't making it easier for me to let go.

At the airport I grab hold of Obie's coat sleeve; he brushes me off; walks away.

"'Girl you gonna make me miss my flight," he says, irritated.

"I know; I don't want you to go," I needle.

"It's not like I have a *choice*, Princess," he replies; I can *see* Obie's getting angry.

"We never have time together," I whine.

Obie spins around to face me; beneath his anger I sense a terrible loneliness.

"I don't like it any more than you do," he goes off, "but *I* have to deal with it, and *so do you*.

Another couple a weeks and it'll be all over. *Right now*: ***I gotta go***."

Obie moves towards his gate; like an *ass* I grab him from behind.

He pushes me off roughly; *way too roughly* for *my* taste.

"I'll call you," he promises as he departs.

Now where have I heard *that* before?

I dreamed about my pretty chocolate baby again. This time he was two years old.

We were waiting at the bus stop, when I got on I left him behind.

Once I realized, I panicked, got off the bus, only: I didn't know where I was.

Lost too, I stand on some strange corner crying my eyes out for my lost baby.

Dionne's shaking hands wake me up.

"You were cryin in your sleep again," she says gently, handing me a tissue.

My face is soaking wet.

A messenger, escorted to my trailer, hands me an official-looking-document; says:

"Princess Davis? You've been served."

I open the damned thing to see what it is;

Albert's parents are suing me for "wrongful death."

After what *HE* did to **ME**???

Nigga **PLEASE**.

My first response is to get truly *pissed.*

Reading on, I see I'm being sued for twenty million dollars.

Daaaamn; this is *serious.*

I'm going to need a lawyer.

He's going to have to hear the whole story.

Depositions will be filed; the *whole sordid mess* will be *all over the news.*

Again.

Then I'll have to endure "vicious whispers" and "snide remarks."

---"Didja hear what that *one* dude, Einstein, did to Princess?"

---"She's a lying slut."

---"**That** bitch *got what she deserved.*"

This is So Unfair.

So, So *Very* Unfair, **Damn It**.

No matter *how hard I try,* **I can't get away from this shit.**

I don't **want** the world to know; I just want to forget-it-ever-happened.

The more I think about it, the more my head hurts.

My vision blurs, the world starts to spin; somebody is screaming *very loudly.*

Oh **shit.**

That's **me**.

5 OB

Curled on her side all Fetal Cess is Barely Conscious.
In the Little Bit a Time it Takes To Get Ready Princess takes a Turn For The Worse.
Blood soaks through both towels I put under her.
Even **Princess** don't bleed **that much** in half a hour.
Somethin is Mighty Fuckin Wrong here and we better Correct It Quickly.
Is there a doctor in the house?
Why yes there **is**, and I'm yellin for Young at the top a my lungs cause **damn it**:
I don't know what else to do.
By the thunderous clamor in the hallway it seems he's bringin Reinforcements.
Young and Mommy get to the door at the exact same time, look at Cess and
Size The Situation Up Succinctly.
"She's Missin," Mommy says first. Young agrees with her.
"Did she pass any clots?" he asks me.
I show him what's on the bathroom sink and he sends Lee to get a plastic bag.
Young rushes Princess to the car.
I grab a few towels so the car don't get ruined but Cess soaks through another
one before we get to the hospital, lapsin in and out a consciousness and mumblin bout the
pain. Young has Princess in his lap, I got The **Only** Death Lock on Princess' hand.
Scared, I pray non-stop til we arrive at the ER.
The doctor's examination reveals what we figured out **way back at the house**:
Princess is havin a miscarriage.
Who knew she was even pregnant?
Did **she**?
Cause she Sure As Fuck ain't said nothin to **me** about it.
If Death comes in three's ain't this Number Four?
And can I volunteer to be Number Five?
Please?
I **sure can't take two more a these**.
The doctor wants to do a vacuum aspiration, which is a little tube attached to a machine
that will suck The Rest a My Child from Cess's Uterus.
Aware a what's goin on Princess comes to, screamin:
"Don't let them do that to me. It hurts."

What am I supposed to do? If they don't stop the bleedin Cess'll **die**.
I done **already Put My Name In The Hat** to be **Number Five** so
Princess Ain't Goin *Nowhere*, you feel me?
In the recovery room Princess is hooked up to mass IV's.
The doctor say she gonna need a transfusion.
I want her to try to Build Up Her Own blood supply but the doctor say
that could take Forever and Princess Need Blood *Now*.
We'll be **damned** if she gets some Crackhead's blood,
so we all line up to Donate To The Cause.
Uncle BB is a Universal Donor but he and Lee never make it through the door.
Homo's Can't Give Blood.
Uncle BB damn near kicked over the table in the lab on his way out.
Next up? Freak.
"How would you describe your sexual orientation?"
"Bisexual," Freak answers, puttin up his palm at me cause that's a label I Don't Subscribe To.
"We can't take your blood either."
"But **Miss**," Freak exclaims with his eyes open wide, "*I* sleep with **girls**."
Jokes he Got but this ain't The Time or The Place.
"Let me ask you this. Have you engaged in oral sex in the past six months?"
"Yes."
"As the giver or receiver?"
"Both."
Whoa.
Freak's got his hand up again.
Not My Business right? I won't say a word.
"Have you engaged in anal sex in the past six months?"
"Yes."
"As The Giver or The Receiver?"
"Both. Mostly The Giver though."
"Do you use condoms?"
"**Not...** *really*."
The screener puts down her pencil and looks at Freak.
"Off The Record Son how much homosexual activity do you engage in?"
"A little some-some," Freak hedges.
I choke back a sarcastic remark.

"Is that your final answer?" she pushes.

"That's My Story & I'm Stickin To It," Freak jokes.

Who he think he foolin? We been on TV Too Many Times.

"They don't call him World Famous Freak for nothin," I quip.

"My **name**...is *LaRocque*," Freak reminds me rather coldly.

"I'm *sorry*; I just couldn't Help Myself."

"You **don't** use condoms but you **want to donate blood. *Why*?**"

"She's My 'Girl and she needs me. She'd do the same for me."

"If you **love** her **you wouldn't do that to her**, and if you **Love Yourself** more than you Love Going Raw you'd be More **Cautious** when you sleep with someone."

"Look at me," Freak smiles, "Do I Look Sick to you?"

"At least three Strong Healthy Looking Young People a week test Positive. That's a **Minimum** Of **Three. Each Week**."

Freak blows her off.

"You see that mirror over there?" the screener points to the wall. "Go look in it."

Freak goes to the mirror and starts Cheezin at his own reflection.

"You see that? **That's** the face of AIDS sweetheart; a young gorgeous face just like yours. By the time someone gets sick enough to show it they could have infected dozens of others."

Funny, but **Freak ain't smilin so hard now**.

It ain't like this The First Time he's hearin this shit either.

He just Hard Head.

My turn.

"Sorry but I can't take your blood either."

"**I'm Not A Homo**," I rise half outta my chair to declare.

"No That Would Be Me," Lee yells from the hall.

Any Other Day this would be *Funny* but *Today*...I'm Just Not Feelin It.

"Look; you know Obie One just like you know World Famous Freak so Let's Skip The Formalities shall we? I ain't slept with another man in over a year; the only woman I slept with except for two One Night Stands is My 'Girl and I *always* wear a condom."

I hand over the results from my last four AIDS tests, which I get monthly.

Screener Chick is *tres* impressed.

"My mother died a AIDS," I tell her. "You Can't Be Too Careful."

"And I Still Can't Take Your Blood. Besides, Husbands Can't Donate anyway. "

Hood pulls me way down the hall away from the rest a the family.

"Did you know Cess was pregnant?"

"She ain't say nothin to **me** about it. I don't think she **knew**."

"How you **know** she ain't know?"

"What the Hell you mean by that?"

"Maybe Cess Knew and she ain't wanna **Tell** You."

"Because..., Hood."

"Well... y'all always **Careful**, right?"

O-*kay*.

I see where this is goin.

"You tryna say that might not a been my baby."

"Basically."

"It was."

"How you know though? Remember Dude at That Party?"

Hood Means Well & All but he **Pissin Me Off**.

Why would he even **Say** That Out Loud?

What good would it do to make me doubt Cess at a time like this?

Who **does** that?

Is that supposed to make this loss **easier** on me somehow?

"It wasn't Dude's baby. Cess Got More Sense than that."

"Why you so sure it was **yours** though?"

"Cause I poked holes in all my condoms."

I don't know what got wider,

Hood's eyes or his mouth, but **obviously** he was Astounded.

"You **didn't**."

"Yes the **fuck** I did."

"What was you *thinkin*?"

"I was thinkin Cess might get **pregnant**???" I crack snidely.

Hood ain't Buyin It.

Twenty Five Bonus Points to whoever can Answer That Correctly.

"I guess I Wasn't Really Thinkin At All."

Ding! Ding! Ding! **That** is *Correct!*

This has to be the Ultimate Obie Moment, but I Bet You already Knew **That** Too.

Hood Opens His Mouth to say somethin Mommy Like.

"Don't," I Terminate this Word a Wisdom at its inception,

"Don't say Nothin Else. You only gon Make Me Feel **Worse."**

As Princess' (dead) Baby Daddy I settle into Cess's room for the night.

With Hood's words Fresh In My Mind I ask Cess why she ain't tell me she skipped her period.

She say she was scared somethin Bad was happenin to her and I believe her.

My head is So Fucked Up right now; very very much so.

First I get Princess Pregnant On Purpose, then I make her Lose The Baby.

It Don't Seem **Fair**.

I know I Was Wrong but *Damn*.

I mean *Really* Though; you feel me?

Clearly I'm **Payin For Somethin** here but **I Demand To See The Receipt** cause *I* think I'm bein **Overcharged**.

A'*ight*?!

I *didn't* Think The Whole Thing Through and it **prob'ly** wasn't Fair to **Do** That To Cess but we woulda **loved** that baby.

I **know** it.

I feel like shit; and Damn It- I'm cryin. Princess is cryin too; in her sleep.

She wakes up at the same time I'm wipin her face dry but falls right back asleep again.

I sure feel like shit.

A full day a Runnin Tests later and Cess is Good To Go.

Anticipatin the Throng a Reporters outside we **try** to Sneak Out The Back but:

Psych;

They Back There Too.

Somebody should Teach These People some Respect.

The Best We Can Do is Duck Our Heads and Run For It.

Since Princess is still weak I pick her up and carry her to the car.

Shortly after we get to the house Princess begins to pack.

Her movie is headin back into production and she's Read' To Go.

I think she **Out Her Fuckin Mind,** very very much so but **you** know Princess.

She prob'ly don't wanna Sit Around Here feelin Sorry For Herself **no way**.

And I ain't Mad At Her.

Every time I look at Princess I feel so bad I could **die**, *always*.

Cess turns her back on me and I wonder if she upset with me cause a what happened.

Reachin out I touch her, apologizin for makin her lose the baby.

Really I'm apologizin for Gettin Her Pregnant in the First Place.

Cess starts to tell me it was All Her Fault but she breaks off, lookin like she wanna cry.

Her head is pressed up against the kitchen wall and her hand is out like Don't Touch Me but it seem like what Princess *really* need is **Comfortin**.

I rub her back with both my hands then lean against her, holdin her in my arms.

Next thing I know we both bust out in tears.

I promise Princess we'll Have Another Baby and I *mean* it.

We'll do it Right and make our next baby Together.

Cess turns around to kiss me and before I know it her tits is in my mouth

and I'm rubbin myself against her stomach.

And we in the **kitchen** with *people* outside.

A lotta good it did too cause when we finish we start cryin all over again.

I **swear** all I wanted to do was make her feel better;

I don't know how it got all Sexual & Shit. I must need my **head** examined

cause I gotta get a grip on **Somethin** besides My *Dick*.

Worn completely out Cess grabs a few hours sleep before our flights leave.

Me?

I can't sleep a wink. Too Wound Up, you feel me?

I'm more worried bout Princess now than I ever been before.

I don't under**stand** this need a hers to Keep Pushin Forward.

Her body's **got** to be tellin her to Slow Down some.

If it was me I **might** be The Same Way but **Who Knows**?

I ain't been through as much as Princess.

I **still** think if **I** was her I'd Take It Easy On Myself for a while.

"I gotta get back to Cali," Freak calls to tell me Late One Night.

"The hospital called and they wanna Discuss My Test Results."

Shit.

This Don't Sound Good.

"If it was Good News they'd a told me Over The Phone, right?"

Riiiiiight.

Freak is HIV positive.

He almost passes out in the floor when the Counselor tells him.

"Does that mean I'm Gonna Die?" he wants to know.

The Counselor explains the different Treatment Options but:

I Can Tell Freak ain't Payin Attention.

"Oh my **God**," he blurts outta the blue,

"Xena… Alicia…*shit…* I slept with Three Or Four Girls on the **Set**. **Oh** *shit*…"
Freak trails off like he suddenly remembers he Left Somethin On The Stove.
He bolts for the door and only my Long Ass Legs enable me to keep up with him.
Outside Freak whips out his cell.
Clueless as to who's on the other line I ease a little closer, hopin to Figure It All Out.
No Dice.
"Hi baby," he whimpers into the phone. "You feelin any better?…Unh huh… You know
how I keep buggin you bout seein a doctor?…Yeah I **know**. . . Well Guess What? My
blood test came back. **I really think you should call**…*I know*…I'm so *sorry*."
Freak sobs the last two sentences then closes his phone.
Now I gotta Back Up Quickly before Freak realizes I'm listenin.
Meanwhile, I gotta break it to Hood who will Not Be Pleased.
"What'm I gon do?" Freak asks me.
Don't know where to go with **That** One Either.
All I can do is let Freak know I'm Here for him.
He ain't hafta tell Xanadi though: Same Thing Happened To Her.
BB almost *died,* always, but it ain't like he ain't know His Girl Gets Around.
You know; I **started** to ask What Else Can Go Wrong but I ain't *even* Goin There.
Not This Time.

"I see **you're** in a Mood," Hood observes.
Very Astute.
Give This Man A Hand.
Princess did **not** take my leavin Detroit well and Frankly Scarlet;
Neither Did I.
I ain't mean to be so **gruff** with the 'Girl though and I Regret it Bitterly.
It's Increasinly More Difficult for me to Leave Princess and
I'm Takin It Out On All The Wrong People.
Like her.
"What do you *want* Hood?" I snap.
"I wanna know what's wrong with you. You missin Baby Girl or somethin?"
What a Dumb Fuckin Question.
"I'm just tired, that's all. **Really. Really.** *Tired*."
A' **Livin**.
"Why you don't lay down a while? I'll call you when your scene is up."

Bad Move.

I shake my head and say:

"I'm Good."

"You sure?" Hood asks soundin Not Too Sure hisself.

"Hood, if I **lay down** I *Might Not Get Back Up*."

"This from the same man who can't understand why Baby Girl won't take it easy. **Both** you niggas crazy."

The look I give Hood Speaks Volumes and Wisely he Leaves It There.

My cell keeps ringin.

Why is Freak callin me Five Hundred Times in The Middle a' A Shoot.

He been Upset I **know** but I- Ain't Got Time For No Convo right now.

Cuttin it off I make a Mental Note to call Freak soon as I get a Free Moment.

Whatever the Hell *that* is.

Not two seconds later **Hood's** phone goes off.

Now I'm gettin A Bad Feelin bout this.

"Hold on, **HOLD ON**," I hear him yell into the phone,

"We finna a shoot a scene. I'll have him call you **right back**. *Promise*."

Glancin over at Hood I see Bad News written all over his face.

That Feelin goes from Bad to Worse in a Eyelash Bat.

I'm gonna Hurl.

Over two hours pass before I can get back to Freak and believe me that seems like a Lifetime.

The first thing I hear is **screamin** in the background.

"*What the fuck is that*?" I demand to know.

"**That's** why I **called** you. Baby Girl's been screamin her head off for hours."

Oh my *fuckin* God.

"What set her off?"

"Beats the shit outta me, I **found** her like this. We could hear her Way 'Cross Set."

"Tell her I'm on the phone. See what happens."

In the receiver I hear the muffled sounds a Freak tryna communicate with a Very Unresponsive Princess.

"No Good," he confirms.

"Where's Dionne?"

"Dionne's holdin Cess. Wasn't much we could do besides that."

"Tell her I wanna talk to her but not if she screamin in my ear."

While Freak is doin all a this I can't help but wonder if I'm to blame somehow.

Maybe Princess is Angry & Upset bout the way I left her at the airport.

I know I keep **sayin** this but:

I **gotta** work on my Attitude.

Sounds a little quieter. Cess still cryin but at least she ain't screamin no more.

"Can you hear me Baby Girl?"

She gives a Stifled Cry that sounds Vaguely Affirmative.

"What's wrong?"

"Ev-Ev-Everything," she cries.

"You got two more scenes to shoot, then Freak'll bring you out here to me.

Can you Hold It Together til then?"

"Maybe. I **think** so."

"**Good,** cause I **really need you to try**. I love you:

very very much so and I'm sorry bout The Way Things Been between us."

"It's Not Just You OB; I can't **do it** anymore. **I'm** Too Tired and

Everything is **Too** Fucked Up. I Can't Catch A Break & I Don't Know Why."

"I know Baby; I really do. Won't Be Long now."

Later that night they mention on E! and again on "MTV News" that Einstein's family

filed a Twenty Million Dollar Wrongful Death Lawsuit against Princess.

The picture is So Much Clearer.

Very Very Much So, you **feel** me?

I could stand a little Break From Reality **myself** Right Bout Now.

By holdin on to wrap her film Baby Girl held on long as she could.

Seein me gave her permission to Let It All Go.

She won't get out the bed she scarcely eats or drinks and her eyes hold a vacant stare.

Dionne refuses to stray from her side.

My movie finally wraps.

I Hate Like Hell to drag Baby Girl out in public in this condition but I gotta get her home.

Her breakdown is all over the news (we can't seem to stay out the papers lately)

and the Hounds Is Out in Full Effect.

I'm *really gettin sick a this shit*.

5 BG

So much is passing by in a fog.
I realize I am screaming; don't know to stop myself: I don't even want to.
With all-that's-going-wrong, why *not* scream?
Sure-can't-hurt at *this* point.
I'm vaguely aware LaRocque is standing over me.
I didn't even know I was on the floor until he walked in.
He's saying something to me; I can't hear him over that damned screaming.
Oh wait...My "*bad*;"
That's-still-*me*, isn't it.
Hold on... I think I can make out what Rocky's saying.
"Cess, come on; pull it together now.
I'm goin through enough-shit-a-my-own and I can't handle *all this too*."
My "bad," *el otro vez.*
I thought Rocky was saying something *important.*
Okay, Rocky's back; this time he says Obie's on the phone.
Oh *well.*
Seems Obie wants to talk to me; he's not into all-this-screaming.
Best I bring it down a notch; what do you say about *that*, Emeril.
Obie wants to know what's wrong.
Damn it, what *isn't* wrong? *You* tell *me*:
I haven't figured that one out yet.
Regardless, he asks me to please-pull-myself-together;
finish this ghastly movie so I can "move on."
Then he says he loves me.
You *figure*?
'Cause he sure didn't act like it at the airport.
But, I'll do what Obie says *one more time*, for old-times-sake.
Then, we'll *see, okay*?
The director gives me another hour or so to calm-my-nerves.
I hardly know the ladies here except for on-the-set-socialization, yet they surround me
with more love-and-kindness than I thought existed among Black women.
They take turns rubbing my head/back/shoulders; bringing hot soup, soothing tea.

I haven't had this much "female attention" since that-thing-with-Einstein.
Each has a story to tell, some of them quite horrid.
I never dreamed so many strong-Black-sisters had been victimized by their men.
A couple even had miscarriages, or were forced into having abortions.
"Survey says:" that's so, so very much worse than losing a baby.
Wrapped in the aura of their overwhelming support, I pour out my rape story.
"You came back to work too soon," LaTrese tells me.
"We *tried* to tell her," Dionne chimes in.
"Especially after losin-the-baby-and-all," LaTrese continues;
"I heard that's why Chante Pierce quit this film. She lost two babies in a row
and when she found out she was pregnant again she went straight-to-bed."
"That and the fact that Dead Nice's wife is layin to *whup her Black ass*," someone adds.
Even I had to laugh at that: he's in this flick too, wife settled firmly-at-his-side.
Full of tea-and-sympathy, I return to the set; wrap up my-two-scenes.
How I do it, I-don't-know: I feel like I'm under water; or **worse**: like I'm in a fog.
The last thing I fully remember is getting on the plane with Rocky and Dionne.
No, that's not it—I remember falling into Obie's arms; he carried me to his car.

Most people don't understand that crazy is a *conscious choice*.
One *literally chooses* to go crazy.
The choice is not-an-easy-one:
It's the choice between the ravaging pack of wolves behind you and the cliff in front of you.
Some choose to stay and fight-the-wolves-off;
all-too-often they end up bloodied/devoured.
Others choose to step-off-the-cliff into the-abyss-of-insanity.
I took the plunge.

You figure.

6_{OB}

Most days we pass layin in bed together.

Neither a us has the mental energy it takes to get up.

I **wanna** say the days go by in a Haze but that would be Slightly Inaccurate.

What we are experiencing is the Mind Numbing Side Effect of Prolonged Inactivity:

Nothing Matters Anymore.

Or maybe **that's** The Cause and a Numb Mind and Inactive Body are The Side Effects.

Whatever.

What's the point a debatin whether the chicken came before the egg

when the end result is the same?

The doctors say that Baby Girl is sufferin from some type a Deep Depression most

likely brought on by the One-Two Punches a Bein Raped and Havin A Miscarriage.

They prescribe anti-depressants that **I won't make her take**.

I could Barely Get Her To Eat much less Shove Some Pills down her throat.

Now, I am not in any Way Shape Form or Fashion against the use a anti-depressants.

BB became a Entirely Different Person when he started his medication.

And lest you think it don't do him No Real Good,

Watch What Happens when he Forgets His Zoloft.

That is **Not Pretty**.

No; I don't make Baby Girl take the pills cause what Baby Girl is dealin with is

Far More Serious and Way Deeper than a mere Chemical Imbalance.

Her soul has been Horribly Wounded; **Mortally** Wounded.

If The 'Girl don't find the Root Cause a her anguish and **Deal** With It her

Mind Will Die and **Then Her Body** and **no** pill **no** where is gonna help her with *that*.

She **already** On Her Way.

We could Lay Here and Fade Away **together**;

Just Another Crazy Couple- Only Slightly More Famous

succumbin to this Black Cloud a Grief, cause Lord **Knows**

I got a Truckful a Mental Anguish a my **own** Parked Out Back somewhere.

But: Who **does** that?

Waitin To Die is some **Easy Shit**.

Don't look like it'll Take Too Long either.

Gettin Better though?

That's gonna be a Hard Row To Hoe
but I Wanna **Live** and I want **Baby Girl** to **Live Too**.
If that is to happen I'm a hafta search Baby Girl's soul, find the wound,
and then repair it. But she has to *let me* **touch her soul** *first*.

Baby Girl been in a State Near Catatonia since she got to Houston.
And *No*: **That Ain't In the USA**.
For those a you Under Familiar With Catatonia that's when
The Lights Is On But Nobody's Home.
I can tell when she sleep and when she wake
but when I talk to Baby Girl it's like talkin to A Crack In The Wall.
I stand in front a her but her eyes don't focus on me.
This is a **Scary Scary** Experience.
Where **is** Baby Girl and Will She Ever Come Back?
Mommy told me she's in a Alternate Environment.
What the fuck does **that** mean? Who **says** that?
I was **Way Too Scared** to ask, besides I think I already know.
And **she gon hafta Come Up** *Outta* **There.**
Pronto.
In the meantime bein in the bedroom's killin us.
First thing I do is somethin I ain't done in ten days:
I Wash My Ass and Get Dressed.
After ten days in bed you **know** what we smell like, *right*?
That's **prob'ly** what Woke Me The Fuck Up:
I can't *stand* Personal Odor.
I couldn't stay in that got damned bedroom **one more day** if I *tried*.
As it **is** I'm a hafta have that bitch **Fumigated**, you feel me?
Once I finish I Wash & Dress Baby Girl.
Then cause my beard done growed in all **Thick** and *Fugly* I shave.
Finally I fix us some food.
I can barely squeeze a can a soup in Baby Girl.
Not that I'm eatin A Whole Lot More mind you,
it's just Important for me to Keep The 'Girl **Nourished**.
Yo, **Hold Up…**
Ain't We Been Here Before?

This is all startin to feel very Ground Hog Day.

Very Very **Much** So.

Like my Dad I always been Slightly Built: Thin Yet Muscular. I been steady
losin weight for months now and all my clothes is hangin off my Reed Thin Frame.

Baby Girl ain't fared but Slightly Better herself but

that's cause she was a Thicky Thick 'Girl to begin with.

Now we both look Smoked Out.

Finished with the Farce a Pretendin To Eat I grab a couple a blankets and
carry Baby Girl down to the beach. After she got raped she enjoyed sittin out here.

Maybe this trip it'll do her some more good.

Radio playin softly beside us we Soak Up The Sun Sand & Surf.

I try to hold Baby Girl's hand but it lies Rigid & Motionless in mine's.

Holdin her hand **anyway** I Pray I'm Makin A Dif somehow.

Do she even know we outside?

I can't tell.

Somewhere round Six That Evenin Hood shows up.

"Oh my **God** Oscar. You **up**," he exclaims, like he Seen A Ghost or somethin.

And what's with this **Oscar** shit?

What's **that** about?

Then the faggot starts Cryin Like A Bitch.

Who *does* that??!!!

"It's Not That Tragic," I assure Hood.

"**Yes it is**," he corrects me. "You ain't been out the bed in almost **two weeks**.
I was scared we was gonna hafta Put Y'all **Away** or somethin."

How you'd love *that*.

Lookin at Hood I try to gauge his seriousness and **yep**:

He's *Serious* a'ight.

"Shawn it wasn't **that bad**."

"I checked on y'all **every day. Every. Day**. Did you even **know** I was **here**?"

I'm busy lookin at my feet, Shakin My Head Shamefully cause I had **No Idea**.

"At least you **better** now. How bout her?" he points at Baby Girl, "She still look the same."

"It's only the first *day* Hood. Give The 'Girl Some *Time*."

"Is that anything like Leave The Girl Alone? Do I Get A T-shirt for that too?!"

"No, you do get The Very Special Deluxe Obie One Beatdown as a Consolation Prize."

"Yuk yuk."

Hood pulls up a chair and sits with us til sunset
when he helps me put Baby Girl to bed on the couch.
"You gon be a'ight though?" Hood asks before he leaves.
"I been a'ight **this** far," I tell him.
"That's Debatable, but Acceptable. For *now*."

I did Way Less Than This layin upstairs in bed but now that I'm Out & About my mind
is gettin *tres* restless. I literally hafta **will** myself to Be Still and Wait Patiently On
The Lord for some sign that my Precious Baby Girl is Still In There.
Remember the promise I made the night Baby Girl disappeared with Einstein?
Every mornin at dawn I read Baby Girl poetry.
I wanna say Maybe It's Helpin Some cause she eatin a little better at breakfast but
For The Most Part she been sittin here listlessly.
I try all kinds a different music seein if I can get a Reaction outta Baby Girl.
No response.
I slip on a disc a tunes from the 70's.
The music reminds me a when I was with my momma.
"Leavin on a Jet Plane" fills me with a regret so Powerful- I'm Moved To Tears.
                    Oh Babe/ I hate to go…
Amazinly Baby Girl starts to sing beside me.
"I'm sorry I left you," I tell her.
"I'm sorry I let you," Cess replies softly.
Finally a Breakthrough.
Thank You Jesus.

Each day brings progress in small increments I call Baby Steps but
Progress Is Progress.
You feel me? So…
I Ain't Complainin.
Anything is better than the way Baby Girl was **before**.
By the end a the week we havin Small Conversations.
Saturday Baby Girl tries the Feedin Herself thing.
Since the beach appears to be Therapeutic we spend most a our time there.
Meanwhile the lawsuit against Princess has to be dealt with.
Uncle BB has a excellent lawyer in NY who'll take the case.

I have him fax me over release forms for "Cess" to sign. Quickly I forge her signature then fax em back. Soon I'm a need Power of Attorney: Baby Girl ain't in no shape to deal with legal issues, 'specially those associated with her rape.

"Have I been gone a long time?" Baby Girl asks me.
"Couple weeks; almost a month."
We sit in silence thinkin for a while until overcome with curiosity I ask:
"Where'd you go?"
Baby Girl Don't Answer and I Don't Press.
We sit watchin the waves so long Baby Girl startles me when she abruptly says:
"It was a nice place. My mother was there. So was yours. Our baby was there too.
At times even you were there. I wanted to stay forever but I knew it wasn't real."
"And I missed you," almost an afterthought this is so quiet I almost ain't hear it.
"I missed you too Baby Girl, and I'm Glad You're Back."
Another period a Silently Holdin Hands later I venture forth with a thought.
"I think you should get some help."
"I think so too," she replies so quickly it makes my head spin.
"I think you should take your **pills** too."
"The Happy Pills?"
I nod my head.
"Will you take them with me?"
Now **that** requires some **thought**.
However…
How come I feel like I don't need them when I spent ten days zoned out myself?
Baby Girl must be Readin My Mind cause she tells me thoughtfully:
"You ain't exactly Well you know."
She Absolutely Right.
Baby Girl continues progressin,
goin from Feedin Herself to Washin Herself Under Assisted but
I still help with her clothes.
She even walkin around the house without me.
This mornin she out on my Rock dressed, but not for this blustery weather.
I'm so afraid she'll Catch Her Death a Pneumonia I rush out with a warm jacket.
As I get closer I notice Baby Girl starin Off Into Space sorta In A Daze.
She done Slipped Inside Herself again; oblivious to me, the weather, whatever.

When I wrap her in the jacket her gaze shifts over to me.

Baby Girl thanks me and then withdraws again.

I ain't sure if it's a Good Idea to leave her out here.

I ain't even sure if I should let her continue to Shift Back & Forth Between Worlds.

I wanna **say** somethin; to bring Baby Girl Out Of It, but I'm scared it might

Backfire on me and I'll end up pushin Baby Girl farther inside herself.

I decide to sit on The Rock **with** her but first I run back to get my*self* a jacket.

Back on The Rock I notice Baby Girl done wrote somethin Over & Over with a indelible marker.

The Lord is my Rock and my Salvation.

I sit behind Baby Girl; harborin her in the shelter a my arms to protect her from the wind.

We ain't been to church in a Long Time, bruh.

They say Pride Cometh Before A Fall.

Well I always been a **Proud** son of a bitch:

proud a My Body, proud a my Good Looks, proud a my Intelligence.

Sunday comes and I wanna go to church but nothin in our closets fits right.

The Body is now Lightweight **Shot**, The Good Looks **might not be** Too Far Behind:

my face looks Drawn & Gaunt and Dark Circles done

Parked They Cardboard Boxes under my eyes.

Plus it Wasn't Too Intelligent to stay in the bed all them days like that *was* it?

Baby Girl always been Proud A Her Looks too but she so Vacant and Wasted now

it Don't Really Matter much to her that we look like a Y2K version a

The Crackhead Couple a The Year.

To *me* that's **worse** than folks **knowin** we **crazy**--

Oh, Pardon Me.

Mentally Ill.

Suddenly I don't wanna go no more.

I don't wanna leave the **house** no more, but that's just The Devil talkin.

Once we get there I'm so **glad** we made it: very very **much** so.

All my fears bout people gettin The Wrong Idea was Under Founded.

What had *happened* was…

I **Completely Forgot** Baby Girl's Breakdown was All Over The News.

The choir sings "I Don't Believe He Brought Me This Far to Leave Me" and

"We'll Understand It By and By."

Lord, I **hope** so.

Right Now I don't Understand Much a What We Goin Through.

Pastor Mclean spoke about the need to continue to Praise Him even in our Darkest Hour. Which I know I Ain't Done.

He said God Has A Plan for us **all** and sometimes He hasta Break Us Down Completely in order to Rebuild Us in His Image.

The parts a us that God finds Under Acceptable- He excises through our Trials.

Is he talkin bout Our Pride or has **Somethin Else** earned us The Lord's Disfavor?

Cause we keep goin through The Same Stuff Over & Over & Over Again.

And Try As We Might: We **ain't** the Good Christians we **wanna** be or even **think** we is.

At the end a service Pastor summons Baby Girl and me up to the altar,

anoints our heads with blessed oil then has the congregation pray for us.

She takin her Twilight Walk Between Worlds again but I hafta hope that the Service and the Congregation's Prayers is reachin Baby Girl.

Wherever she is.

Prayer Changes Things and Monday Baby Girl is a Different Person.

By the time *I* get up she already Up Dressed & Out At The Rock.

And Lo & Behold: The 'Girl **actually remembered a jacket**.

"You hungry?" I ask her.

Lookin right at me The 'Girl informs me that:

"I already ate."

"You want some company?"

"No, I'm thinking. I need to be By Myself for a while."

A Bit On The Wary Side I Back Off and Prepare To Go.

"Oscar?" I hear her call.

Quick.

Somebody tell me.

"When did Obie Die & How did Oscar Take His Place?"

"You let Hood call you that."

"I don't **let** Shawn call me **nothin**. That's Some Shit a his **own** makin."

"Well I think it's cute. Everyone in LA wants an Oscar and you're mine.

Oscar the Grouch."

Ouch.

"Last kid called me Oscar The Grouch ended up in the ER with a broken nose."

"You gonna Break My Nose though?"

147

"As **If**."

"Then can I call you Oscar too?"

Oh FUCK.

You Know The Answer to **That** One.

Remind me to Renew That Hit I had placed on Shawn's head.

Instead a goin to a therapist Baby Girl wants to try Group Counselin at the Rape Crisis

Center of Compton. The inside a this place is every bit as nondescript as the outside.

I'm Pret-ty Much Uncomf'table here just **knowin**

I Don't Belong in this Women's Domain.

The counselor Baby Girl is talkin to signals for me to come over.

"First of all I want to congratulate you both on being brave enough to seek counseling.

Rape is a Traumatic Experience. Attempting to Handle It Alone can be Twice As Difficult.

We also respect your privacy and your Need to Keep This Confidential.

Our Support Groups meet on Tuesdays and Thursdays. Princess you may attend

as often as you like. I Highly Recommend our Men's Group to you Obie.

You'll find it Extremely Helpful."

Okay, see, **now** they really *slippin*.

Obie Don't **Do** the Group Thing.

Lookin Back & Forth at the two ladies I gauge this is somehow Expected a Me.

I am **So Under Happy Here**: Very Very Much So.

Swallowin My Distaste for the whole process I Wrap My Arm around Baby Girl.

"Sure, I guess I'll try it," I lightweight agree. "Anything for you Baby Girl."

There's A **Lotta** That Goin Around lately.

The closer we get to this Thursday Evenin Group the More I Don't Wanna Go but:

I sure can't back out now.

After droppin The 'Girl off I head for my group only:

How come there's only Two Guys Here?

What's **that** all about?

There's at least **six women** in that other room; where's the Men In They Lives?

Feelin More Outta Place Than Ever I move towards a seat.

Instantly I'm recognized.

"Yo; they shootin a movie or somethin?

Ain't they supposed to Get Our Permission before they let stars Observe us?"

Fuck this bitch in his *ass* I think to myself.

"Obie is here for the group," the Counselor explains.

Why Dude is Suddenly Sorry though?

That's what he get for Not Askin Questions before he Opens His Big Mouth.

Who **does** that??!!!

"Did something happen to Princess?" the other dude asks.

Why the fuck they think I'm here?

"It was that **one** dude who Beat Her Up and then Killed His Self, right?"

"Bingo," I confirm.

"Melvin you know we don't go into Particulars here. Just because Obie and his girl are Celebrities doesn't mean we're making exceptions. Princess has a Right To Her Privacy."

Can I Get a **Amen** Though?

Hold On...

Big Mouth is A Nigga Named *Melvin*??!!!

Somebody Slap His Momma.

"What do we call you? Obie One or just Obie?" Mel asks.

"Call me Oscar," I tell them.

6 _{BG}

It's always bright and sunny here, never cloudy, and it hasn't rained one time.
That's why we have a picnic every day.
My mother, Sally is a great cook; she makes the best potato salad I have ever tasted.
Obie's mom, Suzy is a real goof, telling jokes a-mile-a-minute.
I see where Obie gets his sense of humor.
The baby has gotten so big, so fast it's incredible. He runs through the field every day
at breakneck-speed, calling, "Mommy! Mommy!" as he rushes by.
The way he gobbles up his food it's no wonder he's growing-like-a-weed.
Sally *is* beautiful; with her long-black-hair and "chinky" eyes she looks just-like-me.
Each day we spend together brings me closer to total forgiveness.
She told me how sorry she was for not treating-me-better when I was young,
how she hopes she can make-it-up-to-me; I'll buy that for a dollar.
Sally *was young*, after all.
The only person missing is Obie, he's here *sometimes*.
On those super-rare-occasions Obie joins us on our picnics his smile is so bright it
lights up my day; more than the-constant-sunshine ever could.
He's not here much, though; he always has something-else-to-do.
Just like Obie: never-around-when-I-need-him.
Between my-momma-and-his I have plenty of company; the baby keeps-me-busy, too.
At night, before I fall asleep, Obie lies next to me; holds me in his arms;
tells me how much he loves me.
If he's not with me in the daytime at least he's with me every night.
Only problem is: none-of-this is real.
Well, almost none of it. Obie holding me at night is real, I'm sure of it.
I can feel his breath on my neck as he tells me he loves me; sometimes I can feel his tears.
I want to go back to Obie so badly but besides him I have nothing left in that world to go back to.
As long as he's with me at night my world is complete.

No it's not.
I miss Obie more-and-more every day.
It's not his fault he had to leave me: *I* made him go away.
All I had to do was say I-need-you; he would gladly have stayed with me.

It felt selfish to ask O to sacrifice so much; but I couldn't handle it without him.

That's the hardest part: admitting to *myself* I couldn't make-it-on-my-own.

Although I'm steady-missing-Obie, I don't miss-the-world; want no-part-of-it.

My mother loves-me-here; my baby is alive-and-well.

It's always bright and sunny here, never cloudy, and it hasn't rained one time.

That's why we have a picnic every day.

My mother Sally is a great cook; she makes the best potato salad I have ever tasted…

It's always bright and sunny here, never cloudy, and it hasn't rained one time.

That's why we have a picnic every day.

My mother Sally is a great cook; she makes the best potato salad I have ever tasted…

It's always bright and sunny here, never cloudy, and it hasn't rained one time.

That's why we have a picnic every day.

Today, from way across the meadow, come the strains of a song long-forgotten.

I struggle to hear the words; it's "Leaving on a Jet Plane."

That's Obie singing, he's crying too.

It sounds like he's far away; I can tell he's right next to me though.

The meadow melts away; we are sitting on the beach.

We sat here a lot after that "*other*" thing with Einstein; sat in these same chairs.

The wind slices through me, it was much nicer at the picnic; only there was no Obie.

Oh babe/ I hate to go.

The words spring from my lips of their own accord as Obie and I look at each other.

"I'm sorry I left you," he tells me ruefully.

"I'm sorry I let you," I reply.

But I have to go now.

My food is getting cold; I *must* keep an eye on the baby.

It's always bright and sunny here, never cloudy, and it hasn't rained one time.

That's why we have a picnic every day.

My mother Sally is a great cook; she makes the best potato salad I have ever tasted…

Now that I've come out it's hard for me to stay tucked away.

Obie's voice beckons me; I have to respond to it; if only for a little while.

My craving for him is as intense as lust but non-sexual.

I simply *have* to have him in my world.

Since I can't get Obie in here I must venture out where he is.

It's still too cold-and-noisy out here for me to tolerate for extended periods, but I find I'm out-of-my-shell a little more each day.

I can't take missing my baby for too long, so back-and-forth, back-and-forth I go.

Trying to build-up-a-tolerance for an-intolerable-world.

I begin to wonder how long I've been like this;

I'm startled to find it's been a month.

Damn.

Time-sure-flies-when-you're-having-fun, doesn't it?

Obie asks me something; I've slipped away again.

After a while I figure he wants to know where I've been; tell him all about my private world.

That makes it not-too-private any more, but:

What the Hell.

"I think you need some help," Obie says.

For once I agree with Obie wholeheartedly: I am one-sick-puppy.

He wants me to take the "happy pills," too.

We call them "happy pills" because:

they turned Squared from a "miserable wretch" into a "happy person."

Who'd a thunk one day *I'd* need "happy pills?"

I think *Obie* should take some "happy pills" also:

he cries-a-lot, doesn't-want-anybody-to-know.

He doesn't "exactly" agree-with-me at first; I get him to see-it-my-way.

There's a Rape Crisis center in Compton that Dionne recommended way back when "the Einstein thing" first happened.

I wanted to go *so, so very badly*, was afraid the truth-about-Einstein would get out.

I *still* don't want people-to-know, but I *really need help **dealing** with it all,

and I'm not about to sit-and-talk with some shrink.

I make an appointment; feel better about that than I've felt about anything in quite-some-time.

Makes me kind of hungry…

The house was so quiet when I got up this morning.

Obie snores softly; I creep out of bed; wash-and-dress myself; head for the beach.

Something comes over me though; I feel the fog creeping up on me.

When I get to the rock I pray for my sanity: I *don't want to be like this anymore.*

In my pocket is a Sharpie; I begin writing over and over again:

The Lord is my Rock and my Salvation.

I try clinging to this thought, but I'm *cold*; I hear my baby crying for me.

It's always bright and sunny here, never cloudy, and it hasn't rained one time.
That's why we have a picnic every day............
My mother loves-me-here, my baby is alive-and-well.
Can't you see how big he's getting?

There are arms around me, big-strong-arms, they're slipping a jacket on me.
I have to tell Obie **thank you**, for *caring*, know what I'm saying,
but if I stay out here too long the baby might get lost-in-the-woods.
The last thing I feel before slipping away is Obie's big body, wrapping itself around me.
His body warms me like the sunshine in my meadow.
We go to church, I can't concentrate: too-much-going-on-at-one-time.
It's quieter in my meadow.
My dress is baggy on me; I probably look-like-shit (sorry Lord);
I can't bring myself to care. I haven't taken the baby to church:
Sally, Suzy and I spend too-much-time stuffing our faces, cracking jokes.
Maybe they would like to come, too. What should I dress the baby in?
I try to make a decision on an outfit; feel myself being propelled forward.
Back-on-planet-Earth I am still in church: no baby, no meadow.
The congregation prays for me, *and* Obie;
I *literally feel* the Holy Ghost move through me; the message I'm left with is:
"Everything is Gonna Be Alright."

A new and different strength enters my body.
This morning I am up, dressed, manage to eat-something-too; I also remember my jacket.
It's mighty cold-and-breezy in Malibu this time of year.
Crawling up on Obie's rock I'm comforted by my scripture.
Everything-is-gonna-be-alright.
My baby is dead, my mother died hating me,
but the Lord **is** my Rock **and** my Salvation; "Everything is Gonna Be Alright."
I trust in the power-of-the-Lord to see-me-through.
The counselor at the Rape Center tells me how brave I am to come in, seek help.
She don't know the half of it. I'm pret-ty sure the counselor recognizes me;
she's decent enough not to get "star struck."
Obie's off in the corner somewhere looking like a rat caught on a sticky trap;
wondering how the Hell he's going to get-out-of-here.

Survey says: He's *not*.

They have a Men's Group going on; *guess. what*?!

Obie's **going**.

As I walk in the door a hush falls over the room.

Remind me again: *why* did I come here?

I want to crawl-into-a-hole-and-*die,* always.

Seven sets of eyes stare at me; suddenly I feel shy; out-of-place.

See, this is what I *don't* want.

These women shouldn't be in *awe,* treat me **differently**, because I make records.

We've all been through the exact-same-thing; we're all here to learn how to cope.

Then one woman says:

"That guy, your ex; he's the one who raped you, right?"

I *know* she-means-well; but I feel put-on-the-spot.

"*I KNEW IT*," another chick exclaims excitedly, like she won the twenty-five-million-dollar Super Lotto jackpot or something, and *doesn't have to share it with anyone.*

I mean *damn*, what's *up* with that?

Who does *that* anymore?

Questions start flying fast-and-furious.

"Did you think Dude would go off on you like that?"

"Were you ever afraid of your ex before this?"

"How long were you tryna dump him?"

"How could they think Obie would do such a thing?"

"Did he kill himself or did Obie get to him?"

In the heat-of-my-stardom questions pop off like *microwave corn kernels.*

Or bullets from a "clip" on "the Fourth."

Feeling overwhelmed again I drop my head.

The counselor notices; speaks up in my behalf.

"Ladies, ladies, lets give Princess a break here."

You *figure*?

The questions come to a halt; the one-young-lady who has been coming-a-while asks:

"Why didn't you go to the police?"

I examine her thoughtfully; she, too, does not seem "*well.*"

"I didn't want folks all-in-my-biz, 'passing judgment' on me.

I make a living shaking-my-rump.

Too-many-people would have thought I just-deserved-it somehow."

Sister nods her head slowly.

"I know how you feel; even the police pass judgment."

Without provocation she goes into her story.

She reported some dude at her job for harassing her; nothing was ever done about it.

One night while working late he raped her on her desk.

She and her husband went to the police, the police questioned Dude,

Dude said Sister came on to him.

The police said there-wasn't-enough-evidence:

from the angle of the surveillance tapes it looked like two people getting-their-freak-on,

but Sister said they made her feel like a *liar* and a *slut*.

She got fired; Dude kept his job; she went off the-deep-end.

My heart goes out to her; when she starts crying I hug her.

"When you walked in here I was like, **Wow**; I *knew* you'd understand,

'cause they shit *all over* you and Obie."

"**Boy**, did they *ever*. What did I do that was so wrong, really?

What did I do to deserve what he did to me?"

Now *I'm* crying, the counselor's handing *me* tissues.

My grief threatens to pull me under again; I struggle mightily against it.

The ladies assure both me and "sister-woman" that we had done nothing wrong.

We drink lots of coffee, eat plenty of cookies.

Midway through somebody has to break open a brand new box of tissue, but it's all-good.

The counselor guides us in examining-and-defining our feelings;

finishes up with some helpful coping strategies.

Despite my tears I feel better than I have in months.

7 OB

The other cat's name is Fred but they call him Steady.

He here with his sister.

Steady Freddy is supposed to Share but he Ain't Too Good at this.

And I ain't mad at him.

The ball drifts over to my court and I'm bout as Stuck as he was.

"That baby Princess lost," Melvin asks me, "was that Dude's baby or yours?"

Now **why** he wanna ask me some Dumb Shit like that?

I don't even **know** this cat.

"It was **mine** Stupid Ass," I tell him in a voice I hope Conveys a Taste a My Attitude;

"Do The Math."

The Moderator jumps in with Both Feet, Takin Me To Task on the whole Name Callin thing.

While Melvin gets Called On The Carpet for Violatin My Privacy.

I suck my teeth.

Cunt Bastard.

"Sorry Dog," Mel offers. "How did you feel when you found out though?"

"Found out **what**, that she lost the baby?"

"**Nah, *man***; found out Princess had been **raped**."

Melvin's leanin forward in his seat eyein me intently.

Like he tryna Gauge My Reaction before I can Put Some Draws on it.

Who *does* that!?

I'm tryna Figure This One Out and Process Melvin's Question at the same time.

"I passed out," I tell him, slightly shook.

I wanna say more

but the whole Bundle A Feelins rushes back at me from some Under Holy Place.

Unprepared, I can't get the words out and end up holdin my head in my hand.

I feel Beat The Fuck Up.

Wasted.

"I know you love her, dog. It musta **hurt**," Melvin prods gently.

My head tilts Oh So Slightly towards him.

"Why you doin this to me man?" I ask, bewildered.

Tears sting at my eyes. I'll be Good & Got Damned if I Snot Like A Bitch in a room

Not Exactly Full a Black men so I hurry the Hell on outta there.

Out in the hallway I light a cigarette, pause to Compose Myself. The nicotine ain't
Calmin Me Down the way I thought it would. I figured I was Well Past this stage;
very very much so; but the pain is still fresh as the day it happened.
I wanna go **home**; I wanna sit my Happy Black Ass down in the waitin room til
Cess finishes her Group but I can't let her find me out here like this.
What would she say if she knew I dropped outta my session?
Why am I so upset **anyway**?
I Cram To Understand why Melvin would confront me like that,
but lookin at the make-up a my group I'm Feelin His Pain.
Mel's been here A **While** Jack and who knows how many if **any** men been through these doors?
Must be Difficult just talkin to the counselor week after week
without another man to bounce your frustrations offa.
I had the notion the whole point a this Group thing was to learn ways to
help our women get over being raped but maybe I'm wrong.
Finishin my stoag I creep my ass back into the room.
Melvin is still talkin and Steady is still Lookin For The Exit.
Already I know He Won't Last. Melvin's attention swings back my way.
"Sorry dog. I ain't mean no harm. It hit you Hard Like That yo?"
I shrug my shoulders.
"I been puttin so much energy into helpin Baby Girl get over it I ain't realize
I ain't dealt with what *I'm* feelin, you feel me?
When she told me I was **So** Hurt and So **Angry** but I felt like it was **all my fault** too."
"Nah, man; how could you say that?"
"Listen. I ain't **want** her to go off with that Black mothafucka but Baby Girl Got Her
Own Mind, you feel me? I got **So Mad** at her. I said **Fuck Her**, I Don't Care **What**
Happens To Her. Only I ain't **mean** it like that, you feel me? I ain't know Baby Girl was
gon come back all Broke Up In **Pieces** & Shit. I felt **so** *bad* cause **I had let her go**.
I was **mad**…that's **all**. I ain't want nothin **Bad** to happen to her."
"You ever think about killin him?" Melvin asks.
The Counselor gives Melvin a Sternly Worded Warning but I put my hand up.
"Let Me & My Man Mel **Bond** here a bit."
We Two Thug Niggas after all.
"In my dreams I can feel my hands around his throat," I say in a stone cold voice.
"I smell you," Mel replies in the same tone.
The Counselor takes this moment to ask how we could Better Handle the Rage we feel.

Grabbin A Gun and Shootin Someone don't seem like the Appropriate Response.
The Counselor had me listenin to some Damn Good Advice with Rapt Interest.
Why I'm glad I came though?
Imagine **That**.

It's been over a month since Baby Girl Went Slippin.
If rappers go Back To The Lab where do songwriters go?
Cause Baby Girl's **there** yo.
In early times she would sit out at The Rock starin blankly into space,
oblivious to the wind whippin her hair around. Now Baby Girl spends long hours in
solitude out there with her pen and her pad and I **know** she Writin again.
The weather is Exceedinly Rough. I can see Baby Girl tryna shield her pad from the
wind that threatens to Snatch Her Pages & Run. She could actually write in the house
but that rock Draws Her Like A Designer Closeout Sale and after all she been through:
I Ain't The One to tell her where to do her writin.
Times like these when Baby Girl comes in to grab a bite to eat or to Lose It I am
Sorely Tempted to peek at her pad but I don't. When the Time Is Right she'll show me.
"I think you should go back to work," Baby Girl tells me over lunch.
"Why you say that?" I ask; Stunned but Not Showin It.
"You've got to be bored. I'm getting better now; there's not much for you to do."
She ain't never lied.
Since Baby Girl got better it **ain't** much to do 'sides Lightweight Argue with her
(which does my Poor Heart Good actually) and help her move the furniture around endlessly.
Much as it Pains Me to admit it I miss the Excitement a' a Video Shoot.
"What happened to All That Work you had lined up?"
"I dropped it," I answer flatly.
"What does that **mean**, You Dropped It?" she demands.
See what I'm sayin? All that Fire is Comin Back.
"You got sick and I had to bow out," I explain Under Easily.
"Who's running your company, Hood?" she inquires.
I hesitate to tell her but I know I got to.
"I sold it to Barry a while back," I utter quietly between Tightly Clenched Teeth.
"**YOU SOLD WORLD FAMOUS DAVIS**?!?" Baby Girl explodes.
I kinda figured she wouldn't take it well, and she don't.
What a **Reaction** though.

You'd think I Sold Her **Momma**.

Into **Slavery**.

"I can't **believe** it; what the **Hell** was on your **biscuit**?" Baby Girl asks, **Stupefied**.

"Takin **care** a you?!" I say, like what the Hell is **you** thinkin?

"'Girl I Poured My **Life** into Gettin You Better.

What *else* was I supposed to do, Leave You Alone with a buncha nurses?

If I had Let That Shit Go when I **started** to: **None a This** Would a **Happened**."

"Oh **Hell** no."

With her head bowed and her hand up to her nose Baby Girl **looks** as if she bout read' to cry.

Sure enough her shoulders start to shakin Big Time and she sobbin.

"**Why**... are you **crying**?" I ask, stymied.

"Your company was worth **millions**, damn it. It was your life's work."

"You crazy as a bedbug," I tell her; then it occurs to me:

That might not be the Right Thing To Say to a Mental Patient.

"Down the road a piece you're going to **hate** me, I just know it," she snivels.

"What is this, Déjà Vu All Over Again Yogi!? I don't wanna *hear* that shit from you no more.

You fed me that **same bullshit line** when I left to make that **stupid fuckin movie**

and the **only person** I ended up hatin was **me**."

When Baby Girl flinches it Dawns On Me that I'm screamin.

Just That Fast I had forgot how Delicate Baby Girl still is.

"Yo 'Girl, I'm sorry," I say tenderly.

She prob'ly ain't even **thinkin** straight.

"'S okay," she says between tears, wavin me off. "So is your career over?"

"Oh didn't I tell you? I'm your New PA. I'll be Livin Vicariously Through You. **You** know...

Travel The World with you, Be By Your Side, Supply Your Every Need... **that** type a thing."

This produces a Quick Giggle from Baby Girl.

"You're gonna go from being **Obie One** to **Mr. Princess**."

"That's better than bein just Princess' Baby Daddy ain't it?"

Her giggle develops into a light chuckle.

"You'll miss the limelight," she predicts.

"I will **always** be **World Famous Obie**. I'll be that Old As Hell nigga they trot out at

all the award shows and people will say **Daaamn**, Obie One **still** *Alive*?"

Wholesale Laughter escapes Baby Girl.

"And if I miss the spotlight bad enough I can always Tear Up A Club somewhere.

That's good for two or three **day's** worth a Publicity. **Trust** me: I Know From Experience."

159

She laughs so hard she Stamps Her Feet and Wipes Her Eyes.

"You are **so stupid**," she declares breathlessly. "I'm gonna to pee on myself."

"When you get pregnant again I'll run around carryin a can for you to puke in and when you go into labor I'll catch the baby real fast so you can hurry back on stage."

Her laughter dies mid chuckle. For a brief moment I can't figure out What Went Wrong but when I look at Baby Girl's face I know **exactly** what I done.

I done messed around and Used The Word Baby In A Sentence.

Who *does* that??!!!

I mean.... Why I can't learn to Quit While I'm Ahead though?

I can be so **Stupid** sometimes.

Very very much so.

Baby Girl was laughin and **everything**, now she all Depressed again.

Touchin Baby Girl's Long Pretty Hair affectionately with my fingertips I say:

"Can I tell you somethin? The happiest I have **ever** been in my Entire Black Life was on tour when I Chucked All Them Projects and Made The Rounds with you. Wasn't you happy then too?" I tilt her chin up, look into her eyes and ask.

She nods, her eyes brimmin over with tears.

"I want us to be happy like that again. I'm **meant** to be by your side."

"How do you know I'm not tired of being The Park Avenue Princess?

Maybe *I* want to quit; go back to being plain old Baby Girl Davis again; be by **your** side."

As If.

"That's why you out there writin every day? To keep all those beautiful songs to yourself?"

The 'Girl got No Answer for me.

"Don't worry," I try to encourage her, "you'll get Back On Your Feet again and then you'll be Better Than Ever. Watch & See."

Baby Girl gives me a thin weak little smile that tells me she Still Under Sure.

"Don't you **want** me followin you around?" I joke.

"Yeah," she admits, "cause I don't think I can do it by myself anymore."

"You don't have to," I set her mind at ease. "You'll never be by yourself again."

At my wits end I find myself On The Horn with Barry two days later.

"My **Nigga**," he says ecstatically. "I been **waitin** for you to come back to work."

As If.

"What you got for me bruh? I ain't ready to shoot no videos yet," I hurriedly inform him;

"Baby Girl ain't Strong Enough for me to be gone That Many Hours at a time."

160

"**Damn it dog**," he blurts out then Remembers Hisself. "But she gettin **stronger** though, **right**?"

That's right nigga, Come To Your Senses.

"All the time dog; all the time. So what you got for me?"

What he **has** is three days work assistin on some Bullshit Rapper's debut video.

Payin **scale**.

Which makes me a Glorified Gopher but I Take It Anyway.

I'm **bored,** yo.

Goin back to work was a Great Idea on paper; however the Concept a work and

the Reality a' it crash Head On like Two Drunk Drivers the mornin I'm Set To Start.

The thought a leavin Baby Girl By Herself has me a Bundle a Nerves.

I mean suppose somethin **happens**; like she **Slips Off** or somethin?

I tell you, I Got A Good Mind to call Barry and tell him Forget The Whole Thing.

"Go on to work," Baby Girl Reads My Mind, "I'll be Just Fine. Dionne'll stay with me."

"You sure you gonna be okay?" I ask, still Full a Dread.

"Oscar stop worrying so much.

Our baby's dead, my mother died hating me, but Everything's Gonna **Be** Alright

so there's Really No Point in me going back to The Meadow now **is** there."

My Jaw Drops and my Mouth Hangs Open like a Idiot's.

"Close your mouth before you catch flies."

Well Shut My Mouth then.

"**Damn** I feel alive again," I crow.

"You gon take over the shoot or what, yo?"

Before lunch Barry Hands Over The Reigns.

I nearly have a **orgasm**.

Cess is right: this shit is In My **Blood**, like Performin.

"Whassup Obie?" LaTrese croons, her warm body pressin on me.

"Right now girl? It's Makin a Video. How'd **you** Get Roped into this thing?"

"Spliff said This Dude's Gon Be **Large** and I'd do **anything** for Spliff."

Uh **Huh.** And what **ain't** she done? Besides Turn Me Loose.

Now she startin to Rub Herself on me.

I hope I ain't gotta Body Slam this trick to get her **off** me.

"So how's Our 'Girl doin?" she asks conversationally.

"She doin Much Better," I answer politely.

If you **Really Cared** your *pussy* wouldn't be **stuck up on my ass** like that.

"You still Swingin That Thing around?"
And **there it is folks,** my First Proposition a the day.
Many More To Follow I Assure You.
"Nah," I let her know, "I'm kinda Stuck on Baby Girl. You know how that go."
"Lucky Girl," she concludes. "But if you ever change your mind…"
As **If.**
Peelin her Hot Twat off me LaTrese straightens her clothes. And her demeanor.
Now it's time for a True Confession.
Thanks to the Wonders a Anti Depressant Medication,
I Can't Get It Up Anymore.
But I **also** DON'T **GIVE** A FUCK.
Isn't that **Special**???
Now Back To Our Program.
It's not the kinda thing I want to Get Around though so I still **talk** a Good Game.
My Ability To Mack will **never** die but don't you think I should Miss Sex More?
Cause I **useta** Fuck Up A **Storm,** bruh. I mean I was a real Fuck Master General.
Mind you; I Ain't **Dead** just yet.
I still love the feel a The Girl's body next to mine's.
It just don't Stimulate Me Sexually.
It reminds me a how it useta be before the urge to Bone My Own Cousin
became a Personal Obsession.
Take the way I feel now.
The melon scent a Baby Girl's shampoo rises from her freshly washed hair.
She twitches in her sleep.
I press myself firmly against her but as usual, Nothin Happens.
LaTrese's body stirred memories I ain't visited in months,
memories a the heat Baby Girl useta generate in me.
I **craved** Baby Girl's body and the Release it provided.
My **God,** the release.
They don't call it a Climax for **nothin.**
Perhaps I'm givin up Way Too Much to this Anti Depressant thing.
The Payoff is a Mellow Calm that **Surely** was Missin from my life.
I mean it's Better Than Weed yet Won't Make You Hungry, but the **cost**?

It's gettin Kinda High, dog.

7 BG

It's been a few months since my breakdown.
I haven't exactly come-to-terms with all-that's-happened to me,
but I know I'm on-my-way; every day I feel stronger, more-like-myself.
Music is coming to me again.
I've got three songs competing in my head; every day I work on at least one.
Like the *one* song for the son I lost.
Don't know where I'm going with that yet: but it does-me-good to write about it.
I'm getting bored-and-restless, too.
There is only so much one can do in the house; I've done it all: ad infinitum, ad nauseam.
I mean, how many times can I move the furniture around, *n'est-ce pas?*
I love chatting-with-Dionne-and-all, but I miss my-old-life.
Dollars-to-donuts Obie misses his-old-life, too.
He should go back to work, but when I mention it to him he says he *sold* WFD.
And he did this all for *me.*
Who does *that* in the-new-millennium??!!?
He is the *worst*, man; a *fucking-idiot.*
What's Obie going to do *now?*
I swear, I'm reduced to *tears*, which are flowing-like-a-federal-building-fountain.
Obie's got this *brilliant* idea that once I get better he's going to be my Personal Assistant;
follow me around like some-dumb-*dog* or something, snatching crumbs-from-my-table.
Nigga please. What a *crackhead*
Much as I like the idea, and *I like* the idea, I think it's the-worst-thing-he-can-do.
Obie is way-too-*used*-to being his own man to be Mr. Princess.
I'll quit first, maybe then he can buy his company back from Barry.
And what kind of *friend* buys your company out-from-under-you the second there's a crisis?
Who does *that?*
Obie did have me *cracking-up* with his jokes, though.
Right up until the time he mentioned a baby.
Then it felt like he had stabbed me through my heart with a rusty steak knife.
It got so *hard* to *breathe.*
If Obie feels the way he looks then he must be feeling-like-*shit*,
especially since he's (ab)normally so-damned-careful not to say-the-word-baby to me.

O *ought* to *stop dancing around my feelings* like I'm going to *fall apart* again.
It *hurts*; I've learned-to-live-with-it.

He must have thought about it after all.
Barry let Obie assist on a video so he could hurry-back-home to me.
Like I *need* that.
It went so well he worked on another shoot the following week.
You-know-what-that-led-to…
One-lonely-morning I end up at Wisdom In Christ.
I help some of the church mothers clean; man the register at our thrift store.
On my way out, Pastor Julia asks if I'd mind helping out at the school.
Suddenly, I have a part-time-job.
Of course, Obie is *not* enthused.
"You '*pushin yourself*' again," he feels.
"As *If*, Oscar; if you can work: *so can I*."
I'm not *crazy,* you know.

"Out With It, 'Girl. What's up?"
"The BET Awards are coming up soon; I was wondering if I could perform."
O looks up at me in surprise, then a slow smile graces his gorgeous face.
"You think you up-to-all-that, Cess?"
"The video shoot went well; I think I'm ready to get-back-on-stage."
"That's-what's-up. Since 'R U The 1 For Me' is up for four awards, maybe 'the label'
will pay for your performance so we don't haveta come outta-pocket on this, too.
'Cause they ain't paid me for your video *yet*."
That song seemed like it would never die; it's a good thing too;
I was way-too-sick to promote my follow-up single, "Just Because."
It was a so-so single that only did so-so-well.
My new single, "Can't We, Though?" flew up the charts; shot on location in Fort Greene
Park, the video is the most requested clip on "106th and Park" *and* "TRL." To the Label
Execs who *begged* me to stop making those "home movies" featuring Obie One/WFD:
A Big FUCK YOU.
When Obie approached me about the video I was excited; at the same time I wasn't.
First of all: I was self-conscious about my weight.
I'd always imagined myself a slim-size-six, like "regular girls," but, yo:
I looked like bird turd; my "assets" all melted away, along with my "front set."

I was maybe two-steps-away from *Xena*; you *know* how nasty I think *she* looks.

O was looking like a scarecrow his-damned-self,

so we drank liquid protein drinks; hit the machines in his personal gym.

My breasts filled back in, my rump is round-and-lovely once more,

but the *rest* of my body…*yo*, my new body is *buff*, baby.

Not "muscle bound" like a dude's-- *cut:* well defined.

And *Obie*?

If Obie doesn't look good-enough-to-eat, I'm-still-crazy after all-this-time.

The second reason I was so nervous was: I hadn't used my voice for much more than

screaming-my-lungs-out in months. If O looked like a scarecrow, I sure-as-Hell

sounded like one, but O hired a vocal coach to get my voice back in shape.

Not that I needed my voice for a video shoot—it's all lip synched; still,

I wanted to sound my best just-in-case. Besides, who wants to be that *one* chick;

singing along to *her own single* sounding like a *banshee*?!

Who does *that* anymore?

You figure.

'Cause it wasn't *about* to be *me*.

Last, yet by far the number-one-reason? I knew people were going to be

looking-at-me-funny. Let's face it: I was recovering from a "nervous breakdown;"

taking those first-few-tentative-steps out of the-woods;

I wasn't at all sure the woods wouldn't turn around; re-engulf me.

Turns out I worried for nothing.

Last night Obie asked if I missed having sex.

I don't even *think* about it anymore: I haven't had a sexual urge in just-that-long.

That's plain-and-simply-*under-natural* for two people as "highly sexed" as O and I used to be.

I try touching myself; my *own hands* don't feel the same; nothing turns-me-on anymore.

I know it's the pills; Obie doesn't even get hard in his *sleep*.

I throw the whole damn bottle down the toilet.

Of course, *now* Obie wants to talk about the-first-time-we-boned.

All this on no-happy-pills.

It's not like I haven't told him I-don't-wish-to-talk-about-that before.

I could be flying high on the best weed in the world and not want to talk about it.

As far as *I'm* concerned, that crap *never happened*.

Our first *real* night together was San Diego; *leave-it-there*.

O keeps pressing the issue; my steadfast refusal to discuss this has us shouting at we'chother;

apparently O has no idea how much that little "ep" hurt me.

Not the first night.
I was high-as-a-kite that night.

We were both high.
Obie smokes the-best-shit.
Anyway; I was feeling all *mellow*; we were sitting on the couch laughing at nothing at all.
You-do-that when you're high, know what I mean?
Obie was laughing *hard*, with his head thrown back; I thought to myself:
"Damn, he sure is fine."
I put my feet in Obie's lap, but I'm sure I'd done that countless times before.
I'm *sure* I had.
He started rubbing my feet; it felt so ***good***.
He went from the feet to the ankles; at the knees I knew Obie was making-a-move on me;
He rubbed his hands along the top my thighs, his thumbs stroking the inner part;
I started melting in my drawers.
Obie leaned forward; my legs opened automatically so he could get closer.
Then he started caressing my pussy with gentle delicate strokes (the boy is good).
Moving even closer he kissed me in the same way: all soft-and-wispy.
I was *smoldering*.
We sort of nibbled at we'chother's lips,
all while his hands were working under-told-magic in my drawers.
"You ain't had it good in a long time, have you?" he asked me tenderly.
Didn't he know, yo?
He slid his lips down my chin, my neck, straight down between my breasts.
I guess he *had* to stop there: I still had all my clothes on; but my *mind* screamed,
"Keep going."
Not a problem. He slid my panties off effortlessly; lifted me onto him.
Sliding my blouse up, O nibbled at my breasts as tenderly as he'd nibbled my lips.
We fell asleep; when I woke up the next day with my clothes twisted, I was like,
"Oh *shit*; what did I ***do***?"
I fucked *Obie*; ***that's*** what: on my ***couch***.
Who does *that* anymore?
I didn't want to *look* at Obie,
I was afraid he thought I was cheap-and-sleazy; spreading-my-legs, giving-it-up like that.
Maybe he tried to bring it up once-or-twice after that; if he did, I cut him off quick-fast.

Nigga please.

So *who's the dummy* who put her feet in Obie's lap hoping to get *fucked* again?

I didn't even *know* myself anymore;

But whoever-I-was-becoming needed her *ass* whipped.

Fucking your cousin on the *couch* is so, so very *not* cute, don't care *who* you are.

This time we made it out of our clothes/into the bedroom after the first round so:

I-guess-that's-what-you'd-call "progress."

You figure.

Anyway, I woke up buck naked, in the bed, with Obie on my ass like a tattoo.

I started to get up, to see if perhaps I'd left my dignity in the living room,

along with my clothes, but Obie grabbed my hand.

"Don't go, Cess; stay with me."

So I did; I stayed there with my legs wrapped around Obie's waist all day long.

Can't tell you when we finally fucked ourselves to sleep, but I remember *vividly*

waking up at three a.m. Obie was leaning over me; kissing my forehead, he said:

"I love you, Baby Girl."

I love you, Baby Girl: what a crock of **shit**.

The next morning I found a note on my mirror.

Thanx 4 a Great Time.

I'll Call You from Jamaica.

A week later the crying started; it lasted for three solid weeks.

Obie was gone for two months, never called me **one time.**

I wanted to *die,* always.

What was up with that "I love you" shit?

Who says *that* to a girl, then *never calls again*?

Who does *that* anymore?

Eventually; all cried out, I went looking for the pieces of my broken heart;

patched that stupid thing back together with some dollar store super glue.

Consoling myself, I had to admit I'd acted like a skeezer; got treated like one.

I couldn't blame it all on Obie, a dog will burry-his-bone anywhere he can, but:

Did he have to treat me like some chick he picked up in a bar?

This was *me*: **Baby Girl***; remember*?

I thought I was worth *more*-than-that; I really did;

Obie must have forgotten who I was, *right along with my phone number.*

I also promised myself he'd never-catch-me-out-there again.

Now is *that* what he wants to talk about? I don't think so.
I need a pill.

Well, straight from the didn't-I-blow-your-mind-*this*-time file:
Obie tells me he fell madly in love with me that night;
he was afraid to call me after the way I'd blown-him-off the first time;
his heart couldn't take it if I didn't-love-him the way he-loved-me.
Ain't *that* some shit.
All that time wasted because *I* was convinced all Obie wanted was "some *ass.*"
"What did I do to give you that impression,
'Cause obviously I did something 'way wrong,' and very, very *much* so."
"You mean besides not-calling-me? Don't ask me anything *stupid.*"
"*Back it up a minute*, **okay**? The *first* time; *what-did-I-do-****wrong***,
'Cause you wouldn't talk-about-it; you kept actin like *nothin-happened* and…"
"And, I *still* don't want to talk about it, *can't-you-tell*? Nigga **please.**"
In the ultimate what-the-fuck gesture I throw up my hands, shrug, cross my arms.
It must be "Happy Hour:" I *really need that pill.*
"Every time I talk to you, I feel like a broken record; do anything I say make sense to you?
You think it was easy to sit around while other 'cats' got up in your face?
Askin myself: why-them-and-not-me? Why *Einstein*?
I felt like you *had*-to-see I was better-for-you than *any* a them dudes."
Something in the tone of Obie's voice makes me look up.
"I hurt-your-feelings, didn't I?"
"**Yes**," he exclaimed, "you **did; very, very much so**; you **finally gettin it** now."
Stop-the-madness.
I place my hand on Obie's shoulder: my way of semi-saying, "I'm sorry."
My other hand is covering my mouth, trying to *physically* hold the sobs back.
Obie tugs me slowly toward his chest; his arms blanket me with comfort.
"I loved you *so much*, Baby Girl; from-the-very-start," he whispers.
"I didn't know. I was ashamed of myself, I was scared I was just another 'ep' to you,
I was scared you'd lost-your-respect for me."
"What for?"
"No-decent-girl *fucks on her couch,* like a skuzzy ho, with *all her clothes* on."
Obie seize my shoulders, pushes me back; holds me at arms length.
"*Stop sayin that*; it sounds *nasty*. We did not *fuck*…we had *fun*; we had a *'moment;'*

you *wanted* me; and *I wanted you*; it was *good*; I *know* you liked it."

"**Damn,** it was good," I confess; thankful for my darkness.

"The best ever, yo; a'ight? Say-it-with-me-now: Obie. Is. The. Best. Ever."

"OB. Has. A. Big. Ego."

"And a even-bigger-*dick*. I bet I was better than *Einstein*;
you *never* stopped complainin 'bout how crappy *his* sex was."

"I got more thrills from my soapy wash rag. Sex with you was everything I thought sex
should've been but never was. LaRocque is good, not because it mattered to him;
but because if he's good; he'll get-more-ass; it's like…"

Now I'm stuck. How do you describe a sensation and do-it-justice?

"What I'm *trying to say* is… a woman can tell by the way a man touches her whether
he's doing it to excite *her* or to excite *himself.* When you touched me…it was like...
all for me, not to get me to f…get in my pants; I don't know if I'm saying this right…"

"Yeah, I understand you perfectly. It's like, if I 'hook up' with some girl and she goes
down on me, I can *tell* whether she's 'into it' and she enjoys makin-me-feel-good or if
she givin me 'charity head' just 'cause she think it's her 'civic duty' to give-it-to-me.
I *hate* that. Once I stick-my-dick in a girl I'm-gonna-come *regardless,*
even if I 'lay still,' close-my-eyes, and don't-do-nothin *at all.*
That's not-my-idea-a-fun; for me it's watchin-her-get-there-first."

To illustrate his point Obie kisses me deeply; fingers my nipple.

"What that feel like?" he asks me curiously.

"It doesn't," I mourn.

What once would've kindled-a-forest-fire deep inside me, barely-makes-a-spark.

"Nothin at all?"

"The pills have me dead inside."

"Me, too."

Dropping to my knees, I unbuckle Obie's belt; slide his boxer briefs down halfway.
He's limp-and-lifeless in my hand, still "vaguely appealing" somehow.
I kiss his tip delicately; flick my tongue ring across it.

"Hey, baby, you remember me?" I ask the sad-little-thing in my hands.
Obie chuckles a little.

I lick the tip a few more times then take the whole head in my mouth.

"That ain't gon' work," Obie informs me after a while.

"I know," I concede, "It was worth-a-shot though."

He cups the back of my head in his huge-ass-hand;

pulls my head forward until my cheek rests against his navel.

"Are we having fun yet, Oscar? I-can't-tell-anymore."

He chuckles again, softly; it's a humorless chuckle.

I can feel the sadness; emanating from deep-within-him.

"This ain't worth it no more, Cess; I think I'd rather be depressed."

It's been a long hard day. I worked at the church school, helped out at the flea market,

worked on the vocal arrangement for the BET telecast with Dionne, Alicia;

headed to Armani for a fitting. I *know* I've done too much:

I haven't felt this tired since before my breakdown.

Way before I get to "the rock" to work on this *one* song, I plop down in the sand.

As a child I loved building sand castles at Riis Beach with Uncle BB, Squared.

Absent mindedly I start digging around; pretty soon I've got a great-little-sculpture going.

It's a bit "nippy" out here this late in the day; engrossed in my work I scarcely notice.

Miraculously, my favorite-little-feet materialize in front of me;

looking at my watch I discover I've been playing in the sand for over an hour.

Wowzers.

"Whatcha doin?" Obie asks all syrupy-sweet: he thinks I'm "flipping out" again.

"I'm playing in the sand," I reply with a little "artificial sweetener" of my own.

"It's windy out here, Princess," he states matter-of-factly, drops all pretense.

Nigga please.

Like I didn't know that.

"When was the last time you played in the sand, Oscar?"

Obie looks at me like he can't-figure-out where I'm-coming-from,

but he squats beside me; drags his fingers through the powdery granules.

That's right, nigga: anything-for-you Baby Girl.

You think I'm having a-bad-day; I'm gonna milk this crazy shit for-all-it's-worth.

The sand has the same effect on Obie it had on me; inside of ten minutes we are

working on a new sculpture together. Unwinding, Obie has gone from a squat to a full

kneel, gotten sand all over his brand new jeans; down in his Timbs.

He's laughing up a storm; having a good old time;

I can get his jeans cleaned tomorrow on my way to the church.

We step back to admire our handiwork: a huge heart with

O B + BG 4 EVER

written in three-dimensional letters; Obie gives me a mini hug.

"That was 'extra fun,' Cess; I ain't done this in *years*, and I *own* this beach."

Arm-in-arm, we take a leisurely stroll back to the house, then shower together.

Under the running water we trade long slow kisses; I'm almost positive Obie

stopped taking his pills: he's got a little something *working* there.

It's not much, but he's starting to *spring back to life*, know what I'm sayin?

On the other hand…

I am *moaning*; my sexuality no longer a hostage-of-drug-therapy.

Still wet-from-the-shower we take-it-to-the-bedroom.

Obie kneels above me; I'm-not-even-scared.

O can't get it past half-mast; so he puts-his-tongue on me, makes me come.

I want to do the same for him, so I roll over on my knees.

With some very insistent-yet-gentle-coaxing, my friend offers me a "full salute."

I ease myself down on him slowly, try not to move too much;

we don't know how long Obie's erection will last.

Once we get started Obie gets into it;

he sits up; wraps his long arms around me; holds me "mad tight" 'til he has an orgasm.

I feel my own heat rise; I *almost* get there a second time…But it's okay:

Next-time-will-be-better.

Rapt in "the afterglow" we lay side-by-side; fingers-and-legs entwined.

"Since *you* got to talk the other night, it's my turn now," I announce.

"Straight. What you wanna talk about."

"The baby."

Obie's fingers tighten slightly in mine;

I could swear he stops breathing.

"Are we going to do-this-dance *forever*, Oscar; or can we *talk* about it?"

"Put-ten-dollars on 'keep-on-dancing' for the win, please."

"Hilarious, OB."

"Oh, *that* gets a 'OB' outta you."

"Don't change the subject."

"Can-I-live, though?" he quotes the song.

"Hell, yeah, but-you-still-gon'-die," I answer, supply the quote's tag line.

Obie starts to brood; the equivalent of yelling-and-screaming.

"What you wanna talk about *that* for?" he questions me, clearly in a *mood* now.

"Because we-made-a-baby, we-lost-it; now no-one-will-let-me-talk-about-it."

"We-made-a-baby-we-lost-it-then-you-went-off-the-*deep*-end, **remember**?

171

I don't wanna 'go there' again, you finally startin to 'get better.'"

"Talking about it won't make-me-crazy again; not talking about it *hurts*."

"It hurts **anyway,** Cess; it hurts **every single day** I'm **alive***;* why talk about it?

It ain't gon' get-no-*better*, he'll still be…"

"*Dead,* Oscar? Go-on-and-say-it: he'll *still-be-dead*."

"**I don't want to**," he insists between clenched teeth.

He gets *Spanish* on me; rolls over, gives me his back.

Taking a page from the "OB Price Book of Comfort," I run my fingers through his hair;

brush his cheek with my lips.

That's when I notice Obie's tears.

"I didn't know you took it so hard."

"You act like you 'some girl' I messed-around-with who went-out-and-had-a-'bortion

on me. It was *my baby, too*; we conceived that baby *together*, in the heat-a-passion,

and I *wanted* that baby; I wanted you to have my baby *so bad*…"

"I wanted to have your baby, too; only I didn't know it until after I lost it.

I felt *punished*; I *still* feel punished."

"Punished for what?"

"For not having better control of myself; for not listening to you like I should have;

for not being able to admit that I needed you.

For letting you go like an asshole when I knew I was falling apart."

Obie rolls back over, glowers at me.

"It was after I lost the baby; I couldn't *take*-it-any-more, it was all-too-much-for-me."

"Why didn't you *tell me*, Cess?"

"*A*: I'd already made that big stink about 'being a'ight;' *a'ight*?!

B: I didn't want you to think I was some weak-ass-bitch who couldn't-take-care-of-herself.

C: You were *so damned busy*; I didn't want to *bother you* with my *problems*."

"Babe, I *knew* it was gonna be '*overwhelmin*' for you; I *told* you that."

"So that made you-right-and-me-wrong; you *know* how I feel about that."

"You make everything *a confrontation*. Right-or-wrong, win-or-lose, you *always* gotta

come-out-on-top. When you gon' understand we 'workin *together*' here? It ain't no

'I win, you lose' type a thing; if we ain't *both* in-this-to-win-this, *we both lose*.

Ain't that what happened Cess? What *keeps on* hap'nin with us? You gave-me-your-

body then woke up the next morning figurin *I*-had-won and *you*-had-lost, and we *both*

ended-up-losin *years* outta a 'beautiful relationship,' all 'cause you got scared you

might-get-*conquered*; yet you stayed with Einstein's piece-a-shit-ass

172

and *he* tried to make *a 'Stepford Wife'* outta you. What the *fuck,* Princess?!"

"I was not *scared* of getting *conquered*, Oscar, I was *scared* of getting **vanquished**; of putting-my-feelings-out-there; having you dump me for the-next-pretty-face or 'bangin backside.' Einstein wasn't *shit*, true-that; he lacked-the-finesse of knowing-how-to-treat-a-girl, but he never would have left me. For a guy-like-him, I was a-*real-prize*."

"For a guy like **ME** you 'a real prize.' You think I would leave *you* for a hot-piece-a-ass I might *fuck twice* and *forget about*?! You scared if you say 'Obie, *help* me,' you'd be too-much-trouble and I'd kick-you-to-the-curb? So Einstein was your *back-up-plan*?? You **CRAZY**."

"Please don't say that," I squeak; crushed by his overwhelming anger/labeling of me.

"I'm sorry, babe; I swear; but who could I find better-than-you.
Next to Mommy you the strongest-woman-I-know; that means way-more-to-me than a 'pretty face' and a 'great ass,' *both a which you have, by the way*."

"If 'I'm so strong,' why did I *fall apart*?"

"'Cause you a 'natural woman,' not a 'super woman,' and you tried to do-too-much on your own. Even the 'strongest woman' need a-good-man's-support."

"If I allow myself to get used to your help, what will I do when you're not around anymore?"

"*Is there a hole-in-the-bucket-dear-Liza or* **what??!!!**
I AIN'T LEAVIN YOU. I keep sayin the same shit over-and-over but you never hear me."

"You're yelling at me again."

"That's 'cause *you sound retarded; real **stupid**; wassa matter, you need a **pill** or somethin*?"

"Ho, ho, ho, mothafucka: *no*; I do *not* need-a-pill. Einstein was a real 'nerd;' not-that-good-looking; didn't too-many-girls want him. *You*, are *spectacular;* all-the-girls want to fuck you; you can get *any girl you want; **what** the **hell** do you want with *me*?"

"Why do we keep going round-and-round this *same* 'mulberry bush'?
This conversation's gettin *redundant* and it's *borin-me-to-tears*."

"My ass aside; you've dated hundreds of girls *so, so very* prettier-than-me."

"*Who* is 'so much prettier' than you? And *which one* has 'my ring' on 'her finger'?"

Twelve names spring to mind off the bat; I run them down; he acts like I'm not-making-sense.
Maybe he needs Clarissa to explain-it-all to him.
If Obie had even an *inkling* of what-my-fears-are, I'd be a-lot-more-relaxed.

"Hold up," Obie says suddenly. "Every one a those chicks is…I *know* by 'prettier' you don't mean '*lighter*?!' *Please* tell me you don't mean '*lighter*.'"

"BINGO!"

By golly, he *might*-understand-after-all.

"Ohhh, Ba-by *Girl*; you're the most *beautiful girl I've ever seen.*"

"When *I* look in the mirror, that's what *I* see; but how many guys say: I'm-dying-to-fuck-that-coal-black-bitch-over-there? Too-many-niggas knock-me-down then trip-over-me trying to talk to some *busted* yaller chick. Even *Hood* said he wouldn't be *caught **dead*** with a tar-black-bitch on his arm. Plus, I'm *really-fucking-big.*"

"Most men ain't got good *sense*; besides you get *truckloads* a mail from dudes."

"They do *not* want Baby Girl; they want *The Park Avenue Princess*: that woman on TV shaking her 'assets.' Baby Girl is just-another-Black-chic with a 'nice weave' who couldn't get *arrested* in Compton. I couldn't even get 'play' based on *looking* like Princess: those 'cats'' minds went *straight back to Xena.*"

"I don't know *what* was on they biscuits. I *don't* think yaller-is-cute, I *don't* want no yaller-ass-broad and I ***don't*** want no *tiny-ass-broad*, either. How can I make you see that, 'cause this another conversation I'm tired-a-havin. Lay that *shit* to rest; *kill* it; put-it-outta-its-*misery* or we'll never make-our-marriage-work."

"I want to; I want to so, *so very badly*: it's *killing* me."

"This another variation on the 'red dress' theme, right? I'm a see some 'bright chick' and 'magically notice' that you *really, really, really, really **dark***, right?"

"I *know* this, *man*; I look at myself *every day.*"

"Well, *here's-a-hint*: ***I look at you, too***, so I *must* know what color you are by now. You think you gon' look darker standin next to a 'bright' girl than you do layin next to *my*-white-ass???!!!"

Always with the jokes.

"You're trying to make me sound foolish."

"You doin that to your *self,* hon."

Point well taken. Argument over, we wrap up in we'chother again.

"I want another baby, Oscar."

"Where the Hell did *that* come from?"

"Catch up, *damn it*, when this conversation started we were talking about a *baby*, *remember*? How we got 'off topic' I'll-never-know, but what *I* want is your baby, growing inside of me."

"Be*cause*…?"

"Because I love you; because you'll be an *incredible* Dad."

"But we just gettin your career back-on-its-feet again."

"Look; you're the manager/ PA/ major domo/ homie/ lover/ friend guy right? Me: get on stage; you: watch baby."

8 OB

"What's Princess been up to lately?" Barry asks over a Quick Lunch Break.

"She Writin again," I Spread the Good News.

It's More Than That Though.

Because *I* went back to work Baby Girl One Ups me,

gettin a Part Time Gig at the Church School helpin the music teacher out.

Some days Cess spend more time workin at **church** than she spend at home.

I'm angry as Hell without knowin why, but then it occurs to me:

I'm still scared for her.

If the goal is for Baby Girl to Get Better I hafta Let Go & Let God right?

"You think she comin back to work soon?"

"O-**kay**... I Smell A Rat."

"Never that. Officially she still Sick. I wanna be the nigga who gets her in front a the camera again, only I want **you** to shoot it. You Bring Out The Best in her."

What a Lovely Set a Lips to Kiss My Ass with.

"And if you can Guarantee That you'd be The Man."

"Truly though."

"We have a Exclusive Contract **regardless**."

"It's Her Label, *yo*; they On Some **Shit,** askin me to Piece Somethin Together for No Money At All. They fixin to Write Cess Off as a Loss and **that ain't right**. I ain't gon do some Shit Job Video that won't do **nothin** for Cess's career."

I'm listenin pret-ty rapt-ly. It was A Given that if Cess stayed outta The Limelight too long her career would suffer but I figured She Had More Time.

Doesn't everyone?

"I never **seen** a label **willin** to Shelf A Star So Hot. What's The Buzz?" I ask.

"Too Much Scandal. You... Einstein... she Lost A Baby then Lost Her Mind..."

"They think she Ain't Comin Back." I cut in.

"You **Already Know**. And they wanna Milk The Cow before it Drops Dead."

"They ain't even **tryin** to give her a chance. Don't it matter that Cess is sick?"

"All that matters is That Dollar, nigga. **You** Know How It Go."

Yeah I **do**.

But that don't mean I Like It.

"You got a Concept in mind?" I blurt out abruptly.

"No not really but since they ain't developed nothin a they own I figure
they can't complain about what we turn in."

"The Ball is in Our Court Nigga, I say Run With It. What's the budget?"

Barry quotes a figure so low I almost shit on myself.

"What we supposed to do with that??!!

Hire your momma to shoot the video in your livin room with a rented camcorder?"

"I told you dog, they tryna Bury Cess and we can't let her Go Out like that."

"Fuck them bitches. I'll pay for the shoot my **damn** self and bill em."

This is **Bullshit**.

If Princess' Public is Firmly In Her Corner Why Ain't Her Handlers?

This Beautiful Talented Woman Gave Her All to her career.

And made her label a **ton a money** in the process.

Now they treatin her like a Washed Up Old Hag.

After posin some Really Tough Questions to Princess' manager I quickly realize:

He firmly intended to Collect His Check while watchin her career Disintegrate.

Havin a Better Plan I **fire** his ass cause **We** Can Do **Bad** by Our **Damn** Selfs.

He Bitches & Complains but *I* have Power of Attorney so he gets:

A Big Fuck You from Obie One.

Next call: The Clown At Cess's Label.

I Casually Inquire about her next single and the video budget.

His quote is **Slightly** Higher than the figure Barry hit me with.

Either Barry MisRepped or

Label Guy is Scared To Tell Me what they **really** planned on spendin.

My money's on the **latter**.

"You plan on handling the video yourself Obie One?" Label Guy asks Nonchalantly.

Not for the shit **he** payin.

Shrewd Businessmen we are I guess we both Namin The Other's Tune right now.

I might a tipped my hand some but it's All Good.

It ain't like He Can Stop Me.

"How you feel bout gettin back to work For Real?" I approach Cess.

"What does **that** mean?" Baby Girl asks warily.

"You Down to Shoot A Video?"

"You **mean** it?" a bright smile flashes across her face.

"Most Def. Me and Barry was **just** talkin bout that the other day.

You due for a new video and it would Get Your Name Back Out There."
"Who's going to shoot it?"
My hand firmly in the center a my chest I hit her with The Only Kool-Aid Smile.
"Baby Girl? If I don't shoot the video: it **won't get done**."

I try to envision what Cess was thinkin bout when she penned this tune.
The more I listen the more I see Cess sittin somewhere givin herself a Pep Talk.
And what better place to Sit & Think than A Park?
It's Cool It's Quiet & It's Peaceful.
Gradually the storyline comes together for me. Princess heads for the park to sort
through all these Conflictin Feelins she has. She stops at a bench. Sits & Thinks.
Gets Up & Walks Again. Stops At Another Bench to Sit & Think Some More.
Next I hafta set The Pattern a Walkin & Sittin with The Rhythm a The Music.
I figure she'd walk the choruses and sit the verses.
To change it up I want Cess to Under Expectedly find me sittin on the last bench.
I motion for her to sit down and ask her Can't We Though?
What?! I *know* you ain't think I was gonna **not be in this video.**

At first Cess was excited about the video only now she Ain't So Sure.
Finally she confess that she Ain't Too Thrilled with her looks **or** the way she sound.
I look like Jack Schitt myself but that's the Easiest Thing a All to correct.
I also hire a vocal coach to help Cess get her voice back.
In my mind I'm picturin Fort Greene Park.
Cause the Stairs & The Monument's so Visually Stunnin.
I gotta fly up that way anyway.
The lawyer Uncle BB hired to defend Princess is holdin a meetin.
I'm dreadin This Whole Scenario.
The last people on the face a this **planet** I wanna see is The Bells.
They obviously Don't Have A Clue What Went On 'cept What They Saw On TV.
Who wants to be That One to Break Some Poor Parent's Heart?
Not I said the bullfrog.
Every parent Love They Child and wanna believe Only The Best about him.
I can't very well let them break Baby Girl down though.
Uncle BB and Uncle Tommy arrive Right On Schedule.
All we waitin for **now** is The Bells to show up with they Mouthpiece.

This Ain't No Hearts and Flowers Love Story Pt2 by Brooklyn Darkchild

Albert's folks ain't **too** late, just late enough to be considered Annoyin.

Clearly they think they have The Upper Hand and can Afford to Hold Us Up.

Sorry but…

I Don't **Think** So.

Enough Time has Already Been Wasted.

Our lawyer calls all interested parties into his conference room. Everyone settles in but

I'm steady admirin this Big Ass Oak Table, cause I got them oak cabinets, you feel me?

That and I'm tryna Occupy My Mind cause I'm Nervous.

We line up in Camps:

Mr. and Mrs. Bell, Albert's sister Bettina, and they lawyer on one side a the table;

me, Uncle BB, and Uncle Tommy opposite them.

Seated at the Head a The Table our lawyer Mr. Weinberg begins.

"At the heart of this lawsuit lies a terrible tragedy. A promising young man lost his life, and the young lady in question was horribly injured. These most basic of facts don't **begin** to tell the complete story. We're here to present some facts we hope will persuade you to drop this lawsuit. The media has besmirched the reputations of both my client and her fiancé. The reputation of Mr. Bell will only suffer should these facts be made public."

"Let's skip the useless allegations. If you have any supportive evidence I suggest you present it. Otherwise I'll advise my clients to terminate this meeting at once."

They lawyer's a **Indignant** Fuck ain't he?

Over the next couple hours Weinberg hits them with the cell phone records,

house phone records, pictures we took at Princess' house

and the actual clothes she had on that day, none a which I can look at.

It's bad enough I **lived through** that shit.

Just the thought a those clothes makes me wanna hurl.

Pandemonium Erupts at the mention a rape,

as the Bell Family denies the **possibility** that Such A Event could have occurred.

"Ms. Davis states she was raped several times over a ten-hour period and

forced to lie bleeding in **this** spot. She was menstruating at the time but also suffered other fully documented injuries which increased her blood loss."

The doctors' reports was next and Last But Not Least the Good Officer Tyson sent a deposition.

I feel Beat The Fuck Up for like the Thousandth Time

and the Bells look like they been Through The Wringer too.

One lift a Weinberg's hand and a silver tray a coffee and tea Magically Appears.

My Nerves Is Shot so I opt for a Cup a Chamomile.

Goldman decides to Earn His Salary.

"Is there any physical evidence pointing to Mr. Bell as Ms. Davis' rapist?"

"No. Mr. Bell forced Ms. Davis to bathe. Our experts state that because Ms. Davis was bleeding heavily most of the semen would have been expelled anyway."

"How convenient," Goldman states dryly.

Uncle BB had his hands full tryna hold back Lee on the left and me on the right.

Goldman has that These Niggers Sure Are Crazy look on.

He's so **Blissfully** Under Aware that The One To Fear Most is

the Cool Brotha holdin Us Hotheads back.

If BB wasn't the Bad Mothafucka he was he **mighta** *Lost*,

but he uses **Lee's** body to hold **me** back.

"How could you let this bastard talk about Baby Girl like that?" I ask the Bells.

"How do we know **you** didn't do these things Obie?" Bettina fires back;

"You've **always** had a bad temper, for as long as I've known you.

How do we know you're not blaming this on Albert to cover your own shit?"

"Why would I hurt Baby Girl like that? I *LOVE* her."

"*Albert loved her too*. He loved her **so much**. How could you do that to him?

How could you take his girl when **you** Hooked Them Up in the first place?"

"I ain't do **nothin** to Albert. Baby Girl was tired a him **way** before we got together.

That's **his** fault not **mine's**. He ain't want her to go to Cali, ain't want her to be famous,

ain't want her to be **nothin**. That's not **Love**, that's Sickness."

I drop back to my seat so hard the chair groans in agony.

Oh *Well*.

Nothin could hurt more than I do now. The Group Sessions, the Happy Pills,

not even the Passage A Time has dulled this pain for me.

"Even without the physical evidence we have over twenty eye witnesses that state Ms. Davis left the party with an irate Mr. Bell and returned the next morning battered beyond belief," Weinberg declares.

"All those people are her friends and relatives," Goldman counters.

Like a fencing match it's become all Thrusts and Parries.

"Look here," I speak up. "As far as The Media's concerned I'm the Only Villain in this equation. No one knows Baby Girl got raped and we wanna leave it there. I don't mind bein The Bad Guy, I really don't, but I don't want My 'Girl to go through the Shame & Embarrassment a' A Trial. Whatever you believe a lotta people gon be lookin at your boy in a Different Light once this story goes public. At the very least we got enough documentation to cast doubt in any juror's mind. You'll never win so what's the point?"

Goldman Ping Pongs between his clients and Weinberg.

At last they agree to drop the lawsuit.

We graciously agree to pay Goldman's fee.

Uncle BB throws in somethin For They Sufferin.

Weinberg cautions them not to view this as a Settlement or Admission A Guilt.

As If.

Another load off our backs.

Back in Cali the Men's Group is down to Mel & Me again but it's All Good.

My Man Mel is a Great Conversationalist.

Us bein Men this week's topic is sex: a great topic for Obie the Sexless Wonder.

It's been almost a year and Mel's wife still won't Let Him Touch Her.

"I'm tryna be patient. After all this time I can **see** she still hurtin, you smell me?

It's like the whole thang's crippled her. She still cries about it in her sleep.

She scared to leave the house and e'rythang. You ain't have that problem?"

"Nah, dog. Just the opposite. After bein In A Coma for two weeks Princess decides we gotta Do It **or else.** I told her Don't Feel Like You Gotta For Me cause I'm **Good,** but **No**... Princess wanna **Move On** like we could Close Our Eyes and **forget** what happened. Then when we try and Get Somethin Started she balls up in a **knot** like I'm **killin** her. Made me Feel Like *Shit.*

Even now it's too many times Baby Girl'll flinch if I touch her

or she'll Do It but she don't really be **into** it like she was before. I'd rather not Do It **at all** then have Baby Girl do somethin she don't wanna do but if I say somethin she get **mad.**"

"So you're Dissatisfied with your Sex Life?" the Counselor asks me.

"Oh we ain't **got** no sex life. After we cracked up we went on anti-depressants.

That cured All Our Problems, even the Sexual ones."

It was supposed to be a joke but I got depressed just thinkin bout it.

I miss my pussy; it was **good** to me.

"But you became dissatisfied after the rape?"

"Very Very Much So. It wasn't Fun & Carefree no more."

The counselor talks about why that was: Mel's wife couldn't trust again and

Baby Girl was tryna force herself to trust when the last thing she felt was trusting.

"Work on bein intimate again without the expectation that sex should follow."

"Yeah," I confirm the counselor's advice, "take the Dick outta sex.

Keep your draws on. Lay behind her if that don't freak her out. Kiss her and

180

touch her body through her clothes. Make sure she know it don't hafta Progress."

"Why you ain't follow your own advice though?"

"Cause **My Girl** wanted to Climb Mount Everest when she Just Learned To Walk Again.

She acted like I'm a Fuck Somebody Else. It **Ain't** That Type a Party."

"Sounds like you were frustrated," the counselor observes.

"**Word**. We'd start out with Cess lookin like she Stiflin The Urge To Vomit.

It really hurt when she recoiled from me like that.

It hurt Twice As Much when she tried to act like I Was **Imaginin** the whole thing.

I felt like the rapist. I ain't wanna **be** there."

Far into the night now my mind continues to trouble me.

I run my hand over Cess's curves constantly hopin for some spark.

Somethin to remind me: I'm Still A Man.

We both nekked (like it **matters**) and I can't help but admire her Fantastic New Figure.

I should be Reapin The Benefits a this body I Helped To Mold.

Cess musta Overdid It again: she layin here Deader Than Elvis,

twitchin in her sleep and wavin me off.

I try a lighter touch. It's still botherin her.

"What are you **doing**?!" Cess complains, only slightly awake.

"I'm **touchin** you," I say sullenly. "I ain't mean to wake you up. Sorry."

"'S alright," she murmurs, already on her way back to sleep.

My hand is still movin over Cess's body but she don't notice or she don't care no more.

I shake her gently til I'm sure she awake.

"Do you ever miss makin love to me?"

There's a lotta Other Shit on my mind too.

Cess and me got some Issues Clingin to the Periphery a Our Relationship that's like

Way Past Due for a Clean Up.

Number One?

The Start a Our Love Affair.

At first Cess don't Fully Understand what I'm talkin bout but Oh *BOY*.

When it **finally comes to her...**

"We are **so** Not **Going** There Oscar: so so *very*," Cess states forcefully.

"*Because*," I demand, adamant.

"Because there's Nothing To Talk About," she insists.

"You always say that," I utter flatly.

"That should **Tell** You Something," Cess snaps at me.

And We're Off, launchin into The **Only** Screamin Match.

Cess jumps in her clothes and this time I'm Right Behind Her.

"Look, it **happened**, a'ight? *Okay* Then: **End. Of. Story.** Let's Move On."

Princess says this with such vehemence I'm astounded.

"Let's Move On, Let's Move On; that's all I ever hear from you. Why you can't **deal** with shit. You always pushin shit Off To The Side like you can make it Go Away cause **You Say So.** Well everything you called yourself Movin On from followed you like some Irate Nigga With A Brick. Einstein; the baby; even what happened between you and me: it **all came back** to hit you in the head and **almost killed** you. Was it any **better** that way?"

"You don't know **anything about WHAT** I feel or **HOW** I feel it," Cess shouts;

"You wanna **talk**?! Let's talk about how you stayed in bed with me **All Day Long**, told me you **loved** me, then **never fucking called me again.** *Okay*?!

I Love You Baby Girl… What A Load Of *BULLSHIT*.

If you wanted a **fuck** you could have **said** that, you didn't **have to lie.**

I cried for **three fuckin weeks** Obie; I wanted to **DIE**, do you hear me? *ALWAYS*.

If **that's** what you want to talk about All **Righty** Then. Pull Up A Chair & Let's Chat."

I think she mad at me.

Caller, you say what?

I stand with my back pressed against the wall, one leg up; my hands clasped in front a me. My head is hangin down and my lips is pressed together tight.

Cess's anger is Completely Understandable yet Not Entirely My Fault, you feel me?

Be That As It May I still feel miserable.

All this time I knew Cess was angry at me but I had no idea in Hell she was So Damn **Hurt**.

She kept actin like it Didn't Matter; like it Didn't **Mean** Nothin To Her.

Well **Guess** *What*?

Princess ain't The **Only Hurt One** in this room.

"I need to apologize to you cause the last thing I meant to do was hurt you. You wasn't never meant to hear that; I thought you was asleep. But can I tell you a secret though? I wasn't lyin when I said I loved you. I was Feelin You from the **first night we spent together. I wanted** to call you from Jamaica: **very very much so**; but I simply was **not** ready to hear Okay We Fucked. Let's Move On, you feel me? I couldn't **handle** that."

"So you're saying I- Pushed You Away then."

"I'm not gonna Say All **That** now. You could **never** push me away but you sure Backed Me The Fuck Up and a **lot farther than I meant to go** too."

"No shit. That was **not** my intention **believe** that. I was **trying** to **Avoid Drama**."
What **drama**?
What the fuck is she **talkin** bout?
Was it **me**???
Maybe **I** did somethin wrong or put out The Wrong Signal,
but when I ask Cess **what,** all she does is shrug her shoulders and cross her arms.
It's really hard for me to admit how fucked up I was feelin back then.
Cess was just startin to Get Large and Cats was comin outta the **Cracks In The Walls**
tryna Get Next To Her.
She was Flirtin & Datin & Havin a **Good Ole Time** and I had like The **Only**
Front Row Seat for the Break Obie's Heart Show.
Not **one a them** Tired Ass Niggas was worth the Sex Act That Made Them
yet Cess was Giddy With Excitement before each date while payin **me** No Mind At All.
And of course In Between The Jerks there was Fuckin **Einstein**.
What was the Name a **That** Tune, huh?
Oh my *God* I couldn't understand it
and I **definitely** couldn't understand that Ragin Jealousy flowin through me.
I mean **Come On**.
Who **does** that over a girl they only slept with **One Time**?
I admit it stung, so much it's **hard** for me to talk about.
That must be how I finally convey how much that chilly attitude **Really Really Hurt** me.
Why this Makes Her Cryin though?
Cause she **Shamed** a Herself.
As *If.*
For Some Dumb Reason Cess assumed I couldn't Respect Her cause we Did It on her **couch**.
One a us Got Shit Twisted and **I don't think it's me either**.
Is there a Sex Etiquette now?
And So Called Good Girls can only Do It in the bedroom?
When did they give that class?
Was I Cuttin that day?
It musta been one a them All Girl Classes like the one's they show the Period Movies
and give out the Kotex Gift Packs in cause:
I don't know where Cess is comin from.
I'd **like** to say I Don't Care,
but it's Affectin Me Personally here.

As far as I know, two people Wantin Each Other ain't **Never Been A Crime**
and I **know** Cess wanted me **every bit as much** as I wanted her.
She probably couldn't **Deal** With Wantin Me Either.
Who *does* that??!!!
How do you **live** like that?!

I feel so Leaden Inside, so Void and Empty a Any Passion At All.
Playin with Cess's nipple don't Do It for me and it ain't Doin It for her either,
I'm just Goin Through The Motions.
Cess (with her crazy self) hits her knees, unbuckles my jeans and Talks Into The Mike.
That Cracks Me Up every time.
Cess's doin a Whole Lot More than **talkin** to it now;
she starts lickin on me and before I know it I'm halfway in her mouth.
If I wasn't lookin at her would I had noticed though?
My Life is a Livin **Hell** I tell you.

I'm havin the Worst Day In History.
Every little thing is gettin on my nerves and
I'm snapin at just about every person that crosses my path.
You know what this is, don't you.
I'm In A Mood.
While I might a missed the **crap** outta my Love Life I did **not** miss These Moods.
My head hurts and I wanna go home and lay down.
As If.
The Latin King walks up to me, hand extended and grinnin like a fool.
"Come 'ere Dog, I wanna Shake Your Hand," Barry chuckles.
"What the **fuck** son," I snap. "Can't you see I'm busy?"
Like I got **Time** For This Shit.
"Yeah yeah yeah; so what?! I need to congratulate you bruh."
"Cut the Horseshit Barry, who **does** that?"
"**Yo**: that Alfred E. Neuman shit you was on had me **Shook**.
I didn't know if you was the victim a' a Body Snatchin or **what**.
You Skip Your Pill or somethin?"
What a *asshole*. He sure made me smile though.
"Actually I stopped takin em."

"*Good*, cause you ain't **need** that shit *no way*."

That's what **you** think.

Today I'm Gonna Hafta Disagree.

Cess must be havin a Doozy Of A Day herself: she Sittin In The Sand **alone**.

She on That BET Kick now and I think she back to doin Way Too Much again.

Such is the Nature a The Beast:

most Performers is not only Perfectionists but Workaholics to boot.

Cess got her back to me so I can't exactly make out what she doin but whatever it is:

It need to be Shelved Til Spring.

Okay, she cannot **possibly** be out here **diggin in the sand like some kid.**

Worry gnaws at my Sensibilities. I should be keepin A Better Eye on Cess.

Suppose she Not As Well as we **think** she is?

Usin the most Nonchalant Tone I can muster I ask Cess what she doin

but the way she answer me Cess musta Smelled Me Comin.

Fine.

If She Slippin it ain't affected The Sharpness a Her Tongue.

It's Cold, I'm Irritable, & Cess Is Ignorin Me.

She need to Bring Her Ass In The House **Now**.

"When was the last time you played in the sand Oscar?"

There have been *way* too many What The Fuck's crammed into this day.

Now Cess wanna play in the sand like a infant child.

I **know** I need *my* pills;

What's **her** excuse?

Fuck it. She wanna play in the sand?

We'll play in the sand got damn it.

For five minutes.

Damn, this is Lightweight Fun in a Goofy Kinda Way. I peek over at Cess's creation but

I don't wanna make no **Busted Castle**; I wanna make a Monster Heart.

Here **she** come, abandonin her project to help me with mine's.

I throw some sand at her then dart outta her reach.

Cess know she Can't Catch Me; I don't know why she Insist On Tryin.

Outta breath we both collapse next to each other and make sand angels.

This the closest we gon get to snow in Southern California.

The cold is really gettin to Cess so I wrap my hoodie around her and

we finish our heart. I mold some letters on it that say:

OB + Cess 4ever

We got sand everywhere: in our hair, in our shoes, down our shirts and pants.

To the showers … where Cess is Lookin **Gooood**.

Oh Baby **Girl**.

Am I still sandy?

I can't tell cause my tongue is too far down Princess' throat.

Somebody Else must not be Takin Her Pills either cause she moanin up a storm.

Cess feels so good pressed against me with the water cascadin down my back.

I can't get past Half A Hard but **Hey**:

That's Half A Hard More than I had The Other Day.

I might could **Do** A Little Somethin with this thing.

Let's Find Out…

Me and Cess kiss all the way to the bed where she lays back and I hover over her.

We come up for air long enough for it to hit me: Cess ain't scared a me no more.

She smilin at me, but enough a that: I need some more a them Hot Ass Kisses.

I could go on kissin her all night but Cess is gonna blow any second.

My Half A Hard is goin Nowhere Fast so I Go Down on her.

I love the way Cess taste: Fresh Out The Shower; and the Way She Smell & All.

She throws her legs up over my shoulders, buries her hands in my hair til I feel her fingertips diggin into my scalp. It's been a Mighty Long Time since I Been Down Here but I still know the Name a **This** Tune.

Her orgasm leaves Cess breathless and if I can't Get My Self Off--

At least I can still Satisfy My Woman.

Once Cess catches her breath she rolls over and goes to work on me.

She flicks her tongue across the head three or four times which sends little Shock Waves A Pleasure down my spine. Increasin the pressure Slow & Steady with the ball on her tongue ring Cess gets a First Class Salute outta me.

I'm **tellin** you,

This is why I love this 'Girl.

Each time she slides her mouth down my shaft and back up again my toes curl under Just A Touch More.

Pretty soon I got my hands entwined in *Cess's* hair, Ridin The Flow.

When Cess stops I feel like I'm gonna DIE; always;

I reach out to pull her mouth back on me but she just giggles and rolls away.

Lord **please**, I *know* she can't be fi'n a stop **now**.

Don't she **Love Me Though**?

OH, I Spoke Too Soon. Cess just went and Climbed Aboard.

Ride That Obie **Train**, Baby Girl.

She so soft and so **wet**, I **swear** this is what I been missin all this time.

Cess is sittin almost perfectly still but I wanna **move** *damn it.*

I grip her hips, slidin myself into her slowly.

I bend my knees to get better leverage, bracin my shoulders on the headboard.

My palms grip Cess's smooth round thighs movin her up and down for several

long leisurely strokes before I wrap her legs around my waist.

Slow & Steady might Win The Race but this one's Drawin To A Close.

I'm tryna last a little bit longer cause

Cess is deep into it with her head thrown back and her lips parted.

With my Half Ass Start I can't believe I hung in there **this** long.

I nibble on her lips, her neck, the top a her breasts but she tells me to:

"Go ahead Oscar. I'm not gonna come again."

O-**kay** Then.

I'd usually hold back some, save some for the next trip but

I don't think I'm gonna make it another round either so I shoot the whole wad off.

"Next time babe; next time," Cess says, smilin broadly.

Tomorrow is what **I'm** thinkin. I'm a be Better Prepared.

We both pantin this time, **crazy** exhausted. What a way to end a **day** though.

Cess is restin on my chest while I smother her with little kisses.

I'm **so** full a love for this woman in my arms; very very much so.

I can't believe how Blessed I am.

So **why** she wanna fuck it up with Baby Talk?

Cess done blown my Warm Cozy Feelin **straight to Hell**.

But **wait**...

My Mood has Returned to Take Its Place.

Isn't that **Special**???

Cess complains that No One Will Let Her Talk About The Baby.

Pardon **Me** but,

Ain't that cause she **Cracked The Fuck Up???**

Just thought I'd ask cause **Someone** is tryna make me think **I'm** The Crazy One.

Then Cess says Not Talkin Bout It **hurts**.

And **Talkin Bout It will solve...?**

That's what I thought too.

But *maybe*...

I Wasn't Makin Sense again.

Cess think it's **Me** Though, right?

Hold up, hold up: Somethin's Comin Over Me.

It's a...it's a ...

Why *Yes*.

It's a Let's Move On.

The Baby Is **Dead** Now **Let's Move On**.

But of course we can't **do** that because The Princess hasn't **Decried** It yet.

Fuck her Imperious Ass.

I got A Trick for **her**:

You know how she Ain't Wanna Talk before?

Well I- Don't Wanna Talk now and **Princess can't make me.**

What she **can** Make Me Do is Cry and *nothin* should have That Much Power over me.

Knowin I'm Upset & All I turn my back hopin to hide my tears.

Cess tries to make me feel better and that's when she discovers I'm cryin.

A nigga can't keep **nothin** to hisself in this house.

"I didn't know you took it so hard," she says to me.

DUH!!!!

How do you **lose a baby** without it **affectin** you?

Who **does** that?

"It was **my baby too**," Stupid Ass. "It's not like you some girl I messed around with who went out and had a abortion on me," which never happened to me either, "and I **wanted** that baby. I wanted that baby *so bad*..."

I Fucked Around and Put It There without even askin.

You see how far **that** got me, don't you.

Then Cess tells me she knew she was crackin up but didn't tell me.

I swear I wannna strangle her.

She the type who's Always Right.

She'd rather **Lose Her Mind** than admit she might **possibly** have been:

(say it now) *W.R.O.N.G.* thinkin She Ain't Need Me???

You figure, cause I don't know **what** her problem is.

Damned if She Don't Tell Me though.

Princess is Color Struck: she Self Conscious bout Her Skin Tone.

As **If**.

"Cess you can Never be Too Rich or Too Black."

"Why that's something Only Light Skinned People Say though???

Cause no Real Black Nigga would **say that**. We *Know Better*."

The 'Girl is such a Rich Beautiful Shade a Chocolate Brown

she gotta be off her *fuckin* **bird**. Correctin me Cess say **she** know she beautiful

but most dudes push her out the way tryna get at some Busted Ass Bright Chick.

Okay, I've seen that myself.

Most Cats ain't exactly Feelin Her Skin Color.

Every dude Ain't Got Good Sense though.

Most Dudes, myself included, ain't got No Sense At All.

What I **don't** tell Princess is that to a man, every Cat that Scoffed At Her Color

then Got To Know Her wanted to Hook Up with her.

Her personality is Just That Strong.

I ran em all off too cause if they couldn't see how beautiful Princess was

Right Off The Bat then they ain't Deserve A Chance with her.

I hate niggas that think Dark Skin Equals Ugly.

Them be The Same Niggas who say to me:

Why You So White?

Ain't no pleasin some folks; there really ain't.

But Back To The Lecture At Hand...

Princess been The Same Color her Whole Life.

Which I'm **sure** means she was Black As Hell when we Hooked Up.

If her color was such a Big Deal would I had looked at her twice?

I Think Not.

Could somebody tell her that for me?

Since Cess want a baby, which I think is Pretty Damn Stupid right now,

she pulls off her patch.

No Patch + No Pills = Pretty Mean Spirits.

Isn't **this** fun?!

She got PMS and I got A Mood.

After fumin at we'chother for a hour Cess storms off and slams her door.

I throw myself on the couch, Mad As Hell.

Fuck her.

Fuck the **world**.

Flick flick flick flick flick; nothin's on TV and now that my Tude is wearin off

I'm feelin Migh-ty Lone-ly, and I don't mean Horny either.

I float around the livin room then into the kitchen.

Grabbin one a Princess' plates I head upstairs to knock on her room door.

"What do you want?" Cess yells angrily.

"I brought you a plate," I tell her,

"I figure you could throw it at me, we'll wrestle round the kitchen,

I'll drag you down to the water, then we can make Wild Crazy Love in my hot tub."

Silence Resounds for a few clicks before the door creaks open.

Cess sticks first her hand out the door then her head.

Turnin the plate over in her hands she says to me:

"Do I have many of these left?"

"They Open Stock at Wal-Mart. You break em, I replace em."

Cess looks at the plate in her hand intensely for a bit longer

then quietly withdraws back into her room.

With nothin else on my agenda I rest my head on her door and Patiently Wait.

Not five minutes pass before Princess opens the door again.

"Don't you wanna throw a plate? I hate it when you don't talk to me."

Cess chuckles softly.

Reachin for the sides a my jacket she pulls me close to her.

"Let's Skip The Drama altogether.

I've got these Killer Cramps I **know** You Have The Cure for."

8 BG

My period is coming down; so are my Pretty Mean Spirits;
I don't know why Obie thinks this is related to me pulling the patch off.
I only took it off a few days ago.
I think it's got something to do with the pills.
When I took my pill everyday I was on a more-even-keel;
now I feel cranky-and-irritable sometimes without-knowing-why.
It's probably overwork:
I'm carrying a heavy load at the church; trying to fine tune my upcoming performance.
Obie's schedule isn't helping much; I can go over the vocals with "the girls;"
we have to hold off on the dance moves until pret-ty damned late when Obie gets in.
Then I have to be up extra early for work.
O says we should taper down to twice a week.
This represents a 'comeback' for me; everything needs to be **perfect**;
I'm a little worried if we slack off we might lose-our-edge.
Am I obsessing?
You figure.
Okay, I *know* I am; it's *my* career on the line here; no one else's.
Can you blame me for not wanting to fall-on-my-face?
In front of millions of viewers? Black people at that?
I-didn't-think-so.
Anyway, today I'm tired; PMSing all over the place.
To top it off Obie's getting-his-mood-on, so we seem destined to 'bump heads.'
It's one of those arguments where you don't even know what you're fighting about
but-you're-convinced you're right anyway.
At least that's how *I* feel.
For all I know Obie is yelling simply to relieve tension,
I swear he does that sometimes. Overcome with anger I throw a pillow at him.
"*Throw somethin at me again*," Obie shouts menacingly."*See-what-I-do.*"
"Fuck you, *bitch*," I yell back.
My self-control is slipping rapidly; we're definitely not treading-that-path again.

I beat it for my room, slam the door behind me.

Ten-deep-breaths don't do it for me; neither do twenty or fifty.

Hugging my pillow tight I roll over; face the wall.

If nothing assuages my anger I'll have to sit here until it dissipates on its own.

Damn, it's taking-a-long-time.

I've come to two conclusions here; neither of them good.

The first is: I'm as stubborn as a three-year-old in a toy store.

The second is: I will cut off my nose to spite my face.

Take now for instance:

Obie's knocking at the door; I'm paying him no mind whatsoever; knowing all the time
I really want to talk to him. Once I get mad, though, it's hard for me to transition back
into not-mad no matter *how* tired-of-being mad I might be.

Since Obie isn't the-type-to-be-ignored this only makes him knock harder:

It's always a-contest-of-wills between us; most of it my fault.

Through the door Obie claims he has a plate for me to hit him with, after which
I guess we're supposed to beat the shit out of each other then fuck our brains out.

I know it's a joke, it is *so*, so very *not funny*.

Exasperated, I open the door a crack; take the plate.

It feels heavy in my hands, the perfect-weight for throwing;
the crash of stoneware-against-wall is such a *satisfying sound*.

But I-won't-go-there; no, not-at-all.

That 'bad taste' is still-in-my-mouth, know what I'm sayin?

I close the door; examine the plate in my hands again. Obie bought these plates just for me,
to satisfy my need-to-throw-shit without breaking up his good dishes.

Who does *that* anymore?

He must be a-man-in-love.

With a *real **bitch***.

Opening the door I invite him in to cure-my-cramps.

"Do you love me Baby Girl?"

As we lay basking in that "afterglow"thing, this question pops out of nowhere.

Obie is on his back; my head is resting on his washboard abs;

I have to lift my head to look at him.

Cupping the back of my head with his hand Obie pushes me down again.

It's impossible to read his face from this angle.

The hand tracing circles on top of my head seems relaxed enough,

although I sense a little tension in his body.

I try to sit up again; Obie's hand holds me firmly in place.

"Of course I love you, Oscar; I love you very much."

"Sometimes you act like you-can't-be-bothered

and sometimes you act like you-don't-care-if-I-live-or-die."

And sometimes this is even true; except I don't know why.

Obie has advanced past the point where he is afraid to show his feelings;

I'm jealous of that.

He's got that shaking-like-a-leaf thing working.

Remember when that used to bug me out? And I didn't know what to make of it?

Now I know it's just that outpouring-of-love he feels for me.

Sometimes when we make love Obie cries; that's a-little-tougher for me to deal with.

While it doesn't scare me *per se*, it is under-settling; partly because our 'lovin' is so,

so very good it makes *me* want to cry too; but I can't let-myself-go like that.

It's too risky.

Instead of explaining all of this to Obie I cop out by saying:

"You know I'm moody. You should be used to me by now."

"I love you so much, Princess; very, very much so; and I'm startin to feel like

I love you way more than you love me."

Now it's me doing the "circle tracing:"

small delicate circles across Obie's stomach with my nose.

I kiss his navel feverishly several times causing his joint to start swelling.

Obie is not fooled by this maneuver.

"There's *more to life than sex*; sometimes a man and a woman actually *talk*-to-each-other."

Damn.

"I'm not averse to the 'talking' thing; it just doesn't 'work well' for me."

"Do you love me or do you just love that feelin I give you?" he asks me bitterly.

"It's *not about the sex*, babe; that's how I express-my-love for you: with-my-body."

"So, you can only show-me-you-love-me in *bed*."

He rubs the back of my head like he understands; I know he doesn't.

"When we're together, can't you feel how much I love you?" I ask him.

"You still scared I'll leave you? Is that it?"

"I've *always* kept feelings inside; you *know* that. It's hard for me to express how much
I love you, how much you mean to me…Relationships are so *painful*."
I took-that-risk before; the fallout only confirmed that no man is worth putting your heart into;
(maybe) not-even-Obie.
"Is our relationship painful to you, too, cause it's not to me.
You the-best-thing-that's-ever-happened-to-me, Princess."
See, it's *this type of mushy confession* I have a hard time with.
"I don't know how to say what I'm feeling without sounding corny or old fashioned.
You have all-these-pretty-words to express yourself with; but when I feel these things
I get panicky. Something makes me pull back; push-you-away."
"That's *exactly* what bothers me the most. Things'll be going great and all of a sudden
you'll start a fight. Or, like today, you'll clam up and stop talking to me, which I *hate*.
Half the time I can't figure out what I did wrong, and I walk around on eggshells tryna
make-everything-better so you'll *love* me and not *leave* me."
"Now, what-in-the-world would I leave-*you*-for?"
"*I don't know, Princess*; *pick* a reason, *any* reason.
Maybe you'll get tired a my 'moods;' maybe you'll start *believin* I'm tryna run-your-life;
maybe I'll Obie-out-on-you and fuck-up-big-time; maybe I'm *too-damned-old* for you.
There's so '*many* paths' to the 'same destination.'"
"So, *basically,* what you're saying is: you tolerate-my-bullshit because,
you're scared if you put your foot down, I'll-get-mad; bounce-on-you."
"*Basically*; but don't you do the same with me? Don't you put up with my 'moods' and
''tudes' and rebuff-my-help, cause you scared I'll pick-a-chick easier to 'deal with?'"
Exactly.
"So, fair-exchange-is-no-robbery; we *both* make concessions to keep-the-relationship-
flowin-smoothly. All I'm sayin is: I-opened-myself up to you, I gave-you-my-heart,
even though it scared-the-shit-outta-me, 'cause I ain't wanna live-my-life without you.
Can't you at *least* try to let-down-that-wall and love-me-back the same way?"
My eyes are brimming; my mouth is wide open; yet try as I might:
I can't force the words out: my heart has my tongue in a death lock.
Genuine tears soon fall; words spill out with them.
"I don't want to get burnt-up-in-our-heat or 'lose myself' in you."
While I'm busy 'crying puddles' into his bellybutton,
Obie is rubbing my neck, the back of my head, with his hand.
He heaves this tremendous sigh; I don't know what that's all about.

Finally, in the most thoughtful, tender, tone-of-voice imaginable he says to me:
"You have so many fears inside a you. You think they tryna keep-you-safe but
in reality they holdin-you-hostage and you don't-even-know-it. Hopefully one day you'll
be comf'table enough to talk-to-me. Maybe then you can let-that-shit-go."

Disappointment still sits in Obie's eyes.
We messed around again early this morning.
Because of last night I tried to make it 'extra special' for him,
but it-all-comes-back to the eyes, doesn't it.
"I-don't-know-why, but I'm always doing the opposite of what you tell me, just to prove-
you-wrong; yet I always end up hurting myself. Deep down, I know you're right, but *you*
know: in my mind, giving-in-is-the-same-as-losing. I also know if it wasn't for you
pushing me in-the-right-direction, I would be *lost* right now. You mean the world to me,
Oscar Price. Your patience and your guidance have been the best gifts I've ever received.
I don't know how I would make it in this world without you; don't want to find out.
Sometimes, I just hate-how-weak that feels."
Kissing me delicately, Obie says:
"You gotta stop viewin 'givin in' or leanin-on-someone as a sign-a-weakness. It takes
a lot more strength to admit-you-need-help than to follow-your-own-path to 'destruction.'"
"I need your love, too; so, so very badly that, sometimes, I think I might *die* without it."
"Where I'm goin, huh? You can't push me away so you might as well stop tryin."

It happens again.
Obie and I are spooning when he tries to stick-it-in-me.
Needless to say I freak out 'big time,' practically leap-from-the-bed.
"*What's the matter with you?*" O yells in frustration; under-characteristically grabs my arm.
Damned-if-I-know; it just hurt so much when Einstein did that
it makes me scared if Obie comes anywhere *near* my behind with his dick.
What in the Hell is he looking at me like that for?
Please tell me I didn't say that out loud.........................
Oh, shit.
"You are a wealth-of-secrets, Baby Girl," O observes dryly;
"Anything else I should know?"
Embarrassed, I cover my face with my hands.
"Come 'ere," he motions softly, applies gentle pressure to my arms.

I remain rooted-to-this-spot on the edge of the bed.

"Come on, Baby Girl," he says with great tenderness.

When he can't get me to move, Obie comes to me; takes-me-up in his arms.

"You-don't-*know*, 'Girl; how I-had-hoped with

all-my-heart that bastard didn't do-you-like-that.

He did that shit to *humiliate* you; and I *hate* him for it."

"Well, it worked: that was the single-most-humiliating-experience of my life."

"Let's play 'True Confessions.'"

We sit back-to-back; tell our deepest secrets; can't comment on what we hear.

Can't say I want to play-this-dumb-game, either; do-I-have-a-choice?

You-already-know.

"I want you to know I could **never** *hurt you* like that. Remember Utah?

Well, Dude didn't just beat-me-up; he raped me, too. I was too embarrassed to tell

anybody cause it made me feel *weak* and *stupid* and *less than a man*."

Obie sounds like a wounded child; *I* feel like horseshit.

Do you know how many times I said to Obie:

"You weren't the one who got raped?"

I wish I could take-them-all-back; according to the rules I'm not permitted to react.

"Your turn," Obie prompts in a teeny little voice.

If I gotta tell-another-secret, I might as well go-all-out.

"When I was sixteen, I got pregnant with Rocky's baby; had an abortion."

"Me & Xanadi had this 'thing' goin, even though she was only thirteen. It lasted bout six
 months, 'til she tripped out on me and thought she was my 'wifey.' Then, I dumped her."

We are all-confessed-out, yet unwilling to face the other,

neither of us moves so much as a muscle.

Gradually, Obie eases his hands backwards until they make contact with mine.

Linking hands, we sit for quite a while, our backs pressed together,

before I decide to turn around; fold myself around his back.

An almost desperate need for Obie's loving sweeps over me.

My hands travel over his body while my tongue finds a spot at the base of his neck.

Our loving completed, we dedicate the rest of the night to our secrets.

9 OB

Can a person be so right and so perfect it's like you were created to be together?
When I put my hands on Cess's thighs my thumbs fit into the grooves on the inner part,
the very part that makes her so hot. Same with her waist; when I put my hands round it
my thumbs reach her navel just so. The small a Cess's back **had** to have been designed
with me in mind; otherwise it wouldn't be so easy for me to rub myself there.
Her breasts and her behind fit into the palms a my hands like they was custom made for me.
So does the back a Princess' head.
When she's goin down on me?
Dog, it's like Palmin A Basketball.
The Best Part a' All though is the way her I fit into her.
It's a Smooth Easy Fit with Just Enough Room for Freedom a Movement, you feel me?
Deep enough so I don't have to worry bout hurtin her accidentally if I get carried away
but not Big & Sloppy like A Truck's been Drivin Through It or somethin.
I guess what I'm tryna say is: Our Love Life Is Spectacular. Sex really does Bring
People Closer emotionally. I mean, me and Cess **always** been Tight & All
but since we got our Love Thing workin again we Tighter Than Ever.
Kissin her is **so** sweet and **so** powerful it makes me tremble.
I can't help myself and I can't make it stop either. When I make love to her my heart
swells up so much I feel like it's gon **bust** and **sometimes** It Makes Me Cry.
Cess don't make me feel bad bout cryin either; she holds me close and tells me It'll Be Okay.
I know it will; I'm just so Happy and Content and Serene and All That **Other** Bullshit
it overwhelms me sometimes.
I never knew it was possible to feel so much love for a person who's Not Your Child,
and I never in a million years thought I'd feel Love Like This for a Woman.
Not My **Style,** Dog, you feel me?
But here I am.
I'm not used to this Inner Peace shit. I know it sounds dumb but Contentment is some
Crazy Scary Stuff. Chaos & Disorder I can Handle; I was **steeped** in that.
This Love Crap though?
You can't Control It and you Can't Mold It to Fit Your Needs.
The feelin just Washes Over Me for No Reason; either I Go With The Flow or
Get Swept Away. Fortunately I'm a fast learner: I almost got it Down Pat.

At the same time Cess has this Crappy Attitude that's wearin me out.

I swear **some**times Cess act like she don't Love Me At All and **other** times

it's as if she Mad At Herself for lovin me.

Who **does** that?

When I finally gather the courage to confront her she starts kissin my navel.

Nice Try Girlfriend but: Not What I'm Lookin For right now.

Hold That Thought though.

I might **Need** Me Some Head after **this** is through.

Lord That 'Girl took me on a **Journey**. Cess ain't learned to Ride The Wave yet,

she scared she Might Drown in the Depths a her Feelins. *I* been **there**; matter **fact**,

I Ain't Moved Out. But whereas I'm strugglin to Manage My Fears cause I know

most a them's Sorta Irrational Cess wanna Bury Her Head In The Sand hopin that

When She Re Emerge her fear will have Magically Disappeared.

As If.

In the mornin Cess makes a Meaningful Attempt at Openin Up To Me.

I end up all Misty Eyed; touched by her effort.

Perfect body backed up against me, breasts heavy in my hands, hair smellin like fresh melons…

I'm Hot and Horny and Wantin My Baby Girl Somethin **Awful**.

She Breathin Heavy and Grindin On Me so I know She Want It Too.

I'm feelin this position: don't wanna Change A Thing, want it Just Like This.

Baby Girl voices her objections rather loudly however,

divin for the edge a the bed like she Couldn't Get Away From Me fast enough.

Sorry to say I **Lose It** and **yell** at her; askin her what the Hell her problem is.

"Damned if I know. It hurt **so** *much* when Einstein did that…"

Whatever else she sayin gets Lost In The Translation for me.

My stomach drops down to my knees and then does a back flip.

I prayed and prayed, oh **God** How I Prayed My Girl wasn't violated *That* Way.

Now My Worse Fear Done Come True.

You think **maybe** Cess could a been **spared** that indignity?

Einstein put her through *so* much; *Why That Too*?

Cause it's The Worst Thing You Can Do to somebody; the Ultimate Submission Move.

Cold hatred for that bitch Einstein infuses every cell in my body.

Look at her over there; coverin her gorgeous face with her hands.

Baby Girl is so embarrassed she wanna die, always.

I try to get her to come to me but That Ain't Hap'nin so I Slide On Over her way.

With her safely in my arms I do my best to apologize for losin my temper.

I don't blame her in the least for not tellin me; I ain't told either.

Nobody wants to admit to bein forced into that position.

Maybe if I tell her what happened to me it might help.

My heart starts poundin outta Sheer Nervousness. Some things I can't say to people faces cause I don't wanna see they expression, you feel me?

Makin A Game Outta It I get Baby Girl to sit with her back to me, and make her promise not to comment on nothin I say.

Then I squeeze my confession outta my reluctant mouth.

I think she sorta Taken Aback cause she so **still** and so **quiet**.

It ain't every day your man tell you he got raped in a hotel room.

Calmly I remind Baby Girl she gotta tell **me** a secret now.

Boy do she come up with a *doozy*.

Why she tell me she was pregnant with Freaky's baby and had a abortion?

What the Hell is *that* about???!!

How do Baby Girl keep All This Shit *Inside* Herself; and Where Do She Keep It?

Let me not Cast A Stone here cause I got some Secrets a My Own that'll Blow Your Mind.

Like sleepin with Xanadi when she was only thirteen.

To this **day** I can't believe I Stooped So Low. She was a baby.

The 'Girl's Been Mute for a **grip** now.

Hopefully that signals The End a this Experiment.

Cause I don't think My Psyche can Handle **one more confession**.

I'd forgotten what a **bastard** I useta be.

You know what I need?

I need to **Go** To Confession, **that's** what I need.

I need to find me a Real Church. Catholic Style.

I'm Lost In Thought, more bout my **own** shit than bout Baby Girl's.

I hope she don't look down on me for what happened in Utah.

I'd prefer it if she viewed it as another Common Bond we share.

Too scared to turn around but Desirin some Contact I search for Baby Girl's hands.

Once I locate them I weave my finger into hers.

Soon I feel her ta-ta's on my back and her 'cat Warm & Moist on my behind.

Baby Girl's legs come around my waist and up over mine.

Her hands is touchin me: touchin me in All Those Places and All Those Ways

I love so much. This time when we make love it's as Holy and as Spiritual as
Anything Can Be between a man and a woman.
Finally Free I divest myself a all the anguish I been holdin in since Utah.
Then I encourage Baby Girl to rid herself a her torments too.

"Okay nigga: Up You Go."
Don't know **why** Cess called The Latin King or **what** he thinks he's Fi'n a Accomplish but…
I ain't goin **nowhere**.
I couldn't get out the bed this mornin.
Or yesterday.
Or the day before.
"Come on bitch, you Costin Me Money."
"***Fuck* you**."
I ain't been out the bed since me and Cess played True Confessions.
But maybe I'm just Tired and Need a Little Break.
Caller; You Say What?
"If you don't Get The Fuck Up I'm a **bus' yo *ass***."
Okay…Who In The Fuck Is Barry Talkin To???
I'm so mad I **actually** Start To Rise.
"You ***better***," this fool hollas.
"I bet the **only** reason I'm Gettin Up is I can't ***wait*** to Beat The Livin Shit outta you."
"What**ever** nigga; what**ever**. Just Come The Fuck On."

I wrote this little Piece a Shit song.
When I showed it to her Cess ain't Dis My Effort.
In fact **she** showed it to Freak.
"It Needs Work but Me & Cess'll Hook You Up."
Yeah, what**ever** nigga…
Then Cess show me **her** work.
My Black Ass should Stick To **Dancin** & Leave The **Songwritin** To The **Experts**.
I guess we share a lotta the same Feelins and Thought Patterns though
cause a couple a Princess' songs kinda mirror the sentiments I tried to put down.
One song she wrote was about how Einstein **hit her** but I couldn't read that one.
Nearly gave me a Tude.
In the last song Princess describes her Meadow and the struggle it took to let go a

the Mother & Son she Created In Her Mind in order to Reclaim Her Sanity.

That one I read three times.

The BET Awards is next week.

East Coast arrives and once again my household is turned inside out.

This place been quiet for so long I forgot what it was like to have a house full a people

Laughin & Jokin all the time. And another thing…

Why we gotta fight so much whenever we get together?

Who **does** that?

Don't Get Me Wrong now: I don't mind seein my family but *damn*,

Conflict and Turmoil follow them around like Smelly Farts.

I **swear** ninety percent a these arguments is alcohol fueled.

Before The Fam got here the most I had to drink was a beer or two after work.

Young brings Cocktail Hour with him and I'll Be Damned but a drink's been in my hand

ever since. And we been Gettin High too. We ain't done that in a grip.

Now the arguments done started.

Remember when we thought this was *fun*???!!

I tell ya, I didn't miss this shit **at all**.

The same way a group a men will always end up talkin about sex;

throw a bunch a women together and you got the recipe for some Serious Man Bashin.

I catch the tail end a this session cause chicks invariably Clam Up

the minute a man comes into the room.

Most chicks anyway.

Cess in her Growny Grown Folks Mood.

Translation?

She Showin Her Ass again.

"They ain't **made** the man powerful enough to tell **me** what to do," Cess crows.

Dionne and Xanadi's tryna Signal Cess On The Low to Watch Herself.

"Fuck OB," Cess states defiantly. "I was My Own Woman before I **got** with that nigga

and I'll be My Own Woman on the Very Day I Die."

Yeah. **That & A Token** will Get Her On The Subway.

Cess been makin Smart Ass Comments like this ever since Mommy & Them got here.

Explain to me the significance a Cess's So Called Autonomy.

Have I ever tried to Super Impose My Will on her?

No.

So Where's The Beef?

Dionne and Xanadi's lookin at me, Anticipatin a Problem, but I ain't allowin myself to
get drawed up in Some Dumb Bullshit. I sit my Angry Ass down on the couch and
Proceed to Ignore Princess. Besides, "Pardon The Interruption" is fi'n a come on.

"Whassup Obie?" Xanadi asks, her voice drippin amusement.

"Can't Tell Yet," I grouse curtly.

Truly annoyed, I don't even bother turning around.

"That nigga knows better'n to mess with me," Princess remarks,

suckin her teeth and lookin at her nails disdainfully.

Now she takin it too far.

I crane my neck to take a good long look at her and yep, Cess High as Hell.

"You must be out your **damn mind** talkin to me like that," I snap,

"What the Hell you mean I Know Better? **You Don't Run Me.**"

"You don't Run Me Either you just **think** you do. This **my** show, nobody runs it but me."

"The Only Thing You Runnin is your **mouth** Sweetheart

and you **might** wanna **Cut That Out.** Save Yourself Some Trouble."

"Whatchu gon do, **Spank** Me?

You my Lover not my Father; you can't tell me what to do."

"You High, Princess and you talkin Stupid Shit right now."

Cess so high she can't **talk** straight.

"I AIN'T HIGH AND I AIN'T STUPID," Cess shouts.

"THEN STOP HOLLERIN AT ME LIKE YOU STUPID," I yell back,

"And **Yes You Are** High. I can **tell**."

"You just mad cause I won't let you boss me round.

I don't need you to think for me. I'm capable a makin my own decisions."

Oh, see now, we **both** know we had a Nice Long Talk bout her Decision Makin Skills.

Far Be It From Me to **remind** her Intoxicated Ass bout that though.

She ain't even capable a Good English.

Super Heated I sit back down, returnin my attention to the television screen but

Cess done Made Me Miss My Program.

Damn Her to Hell.

Oh Well.

There's always "Sports Center"…

Uncle BB & Them troop in heavy laden with The Spoils a Shoppin.

They all plop down leavin they bags strewn around like wind swept garbage.

Generally makin my livin room look a mess.

As if I ain't already have Enough a' A Attitude Workin.

Lost in Today's Sports Coverage I had almost forgot I was mad at Cess.

Almost.

We really need a Sit Down & Talk but privately; I ain't gon Read Her In Public.

Lee hands out a round a beers.

In Typical Fashion Young has his with a shot a Jack Daniels.

I pass. The commotion behind me signals the return a The Girls.

Where they had floated off to No One Knows but They're Baaack.

I hear Cess in the fridge so I ask for somethin to eat.

Why that start a big ruckus though?

Who **does** that?

If The Fam wasn't here Cess would have No Prob At All fixin me some food.

This must be Another Facet a that Showin Your Ass thing.

Lord I'm gettin sick a Cess's Frontin, you feel me?

I'm tired, I'm irritable, and I ain't ate nothin since Moses parted the Red Sea.

"I don't need this shit," I finally say, and walk away.

"So whatchu sayin though? Cause Anything **You** Can Do **I** Can Do **Better**."

"You think so?" I '180' and ask her.

Evidently Cess is mistook but I don't like bein threatened which is why

I don't correct her.

"I **know** so. You ain't The Only Nigga in town.

They givin a party up in BB's hotel room. I bet I meet **Ten** Niggas there."

"How you'd love **that**," I tell her sarcastically.

"You **figure**?" Cess fires back.

Yes I do.

Only way Cess is leavin is over My Dead Body.

Remote in hand I Post Up on the couch Bidin My Time. Half a hour later Cess bounces

downstairs in a little crop top that barely covers her titties and her baggy jeans saggin

so you can see the top a her thong. Fashionable, yes; *but...*

I Don't Know where the Hell she *think* she goin cause it **won't be outta here**.

I tell her that, she say she grown, I invite her Grown Ass to Go On & Walk Out.

Instead Cess takes a seat.

Minutes Seem To Hang Like Hours while we each silently Hold Our Ground.

With her arms folded across her chest Cess looks like a petulant teenager.

"Cess ain't goin no where," Dionne informs Xanadi. "Let's Bounce."

"No wait," Cess begs them. "Don't leave me. I'm coming."

I don't *think* so.

Her g's is Back On The End a Her Words so she must not be as high as before.

Maybe her Brain Cells will Do A Little Work now.

Cess lookin at me, I'm looking at her. Neither a us said a word to the other yet.

"You gonna make me beg for permission Oscar? Like a **child**?

In front of *everybody* though?"

We ain't Blown The Dust off a Oscar in Quite A While.

Regardless...

"I ain't gon make you do *shit*. You **Grown**. There's The **Door**. Go **On**... **Use It**."

Cess don't Move A Muscle but her Resolve starts to Crumble Visibly.

"You are **so so very Not Right On This Oscar**," Cess whines, on the Verge a Tears.

"*Why?!*" I demand to know. Like I Give A Fuck about her **cryin**; "Why you so busy

tryna act like **You** Runnin **Me** when Everbody Knows I'm In Charge? **Yet**: if I wanna go

out with Uncle BB or my Dad wouldn't I **ask you** first? Make sure it's **a'ight** witchu?"

Bitin her lower lip Cess nods her head reluctantly.

"You know why?" I continue,

"Cause maybe it's **not** A'ight With You; maybe you had Somethin Else Planned or

somethin for me to **do** first. So I Give You That Respect as My Wife."

Cess is embarrassed now cause I done Told Her Bout Herself.

She knew she was wrong when she started this mess so:

what made her think I was gonna Roll Over & Take It?

"That's How Y'all **Livin** though?" Xanadi asks.

"**Exactly**," I confirm. "A relationship is like a partnership and even in a So Called Equal

Partnership someone has to Be In Charge. Cess is my **partner**, my **soul mate**. As a man

I **happen** to be in charge cause that's the Natural Order a things. I ain't make it that way,

neither did she but Don't Get It Twisted: that don't make Cess Subordinate to me or

At My Mercy. Cess **chooses** to listens to me, she know I got her Best Interests at heart."

"Picture Me List'nin to some *man*," Xanadi chuckles.

"Where the choice was in **that** confrontation though?!" Dionne gives her a High Five.

Still Peeved I make One Last Attempt to watch TV.

Ain't hap'nin.

This is The **Problem** With America:

Too Many People All In The Biz Passin They Crappy Ass Judgments On Folks.

Disgusted, I toss the remote to the side.

"May I go to the party Oscar? Please?" Cess asks me softly.

"The Devil Got His Skis On Cause It's Snowin In Hell Tonite," Xanadi exclaims.

If she Know So Damn Much…………..

Why's Her Man In A Hotel Room?

I Just Wanna Know.

Anyway, satisfied I wave Cess on.

She showin Way Too Much Flesh for **my** taste but I trust her I really do.

Cess Jumps Up & Down in gratitude then jumps up in my lap facin me.

With the Heat turned up Full Blast Cess grabs my collar and kisses me deeply.

"You comin?"

Not Yet but A Few More Kisses and...

"Maybe later," I promise.

"I'm not going to do anything stupid; I just said that because I was mad."

"My knew that."

Cess kisses me again, this time slidin in closer.

"If you don't get Offa My Lap the only Party You See'll be In The Bedroom."

"We got a little time."

"How many mornins we said that and ended up flyin down the highway; Late For Work?"

Cess kisses me again: a Long Slow Lingerin Kiss that Sets Me Ablaze.

I slap her on the ass and move her off me.

"Go on to your party 'fore I change my mind."

Gigglin girlishly Cess struts out the door.

I follow her behind with my eyes the entire way.

I Hate It when she leave.

But when she leave?

I love to watch her walk.

The best way to describe this scene is Well Ordered Chaos

but that's how it is backstage at any show.

About a hour into the broadcast Princess and WFD receive our cue.

Five Minutes Doug E. Fresh We're On.

Hurryin to our places we check ourselves One Last Time then get set.

The lights dim.
The curtain rises.
It's Showtime.
Somebody notify The Media....

Park Avenue Princess Is Back.

9~BG~

New York is in the house; Obie-and-I are busting our asses trying to get-some-work-done;
"be entertaining" at-the-same-time. Because it's BET Awards Week there are
no video shoots; only pre-/post-production on several projects.
You'd be surprised how much time that takes up; I know I was.
Plus, there are parties to attend.
This is almost like being on tour or promoting a record:
Too-much-to-do, not-enough-time to do-it-in.
I feel like I haven't slept in a year; and I still have to teach music class at the church.
Obie wanted me to take-this-week-off.
*Nigga **please**.*
Who does *that* anymore?
Jesus is the-only-thing that got me through those-hard-times.
I'll be paying *that* debt *forever*.
Since nobody is all beat-up, in-the-hospital this time, we can actually *party*.
Thanks to Young, "alcoholic beverages" are the-order-of-the-day.
I love my dad, but face it: he's a drunk.
There-but-for-the-grace and "all that:" remember Big Momma, her "nightcaps?"
Young's a *lively* drunk, though, so *it's o-kay.*
Uncle Tommy invariably has the best weed/the best coke on the East Coast.
It's-been-a-long-time since I got high; I'm in the-party-mood so-what-the Hell,
know what I'm mean?
You only live once.

I kind-of-forgotten how hard it is to get up in the morning after getting high all night.
This is so, so very "not fun."
I've never been to work tore up before;
I feel naked-and-transparent in front of Pastor Julia.
Afterwards, there's the-first-fifty of approximately one-hundred-thousand-things-to-do.
If looks are any indication then Obie must have dragged-his-ass-all-day-long, too.
Oh *well*.
Time for a little pick-me-up.

Dionne and Xena share a bottle of Alize: I'm not big-on-drinking.

"If I start this early I'll be wasted by the time the party starts," I inform my "girls."

"You ain't worried about 'that high,' though."

"Nigga *please*. I'm *never* too-high-to-party; but I *can be* too-drunk-to-stand-up."

"Like Obie's gonna let you go to a party tore-the-fuck-up," Dionne comments.

"Obie-don't-haveta *let* me do *nothin*," I snap, offended. "I'm *grown*."

"Riiight," she answers snidely.

"Obie-don't-move-no-mountains in my life," I say defensively.

"Tell that to Obie; see what *he* say."

Why they laughin at me though?

You figure.

'Cause these bitches are so, so very gettin-on-my-last-ass-nerve, know what I'm sayin?

"Obie is gonna *come in here, see you* 'high,' and **flip** on you," Xena predicts.

"And you *know* how he gets about you; he ain't lettin you go-to-no-party 'high' without him,"
Dionne throws in her two cents.

"And *you gon' listen*," Xena begins.

"'Cause *that's yo' man*," Dionne finishes the thought.

"That's why I don't *have* no man," Xena states emphatically. "Y'all go through too-much-shit.
I do what I *wanna* do and *bet'-not-nobody* tell me *diff'rent*."

The thought that Obie might give me a problem pisses me off;

I remember *well* being able to go wherever I wanted without checking with Obie;

I envy Xena's freedom.

Not that Obie would ever tell me I-couldn't-go; I just resent having-to-ask.

Well... having to ask in *front of people*, anyway.

Come to think of it, Obie *would* tell me not-to-go if I was "fucked up;"

he'd be scared something (*some-**one***) might happen to me.

I love how protective O is; hate the way my girls act like Obie is running my life.

"They ain't made-the-man powerful enough to run my life," I let them know.

Xena and Dionne are trying to signal me frantically about something;

in my altered state it takes me a minute to realize Obie's home;

from my vantage point I could neither see-nor-hear him walk into the living room.

Judging from his body language Obie must have heard me.

*Oh **well***.

Xena bullshits with Obie, who lets *some* snide remark pass-from-his-lips.

"That nigga knows better than to fuck with me," I fire back.

Although I'm speaking to my "girls," I'm really addressing Obie; he knows it.

Well, from there it is so, so very *on*. I want to make it clear to him *and* to my girls that

Obie does *not* run-my-life. Sometimes he thinks he's my *dad* or something.

Take yesterday for instance.

I was driving a bunch of us back from rehearsal. The only time Obie is critical of me is

when I'm behind the wheel, then: *watch out*. Well, somebody got too close to me, like

they were going to cut me off; nervously I hit my brakes.

Obie's dumb ass pushes my foot off the brake, steps on the accelerator,

grabs the wheel, steers around the "cat" blocking me.

I *HATE* when he does that.

"Hittin yo' brake like that's gonna cause a *accident*," he yelled at me.

Angry-and-upset, I pulled over to the shoulder, got out.

"*Get back in the car*," Obie demanded, half-way out of the passenger door.

A shouting match ensued; cars were slowing down to watch us:

two celebrity assholes arguing by the side of the road. Obie noticed, too.

"Get back in the car 'fore they break out the 'copters," Obie instructed me.

I got back in the car because we were "creating," but I refused to drive.

"You're my lover OB, not my father," I had to tell him.

I gotta tell him that now, too; Obie says I'm 'high,' 'talking stupid.'

I might-be-*high*, but I've never-been-*stupid*. We hurl a few more overly-loud-words at

we'chother; Obie turns back to his TV; we girls head to Dionne's room.

"Obie is gonna *kick your ass*," Dionne laughs once we get there.

"Nigga *please*," I reply sarcastically.

Xena cracks another blunt, laces it, passes it around.

The smoke carries the tension away, which is good;

arguing with Obie was killing-my-high.

All that weed has me craving something sweet; we embark on a 'refrigerator raid.'

"What we got to eat," Obie asks me.

"Food," I say. "Don't ask me nothin stupid."

"Can a nigga get a *plate* though?" he bellows.

"'Feel free' to fix yourself whatever-you-like," I hurl back.

"*What the fuck is your problem?*"

"What makes you think I have a problem?"

"Any other time you'd a *been* fixed me a plate."

"That sounds like *your* problem, not *mine*."

"Look, if you got a problem spit-it-out already."

"*I don't have a problem.* **You** *have a problem*?"

"*Yeah*: you been actin a *fuckin fool* ever since Mommy-and-them got here; actin all 'funny time;' and won't listen to a-thing-I-say."

"Nigga, please; 'Somebody' forgot to tell you: I. don't. have. to. listen. to. you."

"Yo; I don't need this shit," Obie decides; turns to walk away.

Don't-know-where-he's-coming-from with *that* one, but guess what?

I don't need Obie's ass, either.

"Anything you can do, I can do better," I warn him.

I tell him about the party tonite, let him know

I could meet 'mass' men there; not have to be bothered with his shit.

Obie looks sort of surprised, then tells me I'm not going anywhere.

We'll see-about-*that*.

I run upstairs to get ready.

"*You ain't go-in no-where*," Xena teases me in a singsong voice.

"You figure?" I snap back.

"Obie ain't lettin you out-that-door," Dionne declares.

"Let's see him stop me."

My high is shot-to-shit; I'm quickly realizing this has gotten out-of-hand.

My pride will not allow me to back down *even one inch*, I'll pret-ty much have to press-my-way-through; hope I avoid "losing face." I so, so *very* **refuse** to *lose*.

Who does **that**??!!

"Survey says:" all the girls are baring thong *and* midriff; *I can outdo them, too.*

Since I bulked up for my video I'm-no-slouch in the 'physically fit' department.

Nothing on Dionne stimulates my sense-of-competition; but those biceps of Xena's are out*rageous*, man; so are her abs. Xena might have gotten herself a 'boob job,' but: I've got tits *and* ass, so am supremely-self-satisfied with my look.

I flounce downstairs making a beeline for the door, my girls following closely.

"Don't know where the *Hell you think you goin* but it *won't* be outta here," Obie warns.

FUCK.

Why he couldn't just let-me-go without an argument though?

You figure.

"Think you can stop me?" I taunt Obie; hands on hips, neck popping.

"Somethin like that."

"You and what army?"

"You the baddest-motha-fucka-on-the-planet *tonite*, huh, Cess; ain't that what you
tellin everybody? There ain't *nobody* bad-like-Cess? Well, how you gon' get yo'
'bad ass' to the party on two-broke-legs? Huh? Answer me *that*."
"*Don't fucking threaten me, OB*; I can go *anywhere I want to*;
I'm a got-damn-grown-ass woman."
"You *grown*-all-right: *too fuckin grown* to be actin-like-you-*two*."
"Because I'm not on-your-shit?"
"What **shit**, Cess; what **shit**? What have I done in the past few days
that I haven't done every single day a your life? *Huh*? I thought we was so *over* the
I'm-grown-and-can-do-what-I-want-stage; why you blowin-the-dust-off-it now?"
"Because you persist in telling me what I can-and-cannot do; I'm *tired* of it.
You're my lover OB--"
"Not-my-father," he finishes with me. "So-you-say; but who are you saying that *to*: me,
your *self* or your *dad*? Do you even *know*? Because I'm not trying to be your *father*, I'm
trying to be your *man*, but if you're that got damn grown, *walk on out that door then.*"
I've painted-myself into a corner, my back is against-the-wall;
this is one challenge I'd be a fool to take; if I surrender, my *grandkids*'ll hear about it.
"I'm *so, so very 'not worried'* about you," I boast, try to think-my-way out of this.
"Then walk out the door," Obie demands one last time; returns to his program.
This is *so-not-fair*.
So, so *very*.
Spying a recently-vacated-recliner I plop my ass in it, fold my arms.
This is also stupid:
I'm all-dressed-up-with-nowhere-to-go;
in a "standoff," contesting my betrothed's authority in front of an audience.
Obie has always *been* in charge; always will *be*. Obie's in charge of us all.
I'm not the-only-one who listens to him, either, we *all* do; we *have* to.
It goes deeper than that, though.
I don't pretend to know *half* of what Obie has learned;
neither do the rest of us; we depend on his advice, lean on him for support.
Biding my time, I glare at Obie fiercely; he acts like I don't exist.
Shit gets critical when Xena, Dionne, decide to leave without me.
Begging them to hold on a minute, I crank-up-the-thought-process three notches.
Why, I don't know; simply put, there-is-no-gracious-way-out-of-this-mess.
Really-and-truly, Obie would never hit me/hurt me if I left.

He would, however, be mad-as-fuck for a very-long-time; it's just-not-worth-it.
What I'm doing is being stubborn again; I know it.
But I still-don't-want-to-give-in.
"You gonna make me beg for permission, Oscar? Like a *child*?
In front of *everybody,* yo?"
"I ain't gonna make you do **shit**. I already told you,
if you think you *so grown, walk out that door* then. *Go* on; *there's* the door; *use it*."
I'm-not-going-to-win; I hate it.
"*You ain't right*, Oscar," I complain, close to tears.
Boy does he let-me-have-it then. I want to bury my head in the sand,
I want to disappear; *anything* but sit-here-and-be chastised, but I know I'm wrong.
Raising the white-flag-of-surrender, I humbly ask permission to go.
It was just-that-simple, and just-that-*fucking*-difficult.

They ragged on me "big time" after that.
"Y'all on that **Christian** shit," Rocky laughs. "Wives, obey-your-husbands."
"That's what it say in the Bible. When I get married, my wife's gon' 'obey me,' too,"
Hood pronounces, draws the-*only*-ugly-look from Dionne.
Obie is under-impressed; cops a lightweight Tude.
"I hate when half-ass-niggas quote the Bible and don't know what the fuck they talkin 'bout.
Ain't-no-shame in *obeyin*. If a chick got a man she can't obey, *she* got *the wrong man*.
'Cause, if you can't trust your man's judgment, you ain't got no business wit' him.
Yes, wives gotta obey-they-husbands, but husbands gotta obey-the-will-a-God,
so we all obeyin *someone*, you feel me? Do you *know* the-will-a-God?
Do you *even-know-how* the **rest** a that passage **go**?"
I'll bet *you* could "Name *That* Tune."
"*That's what I thought*," Obie continues, upset. "The Apostle Paul *also* says: husbands,
love your wives like *Christ* loved the *Church*; *love your wives* as you *love your own flesh*.
The same way Christ laid-down-his-life for *us*, a husband should be *willin* to **die** *for his wife*.
And, just like you couldn't *hurt yourself,* you should *never, **ever** hurt your wife*.
If men had-it-together and did like The Apostle Paul said, women wouldn't have no
problem obeyin them: a woman naturally wants to please-her-man. Instead, men wanna
beat a woman over the head with they *supposedly* God-given-superiority or treat-them-
like-shit just 'cause they *women. That*'s what women rebel against. A man with a
good woman who don't treat her right is a straight-up-buster. Treat your woman right,

like she worth-somethin, and ain't nothin-on-the-planet she won't do for you."

Butterflies take up residence in my stomach before every performance;

they've never attacked the way they're attacking tonite.

I've waited for this night forever,

and, that's a-mighty-long-time;

now that it's finally here…

Let's just say I'm a wreck and leave-it-there.

I haven't performed in so *long*; will I do alright? Will the public still accept me?

My records are selling; my publicist wants me to do a round of promos,

so I take that as a positive sign; now, if I can just-get-through-tonite…

As we take our places, a supernatural calm comes over me.

No matter what I've been through, where life may lead me, this is where I belong: *on stage*.

This is not only my-world: but my-universe; Praise be to God.

Up here, I am in-control.

And, this-man-facing-me?

God granted me a "born performer" to share-it-with.

Hosanna in the Highest.

The beat drops, the band begins to play, it is so-so-very-*on*.

The performance runs smooth as silk.

During the dance break the fans in the upper rows start

chanting/signing "O-B-1" over the instrumental with us.

Most of the younger celebrities, many of the older, more staid stars, pick up the chant,

sparking a concert-like-atmosphere.

Rushing center stage I begin to clap my hands over my head, lead the crowd on.

"Come on…Everybody…O-B-1."

Well-over-my-time-limit, they almost have to pull-me-off-the-stage.

But, I *am* a Princess.

And, Obie One is My King.

FIN _{OB}

You know I ended up the Default Winner in the House thing right?

Baby Girl ain't move in with me **Per Se**, she just never set foot in her house again,

not even to reclaim her precious Smooshies.

All the clothes she had in there: the shoes, the purses, *everything*, got auctioned off on eBay.

Baby Girl ain't wanna so much as **look at** anything that came outta there.

And I ain't mad at her either.

Last month we quietly sold the house too.

The proceeds from the auction went to Rocky's foundation.

The money from the house we split between the church and The Rape Center.

The Whole Thing With Freak knocked me on my Hind Quarters for a Long Time.

I went back to work with Barry but most a my time is spent at the church.

One day I stayed to watch Baby Girl sing with the choir.

The next thing I knew I was singing too.

Turned Around Twice and I was Head a The Praise Dancers:

a bunch a kids in the church who Dance For Jesus.

How I got Roped Into Coachin the Basketball Teams--both a them--I'll Never Know

but it's All Good.

I might a Failed Freak but I Won't Be Failin These Kids, Ya Heard?

These days though my Favorite Activity is layin on the couch

with my head on Baby Girl's stomach.

If I'm Still Enough and Quiet Enough I'm rewarded with a movement

or even better a Swift Kick In The Head.

Sometimes if I holla into her belly or shake it vigorously

I can get a **Whole *Crapload*** a movement.

That's right.

Baby Girl married me.

And she's havin my baby.

Hope you Wrote That Down like I told you.

FIN <small>BG</small>

Three weeks ago I finally released my last disc.

Or should I say "discs."

At my insistence the label released two separate CD's:

For da 1, an R&B flavored dance jam and *For The One*, my gospel disc.

The twin-discs set an Industry precedent; I retired anyway.

These-a-ma-days I'm a full-time-music-teacher.

I also counsel at The Rape Center, give voice lessons;

do vocal arrangements for Pastor MacLean and The Wisdom in Christ Choir.

Obie promised Pastor he'd shoot the videos for free;

Pastor insisted on paying *something*; O's doing it for "scale."

After Obie tithes, Pastor will get-his-cut *regardless*.

Oh, **wait**!

Did I tell you Obie and I sing in the choir, too?

My bad.

The hardest part of working at the church is cleaning up my language.

Even after praying over it I still find myself throwing those MF's around like M&M's.

I'd like to tell you I am totally-curse-free-today; I'd-be-lying to you.

I am in "curse rehab," taking it one-day-at-a-time.

O is back to work almost full time at Street People Productions,

he isn't the slightest bit interested in reclaiming his former company.

The Latin King assigns him on a Per Video basis which leaves O's options wide open.

Obie is learning not to over-book himself, it seems to be difficult for him.

Me?

I'm content just being Oscar's wife.

Pregnant is a'ight; it's nothing to write home about, but it *is*-what-I-wanted, *n'est-ce pas*?

And, if I had-to-do-it-all-over-again....?

I wouldn't change a thing.

This Ain't No Hearts and Flowers Love Story Pt2 by Brooklyn Darkchild

www.ingramcontent.com/pod-product-compliance
Lightning Source LLC
Chambersburg PA
CBHW031109260626
47172CB00001B/290